"A genre-busting masterpiece, full of pacy storytelling, wry dialogue and philosophical challenge. It shows a heightened awareness of the promises of language as portals into the deepest reflections. It is funny, beautifully modulated and heart-rending. Róisín Sorahan has written that rare thing nowadays - a book of passion and truth which will enthral and challenge every kind of reader. In contemplating some of life's deepest mysteries, it tells a story that is hopeful, honest and necessary."

—DECLAN KIBERD
Author of *Inventing Ireland* and *Ulysses and Us*,
Professor Emeritus at the University of Notre Dame,
and leading authority on modern Irish literature.

"With forks and turns, and characters that might have stepped out of the pages of Hans Christian Andersen, this is an entrancing book with the timbre of a fairy tale, raising contemporary philosophical questions."

—THE IRISH TIMES

"Sorahan's ability to bring to life some basic tenets of existence and the existential questions many come to feel during the course of a lifetime creates an insightful read on the level of *The Velveteen Rabbit* classic."

—MIDWEST BOOK REVIEW

"Hope and positivity flow from the pages of this lyrical story as we navigate the ever-changing seasons in this magical forest."

—LOVEREADING UK

"A beautiful debut from a talented author."

—MANHATTAN BOOK REVIEW

TIME AND THE TREE

TIME AND THE TREE

A novel

RÓISÍN SORAHAN

IMBOLC
BOOKS

TIME AND THE TREE
A novel
By Róisín Sorahan

Copyright ©Róisín Sorahan 2021, 2024
This edition published 2024 by
Imbolc Books
Vermont, US
www.imbolcbooks.com

For all information, please address Imbolc Books
at info@imbolcbooks.com
Published in the United States of America
ISBN (Paperback): 979-8-9907946-0-3
ISBN (Hardback): 979-8-9907946-1-0
ISBN (eBook): 979-8-9907946-2-7
Library of Congress Control Number: 2024947429

Book cover design by Coverkitchen

2nd edition: 2024, Imbolc Books
1st edition: 2021, Adelaide Books
Printed in the United States of America

For
Mum and Dad

CONTENTS

SUMMER

The leaf fell so softly, that no one heard a sound. It lilted, drifted through the air, then settled on the cheek of the little boy who was curled up sound asleep beneath the Tree that felt its loss.

It tickled the boy's face, making his nose twitch, before it was lifted and spun by a passing breeze. Once more it brushed the child and, though deep in dreams, his mind stirred.

He opened his eyes, and the light crept in. He opened his mouth, and a yawn rushed out. He straightened his arms and his legs and, in no time at all, he was standing upright. He wasn't very tall, not compared to the Tree that filled the sky above him.

"I'm awake," he announced to the forest. He planted his feet in the earth and craned his neck back as far as it would go. "Are you a boy or a girl?" he finally asked.

"I am a tree.

"You were asleep for a very long time," the Tree observed. The child nodded, stifling another yawn and kneading his eyes with his fists. "I'm thirsty," he said.

He followed the Tree's directions to a spring that fed the forest. A wooden mug sat on a stone shelf by its source. The boy knelt by the water's edge, heedless of hands and knees. A small face, with a shock of hair and a missing tooth, returned his serious gaze, before the water splintered his reflection. He reached for the mug, lingering over its weight. It had been unused for some time, so the boy rinsed it clean, then filled it to the brim. The water spilled down his chin and his throat. It tasted of moss and blue glaciers. His eyes sparkled as it washed dreams and webs from his drowsy mind.

When he was sated, he wiped his mouth with the back of his hand and followed the path back to the Tree. It was still early, but the sun had already started opening up the forest's darkest corners. Drones of insects beelined towards the warmth, and dew-dotted damselflies glittered in the first light.

Silver shafts blinked off waxy leaves, deepening the shadows of their dark velvet underbellies. Soldier beetles patrolled patches of cow parsley, whose thousand laced blossoms plotted zodiac designs.

Knees and elbows parted stalks and limbs, gathering burrs and trailing seeds as the boy ducked into the glade, where a ghostly haze still drifted above the clover blossoms.

Soft morning light suffused the space, and the sky, which had seemed so small to the boy in the snatches he had glimpsed through the forest's canopy, opened above him. Ferns edged the clearing, keeping to the shadows, and wild violets basked in the early warmth.

In the middle of it all, the Tree spread its arms wide. It reached towards the North and the South, the East and the West, its broad leaves tilted towards the sun.

The boy circled its trunk, his fingers brushing the thick, ridged bark, finding gnarls and hollows. He carefully selected a foothold and climbed onto its lowest branch. From there he could hear the creaking of the boughs. He closed his eyes and opened his mind. In no time at all, the child's breath joined the rhythm of the Tree's, and there was real peace and happiness and harmony in the forest.

∞

Then suddenly a screech-a-ling siren smashed the silence, and within the space of a heartbeat the moment was shredded.

"Gracious," gasped the boy, as his eyes popped open and he clutched at the trunk to regain his balance.

"Scrawk," squawked a bird, yanking its head from beneath its wing and bolting to a higher perch.

"Time," said the Tree, "is passing."

A mottled round face parted the branches and poked into the clearing. It sported a jaunty brass cap, and was soon followed by a silk cravat, puckered around a flushed neck. After a brief skirmish with the bushes, a belly, which was barely contained by a loud shirt, buttoned waistcoat and checkered jacket, made its appearance, staggering beneath the racket it was making.

Legs, ill-suited to their burden, pushed their way through the undergrowth; while long arms, one of which was decidedly shorter than the other, elbowed and batted at leaves and twigs. A metallic rod, which appeared to emerge from the figure's navel, circled the portly frame with a steady whirr, never stopping, not even for a second.

Time freed his body from the tangle and clamored into the clearing. Pulling himself up to his full height, straightening his hat and clearing his throat, he announced, "It is *hiccup*."

"I can't hear you," yelled the boy, who had covered his ears with his hands. Time steadied his belly and tried again.

"It is nine o' *click-hup*."

The boy shook his head fiercely. "I still can't hear you," he shouted as loud as he could above the din.

Time let out a long sigh, which got tripped up by another hiccup, and wearily nodded towards his rumbling tummy, where one hand was pointing towards his chin and another towards his waistline. "Oh, I see," said the boy. "It is nine o'clock."

The ringing stopped. Time flattened his cap and dropped like a boulder beneath the shade of the Tree. "It's awfully early to be so desperately hot," he moaned, as he wiped his face with a large handkerchief and opened his jacket.

"Take rest for a time," offered the Tree.

Time shifted his bulk and stretched out his legs. "That's better," he sighed, and let his arms fall by his side.

"Well, well, what have we got here?" he squinted in the direction of the boy. "I havn't seen you before."

"I was asleep," said the child.

"That would explain it," Time nodded. "But I am being terribly rude. Let me introduce myself." He puffed out his belly. "I am Time," he announced. "I am all that is past and all that is to come. But, enough about me," he deflated a little. "You must meet my slave. Fool," he roared, "I'm hungry."

∞

A creature, more shadow than substance, slipped into the glade. The boy had trouble seeing it clearly as it seemed to melt away every time he looked directly at it. Its back was bowed almost double from the weight of the cases it was carrying and drab, matted hair fell like a curtain across its sunken face.

It carefully placed the bags on the ground, and then it dropped to its knees before Time.

"Master Time. Tyrant Time. Thy will be mine."

"Enough," growled Time. "I want to dine." He kicked the Shadow, which moaned softly then crawled to the largest suitcase which it started to slowly unpack.

The boy watched as the Shadow took out a folding picnic table and a canvas chair, which it carefully placed in the shadiest spot beneath the eaves of the Tree. It then spread a tablecloth, set out the finest silverware, and finally opened up a large lunch box. The smell of fried chicken filled the air. The Shadow heaped a plate with food and filled a goblet with rich red wine. When the preparations were complete it dragged Time to his feet, settled him in the chair, fetched a cushion to raise him higher, and then curled up at the leg of the table.

"About time," growled the tyrant, before he started gobbling the feast. "Perhaps it's a bit early in the day for chicken," he burped, then continued, "but I've been dashing around all morning. I haven't had a minute. I never once stopped. Until now," he added. "Tree has that effect on me," he mused. "It's always trying to get me to slow down. It is nice here." He looked around dreamily as his eyelids got heavier and threatened to drop. But, just then, the Shadow raised its head and whimpered.

"Quiet, dog," Time spat, torn from his stupor. He hurled the gnawed chicken bones towards the boy. Caught off guard, the child gaped then ducked at the last moment as the Shadow unfurled and shot forth like a lightning bolt. The bones fell to the earth and the Shadow dived after them, scrabbling and growling amongst the roots. It hissed at the boy, shooting him a venomous look, then hunched over its trove, shielding the bones from imagined predators. Its eyes furtively scanned the glade as it rapidly crunched on the scraps, before wrapping the remains in a faded handkerchief and burying them deep in the folds of its lifeless grey garment.

Time beamed delightedly. "Life may be a race, but it can also be a feast, my boy," he crowed. "Stick with me, kid, and I'll show you a good time."

The boy shook his head, mouth tightened with distaste, as he watched the Shadow pack up the case and store the last remaining cutlery. Its back bowed, all energy spent, it moved with painful slowness.

"I don't want your time," the boy's arms were wrapped tightly across his body.

"Nonsense, nonsense," Time blustered. "You don't know what you're talking about. But then, you're young. I find my greatest devotees come to me at the age of unreason. Though there have been exceptions. I have so much to offer. Tell him," he ordered the Shadow, which immediately stopped what it was doing and straightened its back. Its eyes, the boy noticed with a shudder, were circles of darkness, its pupils unnaturally dilated, utterly drained of light.

"Tell him what he is missing out on." Time impatiently pointed at the creature. "Tell him now, Fool."

The Shadow raised its voice, reaching no more than a raspy whisper. "Seconds, minutes fill the hours, always running towards Tomorrow."

"And the rest," prompted Time, who was nodding in mounting pleasure as the Shadow swayed weakly on its feet and intoned dry words.

"A rush of time that kills all thought of can't and care and clinging ties."

"Go on," Time prodded.

"A warm creeping of the skin that builds to a climactic blast."

"Yes…" Time exhaled deeply. "Tell him what happens then."

"Then, there is no hunger, no fear, no feeling and no pain, wrapped in time's blanket, warm and secure, till you nod off on clouds and forget heavy limbs."

"Isn't it wonderful?" Time breathed heavily. "Keep going, there's more. What comes next?"

"Gasping on a dry mouth that sucks for air, your body wracked with vomit and bile and nails tearing at your shell that itches and bleeds, almost as if you were human."

"That's enough," Time interjected. "I think he gets the drift."

The mesmerized boy looked at the Shadow in horror. He wanted to turn away from the shrunken face and fallow mouth that grimaced over barren words, teeth bared and broken.

"You like what you see, boy?" the Shadow sidled a little closer, its garment falling off a wizened shoulder. "Fancy a taste of my charms?" It cackled a horrid, mirthless laugh which ended in a whimper when Time landed a back-handed blow on its mouth. "Shut your foolish trap and cover yourself, dog. No one wants to look at you. No one wants to touch you. You're nothing, and don't ever forget it."

Clasping its robe tightly at its neck the Shadow bowed low and chanted softly, "Time, the master of my life. Time, the shadow cast by death."

"Sing it, sister." Time laughed, clapping the creature on the back and beaming around the clearing.

$$\infty$$

Through a haze of shock and confusion the child focused on the bright spot of red that teetered like a raindrop on the edge of the Shadow's lip. Time drifted, then faded, and all that held the boy in the moment was the slow bleed of colour as it trembled and spilled to the ground. It settled, then soaked into the earth's pores.

"Dolor fin," the Shadow whispered.

"That's right," Time prompted. "But you havn't told him the best bits yet."

The boy thought of offering his handkerchief. But that might mean touching it. His skin crinkled at the thought.

"Get a drink for our guests, child," the Tree nudged.

"I'll time you," Time offered, pulling a stopwatch from his waistcoat pocket. The boy hared off to the river, eager to be free of his fears and misgivings, conscious of time passing. He filled the cup, then, just as anxiously, trotted back as carefully as he could, worried that he might have missed something.

He stood with a half empty mug in his hand, uncertain what to do next. Time was settled comfortably under the Tree, yawning his head off; while the Shadow was tethered at the edge of the clearing, scratching its arms off.

"Four minutes, fifty-two seconds. Not bad, but I'm guessing you can beat that next time round." Time stored his stopwatch and let out a sigh. "Well, what are you waiting for? The water's not going to drink itself." He looked speculatively at the Shadow. "No, I suppose I'll just have to do it myself." He stretched out a languid hand and the boy placed the mug in it.

Time drained its contents in one long slurp. "Not bad. Not bad at all. I'll have another, and be quick about it." Time reached for his stopwatch, as he dismissed the boy with a glance.

The boy wasted precious moments in a sweat of indecision, unwilling to leap to command, yet eager to prove his speed.

"We have another guest," the Tree gently reminded him. The boy spun as he launched into the forest, hair flying and arms and legs wheeling.

"I remember what it was to be young," Time chuckled. "Let's see how long he can keep this up."

"He's not a game for you to play," the Tree chided. "No more than that soul is a stone for you to grind."

"You mean that thing?" Time asked incredulously, nodding towards the Shadow. "Breath, bile and bones are hardly the stuff worthy of crusades. It does nothing. Feels nothing. It's beneath your concern, Tree."

"It bleeds."

"Well, so does a leaf, if you cut it," Time countered.

A breeze passed through the eaves of the Tree, causing a slight tremor. "Not that I would hurt any of your leaves, Tree, you understand. I was just making a point," Time hastily added.

"We share this world, Time. It gives us life, soaks up our blood and cradles our ashes before the flames are stoked once again. It absorbs all the love and joy and anger and pain that we fling about us. It is wrong to be so careless about inflicting so much damage."

Time looked at the Shadow, which was curled in its rags, head lolling to the side, spittle trailing down its chin unchecked. "You're a funny one, Tree," he chuckled indulgently. "The world has forgotten that thing exists. If it knew for a moment it was soiling the earth, it would swallow it whole and save our eyes the assault."

∞

When the boy returned, Time had slipped into a noisy sleep. "How fast was I?" he demanded. The child clasped a sloshing cup, breathless and sweating, hair standing on end and grass and twigs snagged in his t-shirt. Time shifted and snorted, then settled again.

"You were as fast as the wind," the Tree told him.

The boy smiled broadly. "What was my time?"

"Time, did someone mention time?" Time jolted awake, arms flailing and legs kicking out at imagined enemies. "It's time. What time? It must be lunchtime." He consulted his belly and blushed slightly. "I think you caught me a little off balance there, boy. I'm ahead of myself. But it's certainly close to elevenses."

He eyed the cup that the boy was holding. "Not my idea of a decent snack, but it will wake me up." He stretched forward and tugged the mug from the boy's hand. He swallowed a mouthful. "But it wasn't for you," the boy objected. Then Time tossed the rest. "Don't waste your time on that thing, child, it's not worth it."

He looked bitterly at the Shadow, which rocked on its haunches, painfully dragging air through a wasted throat. "Time is a precious gift. I can give you as much as you'll ever need. But even that won't be enough for you. All you will do is take and take and scrabble in the dirt begging for more.

"Never for a moment would you think of saving it up, keeping a little for tomorrow. As though the future were a sure bet. Lord knows it's just about the last thing you can count on. I've spent aeons chasing it down, and I've still never managed to corner it."

"It's okay, Time," the boy tried to reassure him. "I don't want your time."

"Don't be ridiculous, child. Of course you do. You just don't know it yet. Give it a couple of years and you'll look back on this period of your life as smells of summer flowers, blue evenings and bird trills. You will ache to have this time back, when you hopped from one leg to the other, unbalanced by a mug of water. You'll try to remember Tree's words but, over time, you'll stop hearing its voice as a medley of louder ones fill your mind. And you will remember that you were happy once, without ever really knowing why.

"Of course, this means nothing to you now. But I promise you that it will. I have seen this a billion times, and more, before. Nothing surprises me anymore. The best you will ever be able to hope is that the future weaves a promise worth sacrificing everything you have for. And when that runs out on you, that the memories you have can keep you warm when the winter comes. For the winter will surely come, no matter how much you rail against the fates and bargain for more time. Isn't that right, Tree?"

"Every life has its seasons. As each season passes, it enriches the one that follows. Without winter, there would never be spring. The cycle turns, as it always does. Yearning and grasping get you nowhere."

"Well now, Tree, that's not exactly true. I live my life on the heels of the future. I admit it's gotten the better of me so far, but one of these days, mark my words, that will change."

"The future is a phantom, Time. It only exists in your cravings. All that we have are our memories, and the moment, and the motivation to get up when we've fallen, to try again and do better."

"You're such an idealist, Tree. I admire you for it. But the world's ruled by realists. Open your eyes and look around you," Time instructed the Tree. "The present moment is nothing more than a stepping-stone to the future. Of itself it has no more significance than a boulder in a river. The eye only registers its presence as a means to get to the other side. The best the moment can offer is the chance not to get soaked."

"If you live like this, Time, you exist suspended in air. Hounded by what you've lost and driven by what you seek. Where you've come from recedes into the distance, and where you're going stays tantalizingly one step ahead. You'll keep reaching and reaching until you topple, and when you touch the ground, you'll discover that you've turned old, and disillusioned, and that everything you did was driven by a lie."

Time leaned forward, anxiously touching the Tree, slightly breathless, "It's not a lie. I've seen it. How else could I make the promises that I do? Do you think I would have so many followers if what I offered them wasn't so wonderfully sweet?

"The rush of chasing Tomorrow cannot be understood until you've tried it for yourself. Look at that fool. Do you think it would suffer the deprivations and torments if the reward did not compensate? It would do anything for me, for a single drop of what I offer."

"You deal in ghosts," the Tree admonished.

"I trade what's needed," Time countered. "People yearn. I just give them something to wish for. What is more delightful than the promise that this will all come to an end, and that tomorrow may be better?"

"But this is really nice," the boy interrupted.

Time lay back and lazily looked around him. In the silence the forest burst into song. Sparrows languidly chirped and chattered, while distant birds of prey let loose battle cries that were carried on warm air currents. Bees pollinated the purple orchid patches that speckled the earth, humming while they flitted from petal to stamen. The sun rose higher in the sky, shortening shadows, and breezes spun dandelion seeds on heady adventures.

Time sneezed.

"You have a point, child," he conceded.

∞

The boy hung by his legs from a branch of the Tree. "The world looks funny from this angle. Your clock's upside down, Time."

"Don't be ridiculous!" Time chided him. "You can't make jokes about such important matters. If you fall from that branch and break your neck, that will teach you."

"If your second arm fell off would time stop?" the boy asked.

"Where did you find such a brat, Tree? In my day children were seen and not heard. That's the way I liked it. Isn't there somewhere else you can dangle like a bat?"

The boy flipped upwards, grabbed the branch and pulled himself up to straddle it. He looked down on Time. "I'm only asking."

"Time never stops," Time snapped.

"Even when you're sleeping?"

"Of course not."

"What about when you're playing and having so much fun that you forget about everything else, even that you're hungry?"

"I would never miss a meal. My body clock is a finely tuned instrument. I listen to its melody and sing to its demands." Time's tummy rumbled on cue.

"Fool, I'm hungry," Time roared.

The Shadow leapt from its crouch.

"I don't understand how the arms on a dial can split a day into pieces," the boy continued to quiz Time.

Time looked horrified, "Have you taught him nothing, Tree?"

"Tree teaches me tons of stuff," the boy jumped in. "Tree has taught me that time and change are part of everything."

"Well that's a relief, anyway."

"But in the forest time seems different," the boy continued.

"What on earth do you mean?" Time asked. "Different to what?"

"Well, different to your time." The boy delved in, "Your hands seem to carve everything into tiny parts. Each bit is exactly the same size as the one before and the one coming after. I can't even break a chocolate bar into two even halves. One side is always smaller than the other, no matter how hard I try." The boy looked a little distracted for a moment, before he raked in his thoughts. "But, here in the forest, time sometimes passes in a blink, while at others it stretches on and on. It doesn't pace itself, but it doesn't exhaust itself either. It follows the flow of the day and curves, depending on the changes that are taking place."

"Oh, that's nonsense," Time assured him. "You lack a decent routine in your life. What utter rot. Time curving!" He patted his paunch. "I really must talk to Tree about your education. You wouldn't happen to have one of those bars of chocolate, by any chance?" The boy shook his head.

Time sighed, "Time is not something that you can shape or bend. It follows a straight line and it never, ever stops. I stand at the front of a very large army that marches to my steady beat. Every second is in perfect step. The minutes line up smartly behind, followed by the hours and the days. The years and the aeons take up the rear. Every soldier knows its place. No squadron falters. My army stretches far past infinity. Its movements are perfectly choreographed and utterly predictable. Each step, inevitably, is followed by another."

"It sounds very grand." The boy was impressed by Time's show of strength. "But I wouldn't like to get in its way. I think it might run me over."

∞

"You need to step back, child. This is not for the inexperienced," Time cautioned. The Shadow hunched behind Time's back, sweating and straining as it struggled to turn a lever.

"A little tighter," Time panted. "Yes. Yes. That's it."

"What's going on?" the boy asked the Tree.

"Time didn't think he was wound up tight enough."

The boy laughed and turned from the spectacle to clamber up the Tree's branches. Very soon the earth seemed very far away. Seen from above, the antics below hardly carried any weight of importance. Leaves shredded the boy's view and tore the scene into small fragments. Snatches of colour, drawn from Time's wild shirt and plum face, lit up a pattern quilted from greens and earth duns.

"Don't stop. Faster. Faster." Time's voice barely carried to the boy's ears. He pulled himself up to a higher branch, where the soft wind snatched at his tangled hair. Cocooned in the Tree's arms he couldn't see Time's sleeves rolled up and his buttons loosened.

"Yes."

Time moaned in pleasure, and then wheeled on the Shadow and kicked it away. "That's enough." His face puffed and glistening, he sprawled on the ground, breathing heavily. In moments he was snoring loudly.

The Shadow watched his chest rising and falling from a cautious distance. It stared intently at Time's spent form, lying vulnerably on the earth. Without realizing that it was even moving, it reached out and gathered an awkward stone to its chest, around which it wrapped its arms and its heart. It inched a little closer. Close enough that it could have pinched Time's nose and sealed his mouth, if it had a mind to. It drew nearer.

The boy was nestled in a branch, humming to the Tree's tune. If the Shadow craned its neck back it could make out the boy's shoe, a leg, a mouth, wild hair. Even from the dirt it could see the child's eyes widen and his mind leap forward to follow the Tree's teachings. Time slept on. The Shadow alone seemed aware of the cruel sunshine. It was always alone. A head would probably crush as easily as an egg, it thought. If the stone were dense enough.

The Shadow leaned forward. It felt Time's sour breath upon its face, rising and falling in hot, acidic waves. Bile rose in its mouth. The stone began to sweat, and the Shadow's heart beat a little louder. The waves came faster and faster. Hardly leaving time to retreat. Soon the spray was thundering in its ears. The noise roared and its body bucked. It dropped the stone that it might cover its ears and retreat to a quieter space where nothing mattered, and the only sound was the tick of the clock as it beat another nail. The din subsided to a whine, and slowly dropped in pitch until, finally, all the Shadow could hear was the wind softly rustling the leaves of the Tree.

The boy's eyes were closed. Time had turned on his side. The Shadow looked at the Tree and the Tree looked back. The Shadow ducked its head, its eyes lowered, its face hot. "I see you," the Tree murmured. There was nowhere it could hide. Even if it had wanted to. Perhaps the words were just a cruel trick of the wind, it thought. It turned its back and retreated to the shadows.

∞

Time stirred in his spent sleep, a hand cradling his cheek. His mind, emptied of images and dreams, soaked up drifting sounds. The child's laughter flittered across his consciousness. A bird call carried a great distance. The Shadow watched him from the bushes. The Tree sheathed him from above. He sank an inch deeper.

The life of the forest continued around him, oblivious to Time in its midst.

An ant climbed the crevices of his face, weighed down by the segment of a leaf at least five times its size. It was followed by another and another, all grimly determined to overcome this unforeseen obstruction in their path.

A sigh escaped. "Shut it," a leader growled. "I thought the scouts had checked out the route," a petulant voice carried beneath its burden. "You can lodge your objections with Her Ladyship when you get back," another snickered. "An excellent suggestion," the growl melted to a purr. "Er no, it's alright," a voice stuttered. "Her Ladyship need not be bothered by my mumblings." "We could have just gone around," someone muttered. "Who said that?" the leader demanded. The ants lowered their heads and soldiered on.

Time yawned, sat up and scratched his face. The ants scattered.

"Get off me," Time roared as his defenses rose. "I'm under attack. Help me." Leaves, crumbs and twigs were dropped as those that could took flight.

Time leapt to his feet, brushing at his neck and his head, stamping and hopping from foot to foot, swatting and squishing with frenzied abandon.

The Shadow launched from the margins. The Tree muttered from above.

"Get them off me." Time flailed his arms, batting at foes, as the Shadow deftly brushed off his jacket and murmured in soothing tones.

"You were supposed to watch over me," Time accused the Shadow, hurt softening his voice. The stone lay between them. Ants crouched in the long grass. Nothing moved.

"Get out of my sight," Time turned his head. "I can't bear to look at you. You're a blot on my vision."

"Sorry, Master," the Shadow backed away, its eyes fixed on the ground, tracking the edge of the Tree's shadow.

∞

"Now tell him the other one," prompted Time from the shade of the wings. He almost thought of standing up, he was having such a marvelous time.

The Shadow stood uncomfortably in the centre of the clearing, bearing the brunt of the summer sun.

"It's alright, Time," the boy assured him. "I'm pretty sure I get your point. Life is all about living for tomorrow." He knew he shouldn't have sniggered at Time's plight with the ants. Well, he thought, he was paying for it now.

"Tomorrow is the tease that strips our wanton thoughts of other needs," the Shadow recited.

"Go on," Time poked the Shadow with a retractable pointer that, stretched to its full length, just about reached the creature's ribs. Time brandished his weapon like a baton, humming tunelessly to music only he could hear. He smiled contentedly as he poked and prodded his charge. A swathe of dead ants lay emptied at his feet.

"Tomorrow is the thrill that dangles just beyond our fingers' grasp."

"Do it on one foot," Time worried the creature.

The Shadow lifted its left foot. It swayed precariously, then raised its bony arms to steady itself. "Tomorrow is the whispered taunt that goads the lost souls towards the ledge."

"Dance, Fool," Time demanded in a sharp, mean voice.

The Shadow billowed and swayed and shifted its weight to its other foot. "Tomorrow is the taste of death served as the main course at the feast."

"Look at that. My slave's a dreamer and a dancer." Time laughed uproariously and swiped the pointer in time to the rhythm of its gasps.

"It's alright, Time. Stop it. I get it." The boy stood on solid feet, red faced, fists clenched.

∞

"No need to get snippy," Time admonished the child. "I'm only trying to fill in a few gaps in your understanding." Time looked pointedly at the Tree, "I'm not criticizing you. I just think it's important that you get both perspectives. The Tree has a tendency to be a little lax in its observance of time."

"Not at all," the Tree countered. "I am always conscious of the passing of time. I simply choose not to measure the moment. Instead I live it, fully and wholeheartedly. I reflect on the past, but I do not mourn it. I prepare for the future, but I do not crave it. I exist in the present, but I do not time it."

"Of course you do. Every life is accompanied by the steady beat of the metronome. Even yours, Tree."

"I prefer my own rhythm."

"It's that kind of crazy talk that's filling the boy's head with nonsense. You wouldn't believe the number of people who think that they can treat time as their own personal pendulum. Time doesn't come with an à-la-carte menu: 'Oh, I'll have the hours, but hold on the years.' Tree would have you believe that time is something that you can shape to your own needs. That, my child, is balderdash."

The Tree responded, "Time is nothing more than a tool to help us understand the importance of the present. Time marches on. We get older. It is inevitable. This knowledge should help us to make the most of every moment that we have, rather than squander the seconds in a vain attempt to retrieve the past or grasp hold of the future."

"I don't give a jot about the past, Tree. Time's lure lies in what's ahead. The future stretches before us, draped around corners. Of course, it always recoils from my touch, but I cherish the hope that one day I'll catch hold of it."

"Dogs that chase cars most often end up under wheels," the Tree cautioned. It continued, "Life passes, at times so fast that we don't even mark the years flying past. At others, time traces patterns on the sand in slow, languid arcs and we notice, for the first time, the velvet tip of a starling's wing and wonder if it was always so beautiful. If we don't pay attention to what's important in life, and give undue heed to Time's marching squadrons, we end up shuffling in step from that which is past to that which has yet to come, filling the precious moment with the thud of boots stomping in unison to a dead beat."

"There's nothing wrong with a bit of order, Tree. We weren't all meant to weave daisy-chain necklaces and dance in abandon around stone circles. Some of us prefer to keep our wits about us, and our eyes on the prize," Time retorted.

∞

"What's the prize?" the boy's eyes were alight with excitement.

"If, and I stress if, you win our little game of time, you could be the proud recipient of a beautiful time piece that a grandfather clock gave to me when I was your age." Time gave a little flourish then produced a pocket watch from his waistcoat, like a rabbit from a hat. Encased in silver metal, hanging from a chain, he dangled it in front of the boy who snatched it from him and snapped it open. "Ooh, its numbers glow in the dark," he marveled.

"It's of the finest quality. Crafted by some of the world's most skilled artisans," Time elaborated.

"Made in China," the boy held the watch to his face, as he read the insignia.

The time piece felt smooth in the palm of his hand. "I've never seen one of these before," he confessed. Time shot the Tree an angry glance. "Shocking," he muttered under his breath.

"Don't worry, boy," he breezily bustled. "Take a good look. See how the arms move smoothly. Note the elegance of the dial. It's cradled in the finest titanium. It will last several lifetimes. Long after you're forgotten, the arms on this watch will still be keeping pace with my army."

"Then shouldn't this one be moving?" the boy asked, pointing at the second hand which hadn't budged since the clasp had been opened.

Time grabbed it back from him and looked at it closely, before flinging it to the ground. "Inferior quality. Things aren't made to last anymore. I got that watch just last week. It cost an arm and a leg. You can't trust anyone. They'll tell you anything that comes into their heads, if they think it will benefit them. I was cheated by a ruffian with a few glib lines who was selling junk by the side of the road. I should have known not to listen to him. He was a horrible, bony thing with rat eyes. All that nonsense about his failing health and starving family was probably a lie as well. I'm too soft-hearted for my own good. I can't believe that I exchanged a few crusts of bread for that worthless piece of rubbish. I was robbed. Robbed, I tell you!"

Time stormed and stomped around the clearing in his rage. "I almost went hungry myself that day, saved only by the fact that the Fool had packed a roast for my lunch. It was just a stroke of luck. It could easily have gone the other way. Still, I don't mind saying that I would have relished a few pieces of bread to mop up the gravy."

"It's still a nice watch," the boy remarked, recalling the feel of the metal in the palm of his hand. "It doesn't matter that it doesn't work. We can pretend that it does. I think it would still make a fine prize."

"I don't want to play anymore," Time paused in his pacing and pouted. "What's the point of winning if the prize isn't worth the effort?"

"You mightn't win," the boy smiled. "I'm really good at games."

"Of course I'd win. I always win. It's boring, it's so predictable. The pattern is always the same: the Shadow and I roll the dice to start; the Shadow always leads for the first three innings. It has a very dexterous wrist, for one so useless. Then, just when it looks like all is lost, the Fool makes the usual wrong turns and false pitches and I streak towards the finish. It happens every single time. I'm a master of the game. Of course, I'm not in it for the money, or the admirers, though I've refused any number of suitors, in my time."

"What then?" the boy asked.

"It's the glory I'm after."

"Then, in that case, let's play for the honour of winning," the boy suggested. "Besides," he grinned, "it might be fun."

"Lord, he's young," Time rolled his eyes at the Tree. "The honour, you say?"

"Well, really, the fun," the boy clarified.

"You can't eat honour for your lunch. Glory doesn't fill your belly when you havn't had a morsel since breakfast time. If I play, it's for a decent stake. Or a juicy steak, which would go down nicely, thank you very much."

"We could play for buttons," the boy suggested.

"Let's see what you've got." Time's interest perked up. The boy pulled a handful from his pocket, from which he extracted a couple of pebbles and an elastic band.

Time looked them over. "Rubbish," he pronounced.

"They're nice," the boy countered.

"Oh, stop pestering me. Your buttons are tarnished. The watch is useless. The day is ruined." Time flung the watch to the ground.

The boy brushed aside Time's petulance and knelt down to retrieve the prize from the dirt. He rubbed it on the front of his t-shirt and held it at arm's length. The sun glinted off the metal casing, emitting sparks of light.

"Pretty," the boy breathed.

"Argh," Time yelled. "Are you trying to blind me?" He grabbed the watch from the startled boy's hand, dashed it to the ground once again, and stamped on it with a heavy boot. The watch shattered beneath the force.

In the aftermath of the violence there was a moment of ringing silence, which was finally broken by a whimper from the Shadow, rapidly followed by a hoarse gasp from Time.

He flung himself to his knees and gathered the springs and shards of the dead watch, which he cupped gently in his hands, like a broken bird. "I should have known," he almost sobbed. "It's tin, not titanium. Everything he said was a lie."

The Shadow streaked to his side. "Let me see time's innards. I want to touch it. Let me taste it." Its tongue flicked out to lick the shattered drops of metal.

"Disgusting creature!" Time shoved the Shadow aside with one arm, protecting the remains with the other. "Have you no respect?"

"I want to see what makes it tick. I want its secrets. Give it to me." It reached out imploringly to Time, its fingers quivering.

"Give me." Its eyes bored into Time's hands.

"I need it," it moaned.

Time looked at the Shadow with unveiled revulsion. "Get away from me. You disgust me."

He kicked at the creature, then gazed at the broken watch for one last time before thrusting it angrily at the child. "Here, it's yours. You've won. Are you happy now?"

The boy shook his head. "I just wanted to play."

"So, how do we play?" Time asked the boy, who was shuffling impatiently from one foot to the other.

"Oh, it's dead easy. I say: 'What time is it, Mister Wolf?' Then you blow on the dandelion seeds like this, see." The boy blew on the feathery dome, scattering a cloud of seeds. "It's one o'clock," he boomed.

He blew a second time, "two o'clock." Then he blew a third time with all his might. Two more seeds clung stubbornly to the stalk. "Three o'clock." He blew again. "Four o'clock." Neither seed budged, so he gave it another go. "Five o'clock!" he announced in triumph, as the final two seeds soared then dallied in the air. "Now, you have to chase me."

The boy ran off in all directions, giggling excitedly, his hair flying.

"You'll never catch me, Mr. Wolf!" he taunted from the clearing's edge.

"Is he talking to me?" Time asked the Tree. "He does know that my name is not Wolf, doesn't he?"

"Come on, Time, I'm over here."

"Oh, he does mean me. Is he a little soft," Time tapped his skull, "you know, in the head department?"

"He's a child, Time. He loves to play," Tree said.

"It's a damnable waste of time, if you ask me."

"Why is it a waste of time if it makes him happy? You could learn a lot from the boy, Time."

"Are you going senile in your old age, Tree? It's an idiotic game. If I understand the rules correctly, and I believe I do, it involves scattering some seeds and bellowing out the hours, then haring around in the hot sun in pursuit of a wraith who can't, as far as I can see, even tell the time.

"If that weren't bad enough, would you have me lower myself to deciphering the hours by a dandelion stalk? It's hardly scientific, Tree. We've moved on from the days of the dial and the shadow. The magician behind the curtain has been given his marching orders. We live in a digital era, don't you know, where time has become a commodity. I can't squander my precious time playing foolish games with a scatter-brained child. What would people think?"

"People would get by, as they always do."

"Come on, Time, I'm over here. If you run now, you might be able to catch me," the boy poked his head through a bush.

"I have standards to maintain. If I let things slip, my army would fall to pieces. It only takes one false step and, before you know it, the hours are toppling on top of the minutes, the seconds are loitering by the roadside talking with the natives, and the years are throwing chocolate to the children."

"Would that really be so bad?"

"Well, yes, it would, particularly if it were good chocolate. I rather like the Belgian sort myself. Tree, the last thing I need is a band of ragamuffins skipping around and yelling at the cadres to chase them. If the ranks ever broke, imagine the chaos."

"Time would still pass, as it always does. It need not be a thing of violence and dread."

"Fear keeps people in line."

"Freedom and fun keep spirits alive," the Tree responded.

"Life is a serious business."

"Certainly. But there's nothing to be gained by taking ourselves too seriously. Life rolls past, regardless of your position in the world."

"People expect certain things of me, Tree. I can't let them down. I have the dignity of my office to maintain. So, if the hoards stand by the roadside expecting a military parade then, by gum, that's exactly what I will give them. By the sound of things, you would have me rock up at the head of a circus. Where, I ask, is the fun in that?"

The Tree chuckled.

"Come on, Time, I'm waiting," the boy hollered.

"I don't know what's so funny," Time snorted. "You know, Tree, sometimes I think you judge me. But I don't know what you want from me."

"I would have you cast off the burden of others' expectations and be yourself, Time. You might be surprised at how good you'd feel."

"Mr. Wolf, you can't catch me," the boy needled.

"Perhaps a little fun would do me no harm at all, but don't expect me to run," he raised his voice for the child's benefit.

"Get him, dog." Time pointed at the boy and the Shadow broke its leash and leaped forward, baring its teeth.

Seconds later the boy screamed and was dragged back to the clearing and dumped at Time's feet.

Time rubbed his hands together, chuckling. "You're right, Tree. I havn't felt this good in years. I should have listened to you earlier and played along." He plucked a stray hair from his sleeve.

"That wasn't funny." The boy fought against tears that stubbornly swelled in his eyes.

"Wasn't it? Well don't blame me. It was Tree's idea. You wanted a wolf, I sent out my dog. There's no pleasing some people," he muttered.

$$\infty$$

"I don't want to play with Time anymore," the boy whispered to the Tree. "It's no fun."

"Fun! You want fun?" Time rubbed his hands together. "Then wait till you see this. Don your hat, Fool, we're going to the races."

The Shadow rummaged in the bags and finally produced a bonnet with a wide brim, bedecked with plastic flowers. It dangled it from its fingers like someone else's dirty underwear.

"Stop doddering like an idiot and put it on. It's not going to attack you," Time admonished.

The Shadow placed the item on its head and lowered its eyes in silent humiliation.

"Look at that. The pastel shades quite bring out your colour," Time smirked, as the Shadow seemed to diminish even further.

"What do you think, boy?"

Time bent over double on his deckchair to hold in his laughter, while his hands beat a drumroll on his knees.

"Oh no, what now?" the boy looked towards the Tree. A breeze lifted the Tree's leaves in as close to a shrug as a tree can muster. "Another routine, I'm afraid. I'm sorry to say that I've seen this one before."

"How does it end?" The boy drew in his breath.

"Not well. Brace yourself," the Tree warned. The boy steadied his feet and grabbed a branch for support before Time's storm of laughter subsided.

"Well now, if we're all ready?" Time wiped the merriment from his jowls. "Let the games begin."

The Shadow bent down and opened the case once again. It took out two sets of binoculars. One it gave to Time and the other to the boy. It then settled on its haunches and raised its voice to the excited pitch of a sports commentator:

"The horses are lined up in the stalls. It's going to be a thrilling race. On the inside we have a *Stitch in Time*, a nine times runner-up in the Timeless Cup. *Must Dash*, a lively horse, is 10 to 1 at the bookies. *Fool's Errand* is being ridden by Time. *Past Times* is on the outside. But the unbeaten runner and the bookies' favourite is *Tomorrow Never Comes*.

"The bell's rung and the horses are off. *Must Dash* has made a good start from the stalls. The horses are coming up to the first bend. *Past Times* is already lagging behind. Its jockey seems to be having some trouble. What's this? *Past Times* has turned around and is running back towards the stalls! The stewards are on the track and they're chasing him down. The horses have reached the third bend. *Past Times* is out of the race. But it's all to play for as *Fool's Errand* has pulled a nose ahead of a *Stitch in Time*. Time is really cracking the whip. *Fool's Errand* is now moving comfortably into second place as it takes the bend. *A Stitch in Time's* hopes are unraveling on the straight. There are just two runners left to watch: *Tomorrow Never Comes* and *Fool's Errand*."

The boy and Time were both on their feet, binoculars pressed against their faces. "Come on, Fool," they roared in unison.

"With just one more lap to go, the finish line is in sight. *Tomorrow Never Comes* is keeping a good lead. He's stretched ahead a full stride. This horse shows no sign of tiring. But wait, what's this? I don't believe it. Time is leaning forward in his saddle. He has a hold of *Tomorrow's* tail. He's trying to slow him down. *Tomorrow* has shaken him loose and is racing towards the finish. *Fool's Errand* doesn't stand a chance. *Tomorrow Never Comes* has past the post. Ladies and gentlemen, *Tomorrow* has won the race." The Shadow gulped a deep draught of air.

"What a finish. This horse has never shown better form. I'm waiting for confirmation, but I think that it may have just broken its personal record.

"Time is standing outside the winners' enclosure. He is looking explosive. His performance today will certainly be the subject of an inquiry. He has thrown down his whip and, in a most unsporting manner, is kicking *Fool's Errand*. The stewards have surrounded him and are dragging him from the arena.

"Attention is back on *Tomorrow Never Comes*, which is nowhere to be seen. The cup is sitting on its stand, but it seems that it will not be collected this year. The disappointed spectators are filing out of the terraces."

The commentary stopped as Time flung himself back onto his chair and threw his binoculars at the Shadow, which obediently packed them securely in the heavy suitcase, along with the hat.

As Time turned to the Tree his face softened and his eyes took on a wistful look, "One of these days we'll catch up with it," he said. "It was almost within my grasp. We just need to run a little faster."

∞

"All this running is leading you nowhere," the Tree cautioned.

"Tree, I'm not like you. You know I can't sit still for any length of time. If I stay in one place for too long, I fear I'll shrivel up in a rocking chair and count out the days saluting magpies."

He shifted his bulk more comfortably. "I can't just relax while my bones are picked clean by carrion. What sort of message would that give? I have things I need to do. Places I need to be. People are counting on me to tick off the seconds until I pass by."

"You are squandering your life in pursuit of something that isn't even real. The future is a phantom, Time. It simply does not exist."

"Nonsense, Tree, of course it does. It has to. Otherwise, what is there? Tomorrow is just about the only thing that does make any sense. Without the dream of something better, we might as well scrabble in the muck and forget that there even is a sky.

"It's okay for you, Tree. Your life is made up of roots and horizons. You belong to the heavens as you do to the earth. The rest of us have to make do with tin and shoddy workmanship. It's hard to have faith in anything, least of all in ourselves and certainly not in each other."

"Then undo the knots that tie you to anchors." The Tree's gaze grazed Time and the Shadow.

Time looked at his feet, his face hidden. "It's not that easy. People need me."

"You're riddled with time-worn excuses," the Tree admonished. "People don't need a pack of empty promises."

"They're not empty promises. Tomorrow's out there. I can feel it. And it will be better than this sorry substitute for an existence." He wrinkled his mouth in a grimace as though he wanted to spit a glob of bile. He swallowed hard, "I'll prove it to you, Tree. Mark my words. I will run a little faster and waste less time garbling nonsense. I will grab hold of the beast and drag it screaming to your feet. I will cut its throat and pour its blood over your roots. You will feel the surge of ecstasy that I have been chasing. Then you will know that all of this was worth it."

"No thanks, Time. I don't want your sacrifice."

"You say that now. But when I have it on its knees, you'll beg, like everyone else, for a taste of Tomorrow."

"So, I too feature amongst your blind fantasies?" The Tree looked bemused. "Keep your gift, Time. There is no place here for a future gained by a whip and a past tied up by a chain."

"I would never sully you in my reveries. I just want you to believe in me, Tree."

"I have never lost faith in you. Time gives meaning to endings and beginnings and encourages us to dive into the chasm that lies between."

"I'd prefer not to be wrapped around that dark hole, thank you very much," Time sniffed. "I'm either counting backwards or marching forwards. Otherwise, how would we get anywhere? Who on earth would choose to be stuck in the interminable moment? I'm a man of action, Tree, and the future's my quarry.

"I'd have caught up with it by now if that useless Fool hadn't poked holes in its feet with endless excuses." Time spat a dart of fury at the Shadow, which cowered at his spite and pulled its bare, broken feet beneath its shroud.

The Tree considered the creature, which seemed to ache beneath the gaze in its longing to disappear.

Time caught the look, "Must I tell you again? Don't waste your love on that one, Tree. It's nothing more than a corpse dangling at the end of a rope."

∞

The Shadow picked at its halter then settled again, its shoulders hunched and its knees drawn tightly to its chest. Through the shards of its limp, grey mane it caught glimpses of the child as he ran hel-ter-skelter amongst the bushes and trees, tumbling in a heap in the long grass, overcome with a fit of giggles, then jumping up as though his short trousers had been set on fire. He tore back to the Tree for deep breaths and gulps of water, before dashing off again. Though following seemingly random trails, he never once strayed towards where the Shadow huddled. Yet the creature saw the stains the earth had seared on the child's knees and caught the sweet smell of sweat and summer clover in his tangled hair.

These images played before its eyes, yet seemed frozen over a vast distance and pieced together like strips of a torn picture. The Shadow retreated further into its darkness to watch the old reel sputter out a summer that seemed to engulf the child in a heady adventure that involved long, sunny days, choc ices, freedom from chores and tired lists, games played amongst cow parsley, bedtimes that stretched as the sun loitered over the horizon, finally ending in soft beds and dreamless sleeps. Or perhaps that was someone else's memories. The Shadow could never really be sure.

The Shadow closed its eyes and pressed its bony fingers to its lids. Stars spangled and wavered before its vision. All seemed quiet for a single moment. Then the child's voice rippled across the clearing.

"I can hear it." The Shadow strained to pick up the thread. "Of course you can," Time's voice verged on the indignant. "What did you expect?"

"Well," the boy foolishly didn't even hesitate, "I thought you might be empty."

Time choked as the boy reinserted the earpieces and placed the head of the stethoscope once again against his chest.

"I've never heard a clock up close before," the boy explained.

"My ticker's a marvel," Time informed him. "Never misses a beat."

Neither did the boy, "So you're real, then." The Shadow couldn't tell if it was a question.

Time seemed to hold his breath, as though waiting for an explosion. "The ticking's getting faster," the boy excitedly informed the spectators.

The Shadow couldn't remember packing the stethoscope. But it couldn't remember a lot of things. It watched Time's face get redder and redder. Time itself seemed to go faster. Tick tock. Tick tock. Tick tock. The boy didn't know the danger he was in. The Shadow's heart stuttered and sped up. Time was rocking on his feet. If the stethoscope had been left behind this would never have happened. It was all the Shadow's fault. Everything was its fault. It was a fool. A cloud flitted across the sun. Suddenly it felt cool in the glade. It shuddered as it heard the whip whistle across its shoulders, stripping its skin. Another memory. Its own. Of that, it was certain. It looked at the boy and at Time's twitching fingers, and it felt fear for another.

Tree laughed, "Time's as real as I am." The cloud passed and the shadow lifted.

"You have a heart, too?" the boy asked.

"Of course," the Tree replied. "Without it I would lose hope, wither and eventually die. It's the heart that keeps me going. It's what links me to all other living creatures and allows me to play my part in the world we share."

"Can I listen to it?" the boy asked.

"Place the stethoscope against my bark and listen carefully for a murmur beneath my skin. It beats strongest in spring when the sap rises faster and my limbs and joints crackle and creak and stretch a little further. Even old things like me have their growth spurts. It's fainter in summer, but you should be able to hear it nonetheless."

The boy placed the metal circle against the thickly veined bark. "Move it to my North side," the Tree advised. "It's thinner there. Now, hold it steady."

The Shadow held its breath. Could a tree really have a heart, it wondered, while it, a creature of flesh and blood, had none?

The boy's eyes popped open with sudden excitement. "I can hear it." The Shadow breathed out.

"It sounds nothing like Time's heart," he informed the clearing. "Time ticks along with a steady rhythm; Tree crackles and gurgles like an excited stream." He listened intently for another few minutes. "I can hear you grow."

Time looked smug, "Well, that's your problem right there. You need to get that heart of yours under control, Tree. Keep this up and you'll spill your love in all directions, sparing no one. You will ache and moan and feel the pain of disappointments. You will give and give and seek nothing in return for all you offer. My heart, on the other hand, is perfectly trained and contained. It takes no risks nor wastes its affections where they are not deserved. I live as I please, heeding no one but myself."

"I would as soon cage a bird as I would contain my heart," the Tree responded.

$$\infty$$

"How do you get the birds to nest in your branches?" Time asked. "This music is as lovely a thing as ever I've heard. I would like to take this little piece of forest with me when we leave."

"I neither court them, nor plead their return," the Tree responded. "They come as they please and leave as they choose. I am grateful for their song and they appreciate my shelter."

"Well, that will never work," Time assured the Tree. "If we want to capture one of those nice singing black ones, we'll need a plan. I have the prettiest cage you've ever seen. Its gilded bars and hand-painted water dish will perfectly set off the metallic gleam lighting up that one's feathers. But look at its scheming little yellow-rimmed eyes. I can tell that it won't be easily fooled."

The boy followed Time's pointed finger. Beautiful music spilled out of a bright orange beak. The boy had heard the sound throughout the summer, but hadn't really listened, or wondered about its source.

Time looked speculatively at the boy. "It's too high. I could never let you climb all the way up there. I'm sure you're big for your age, but you wouldn't be able to make it. I think I'd need an older child to go up and entice the bird into my net."

Time snapped his fingers and the Shadow darted to the case and pulled out a bird catcher which was attached to a long pole.

It handed it to Time, who looked the boy up and down. "No, no, it would never do. It's far too dangerous. I would need someone who's a really fearless climber."

"I could do it, Time. I'm really good at climbing. Aren't I, Tree? I'm old enough. Please, Time, let me have a go," the boy pleaded.

"Well, I'm really not sure about this. But if you're going to insist," he trailed off.

The boy took the net from Time and headed towards the bottom branch.

Time smirked a thin, mirthless smile before turning to the Shadow, "Get the cage, Fool. And be sure to shake out the old, stale feathers."

The boy climbed slowly, hindered by the long pole.

"Careful now," Time cautioned, as the Shadow rummaged for the cage. "You don't want to scare it off."

The bird sang its heart out, as the boy inched upward.

Time looked at its clear, sharp eyes and rubbed his hands together gleefully before testing the lock on the door of the cage.

"What's that for?" the boy called from his perch, as he rested a moment.

"For the bird, of course," Time shouted back. "It will make a lovely little home for him, don't you think? I'll take care of him and he'll never need worry again about rising before the sun to root out the early worms."

"It's nice, alright," the boy agreed, "but it's awfully small. He won't be able to fly in there."

"Why would he want to fly, when the Fool will carry him on its back?"

"I'm not sure about this, Time," the boy faltered. "If he can't fly, what will he do?"

"He'll sing. More beautifully than ever. There's nothing like heart-ache to add feeling to a tune. I've bred birds in my time, but domesti-cated fowl are nothing compared to the wild ones. Timid, stupid little things, they live in terror of their cage door being opened. Faced with the choice of flight or captivity, they'd rather perch on a swing and beat their heads off their bars.

"But this one will be magnificent. It will be tormented by the mem-ory of freedom and flight. It will struggle and fight and each note will be torn from its throat in anguish. The light in those nasty eyes will fade as hope diminishes, and it will pluck and tear at its skin. It will litter its cage with its excrement and feathers and stink the place up with its grief. It will pine and writhe and its suffering will culminate in one last perfect note, before it fades away. That, too, I will claim.

"Indeed, it is only right that I own the beauty, if I am to be the cause of the pain that inspired it. Make no mistake, child, one cannot exist without the other. Great art requires great suffering."

The net slipped from the boy's hands and spilled to the ground. It was only then that the child realized that the singing had stopped, and the bird had flown.

$$\infty$$

"No one appreciates the lengths I go to bring a little beauty into the world." Time sullenly stuck out his bottom lip.

"You would have killed it," the boy accused him.

"You would have trapped it," Time reminded him.

The boy hung his head in shame.

"My plan's in shards." Time kicked the awkward stone. "Ouch. That hurt. Who put that there?" he demanded, as he hobbled back to his seat.

"Master's in pain," the Shadow fell to his knees and began to loosen Time's shoe.

"Perhaps he can write a sonnet about it," the Tree wryly suggested. Time threw it a withering glance, before sitting back comfortably, as the Shadow set about rubbing his foot.

"Pain is part of life," the Tree commented, "but there is no reason to woo it so that it simpers and simmers and spills over everything that is joyful and good. There is pain enough in the world without you adding to the scales for your own amusement."

"That's harsh, Tree," Time looked hurt.

"I don't speak to wound you. I seek to help you open your eyes. Your cravings are blinding you, Time. You no longer see what is before you."

Time looked around the clearing. "I can see perfectly well. There were suggestions that I might need glasses for close reading, but that was just speculation. You know, it's probably time we got moving." He peered at his wristwatch, drew his arm close then stretched it away from him, tilting his head back. "We probably have a few more minutes to idle. It was hinted that spectacles might give me a certain distinction. I did toy with the notion of a monocle. But I see no reason to acquire such items for vanity's sake. Perhaps when I'm a little older and the eyesight's not as sharp as it once was. For now, Tree, I can see an ant on a hilltop."

47

"But not what's at the end of your nose," the Tree remarked.

Time squinted as he peered down the length of his face. "There's nothing to see, Tree. Oh, butterfly," he pointed. "Nothing gets past me." He looked speculatively at the Tree. "What are you angling at, anyway? Have you done something different that I haven't noticed?" He gave the Tree a good once over. "Those leaves aren't new, are they?"

"The same ones I've had since spring."

"You're looking well. Summer suits you."

The Tree sighed. "The season will soon be passed, and you will have missed it in your rush towards autumn."

"Shame on you, Tree. You would misrepresent me to the child. I have nothing against summer. In fact, I rather like it, though I'd prefer if it wasn't so hot. Indeed, who wouldn't enjoy it? It's the season of cool drinks at 11 and sundowners at nine. It would be perfect, if it wasn't for the sun, the pollen and those pesky flies." Time sneezed sharply, three off-key trumpets blasted in quick succession.

"They don't give me a moment's peace. They're constantly buzzing around my head, drunk on my fumes, dive-bombing my glass." His voice took on a petulant tone. "I don't know what they have against me. I've tried everything. I've even reasoned with them, but they simply won't be stopped. They're like kamikaze fighters, determined to destroy my tipple, so they might perish in the flesh of a few ripe cherries. And don't get me started on the midges!" He swatted at the air above his head. "One sniff of my sweat, and they're worse than a shoal of sharks on a feeding frenzy." Time patted his damp forehead with his handkerchief. "Lord, it's hot. Will this damnable season never end? Fool, my fan!"

The Shadow unearthed a fan, made of swan's feathers, from one of the suitcases, and hovered at Time's side.

"Put a little effort into it," Time snapped.

"You see what I have to put up with, Tree. I have to do everything for myself. I've been run off my feet this last while. I havn't had a minute's rest or a moment's peace from that one's moans and mutterings." He jerked his head at the Shadow, which fanned a little faster.

"Perhaps you should listen to what it's trying to say," Tree suggested.

Time looked incredulous. "Next you'll be telling me to plot sense out of the stars. You're losing your edge, Tree. Perhaps all those leaves are cluttering your brain."

"Time, you and I have known each other many, many years. Over this time, I have seen great changes in you. Your obsession with Tomorrow is clouding your judgment and sharpening your cruelties."

"Tree, you know me well enough to know that I'm all bluster. I wouldn't hurt a fly." Time swatted at his neck. "Got it!"

∞

"I'm far too soft for my own good. You've seen how the dog practically orders me about, always prodding me to do its bidding. I don't know who else would put up with its constant whining. I should have put it out of its misery the moment I clapped eyes on it." The Shadow trembled beneath Time's tirade.

"It won't leave me be. It's always there, staring at me with those holes of eyes, its tongue hanging out for whatever scraps I might drop. I can't eat in peace, knowing it's watching me. I can't lounge at ease, knowing it's timing me. It's an empty, hollow thing that dogs my every step."

"It's just an idea, but you could take off its leash," the boy proposed.

Time practically snarled, "It would tear your throat out as soon as it would look at you, boy. Don't be fooled by its apparent passiveness. It never, ever sleeps. It's always watching. Waiting for an opportunity to drain my marrow and grind my bones."

The boy looked at the Shadow, which seemed to have shriveled to a dry husk of misery, its eyes downcast.

"Maybe it's just not happy," the child suggested.

"Happiness. Is that the sort of drivel the Tree's teaching you? This universal obsession with happiness is driving us all insane. I don't care what Tree has told you, make no mistake, boy, happiness is the ruination of the world. Of course, it's all anyone ever talks about these days. Every second person you meet blathers on and on about it. It's nothing but happiness this and happiness that, as though life held no other promises. Mark my words, it's just a fad. It will wear itself out and people will wake up to the truth that it's nothing more than a fine cloak draped over a rotting body."

Time suppressed a snigger as he pictured the sagging gut and shriveled prunes hiding their ignominy beneath a gossamer shroud, trailed by the dirt-filled claws and dripping teeth of a roaring mob, incensed at having been duped.

"Don't be fooled, child. Happiness is a knife wrapped in silk, gliding across the belly. It always hurts. It tricks you for a time that life is kinder and more beautiful than it really is and then, just when you believe it, it's thrust into your gut and given a good old twist before it's snatched away again. You're better off never having felt it. It makes everything else taste of dust, and leaves you craving what you can't have. Before you know it, you're on your knees at the end of a whip, trading your soul for a snort of oblivion."

"It's not happiness, but craving that's the problem," Tree interjected.

"Here we go," Time sighed, shooting the boy a look. "You just had to bring it up, didn't you?"

The Tree ignored Time's eye-rolling and continued. "Craving is at the root of all suffering. The knife that you speak of is the point of desire that sharpens thirst and denies satisfaction. Yearning after that which you do not possess, aching to be who you are not, and grasping towards a future that does not exist, leads to despair."

Time fidgeted in his chair. "All right then, we should probably get going. We've taken up far too much of your time already."

The Tree continued, "Disappointments become gut-twisting anxieties, and days become colourless voids.

"Happiness is a state of fulfillment that is noble and that should be sought. But it can only be achieved by understanding that joy and pain are both part of life. They are temporary and they pass. One who has achieved happiness experiences both with equal equanimity and neither scours the night sky for sunlight, nor hunts for the moon at midday."

Time rooted in his pockets and found a sheet of paper. In another he unearthed a straw. As quietly as he could manage, he tore the paper into small scraps and scrunched them into bullets. Loading his straw, he took aim.

"Oi," yelled the boy, grabbing his neck. "Tut," muttered Time. "Would you be quiet. I'm trying to listen to Tree."

"Craving severs our connection with the world and our place in it. It devours happiness and creates an emptiness that can never be filled."

Time became uncomfortably aware of his earlier snack of roast chicken and wine. His stomach gurgled and fumed. He couldn't hold it in any longer. He let out a mighty rift. The gas formed a dense cloud around him. He drew in a warm, secret scent of putrid eggs and rotten berries. "That's disgusting."

The smell seeped around the clearing. "It wasn't me!" the boy hastened to defend himself. Time waved his hand in front of his face, fanning a splutter of coughing, then flung a filthy look at the Shadow. "Revolting creature," he grimaced, loud enough for all to hear.

The Tree impassively continued, "Searching for what you don't have means that you lose sight of all that you do. Once we recognize that the past is gone and the future is a false promise, we become what we were always meant to be: masters of the present. And, like the moon, even a shadow can come out from behind the clouds and shine."

The Shadow raised its eyes and looked directly at the Tree. The boy thought that he saw a flicker of awareness in its eyes. However, the moment was so brief that he could not be sure.

The Shadow seemed to shake itself and then crawled towards Time. "Master," it whined, "we must hurry. We are running late. There are people to be seen and places to be visited. The future lies ahead. There is no time to lose." Time kicked it away, but arose, nonetheless.

"My friends," he said, "I must take my leave of you. There is not enough time in the day, and certainly not a drop to be wasted. We must indeed hurry and be on our way."

"Move out, slave," he commanded. The Shadow picked up the bags. Time picked up his whip and, as suddenly as they had arrived, they were gone.

∞

"Tree," the boy looked worried, "should we follow them? What if they catch up with Tomorrow and we miss it?"

"Chasing the future is like trying to catch a cloud with a fishing net," said the Tree.

"There is no past and there is no tomorrow," the Tree instructed. "What we have is this single moment. Once it is lived, it too is gone. Consider the baby you once were. Now compare that to the boy you have become. Every breath you take that boy is also changing."

"But I don't want things to change," the boy interrupted. "I want to reach my next birthday, and after that I want everything to remain just exactly as it is."

"That is not possible," said the Tree. "To live is to change, to shine and to fade away like a star at dawn. Nothing remains the same."

"You do," countered the boy.

"Not at all. It is summertime now, and my branches are filled with leaves. Come autumn my leaves will fall, and I shall feel each one shiver off my limbs, and I shall know that another season has passed."

∞

"How old are you?" asked the boy. The Tree thought for some moments and then replied, "I am as old as time. Possibly even older."

"How can that be?" asked the boy, who was very puzzled.

"We are as old as our memories," said the Tree, "and I carry the memories of all that gives life to this world."

The Tree explained, "Every living being is a part of the world, as the world is part of them. We are all born with this knowledge, but many forget it or simply lose it along the way. My roots are held firm by the earth. They carry the memories of water through my capillaries, as your veins carry blood to every atom of your body. The fire of the sun gives me energy, and this energy enables me to absorb carbon dioxide from the atmosphere and breathe out oxygen in return. The world nourishes me and helps me to grow and, in this way, my roots stretch a little deeper, and my arms reach a little further every year. I neither fear, nor measure, the passing of time, as it holds no power over my memories."

The boy sat beneath the shade of the Tree. He breathed in, and he breathed out. Time passed. The boy changed and he got a little older. And maybe even a little wiser. Though perhaps not very much as, later that evening, he climbed to the topmost branch of the Tree with his fishing pole.

"What are you doing?" asked the Tree.

"I will catch you a cloud."

"Good," said the Tree. "Experience is the very best of teachers." The boy swatted at the sky till his arms ached and the light began to fade.

He finally climbed down, weary and defeated, and threw himself on the earth amongst the late summer flowers. In a little while his breathing quieted and his mind unwound and stretched out. His pole lay abandoned in a cluster of ferns, forgotten for the time being, as he cradled his head on his arm and watched the clouds drift past.

The first evening star hung low in the sky while a parade of cotton animals, their toes dipped in floss, flitted through the boy's imagination. The sun slipped beneath the horizon and the day came to an end as a leaf fell off the Tree and drifted slowly to the earth.

AUTUMN

The boy lay under the Tree looking at the spaces between its leaves. "How many leaves are on a tree?" he asked. "You might as well ask how many stars are in the sky," the Tree responded.

From the distance of the earth, they all looked the same to the boy. But, up close, their veins traced swirls as intricate and unique as a fingerprint.

As the summer waned to autumn, the Tree explained that green would seep from its leaves and that its growth would slow to conserve its energy as the days shortened and the light, necessary to produce its food, would dim.

The boy looked concerned. "Won't you be hungry?" he asked.

"Not at all, my body has stored all that it needs. As autumn wanders through the forest, with its warnings of winter and promises of spring, my heart will settle into a quiet murmur and my mind will retrace my memories. It has lots of ground to cover and many new thoughts to track. I like autumn," the Tree confided. "It dusts off the old cobwebs and gives me space to think."

Dressed in a wooly jumper and a brightly woven scarf, the boy ventured a little deeper into the forest. The early morning was his favourite time, when his breath lingered in the air and the low sun glinted off silver spider threads that criss-crossed bushes and branches, ready to snare the unwary.

He walked with his hands buried deep in his pockets, breathing in the rich, woody smell of damp leaves, crackling tinder twigs beneath his boots. The Tree told him that autumn was the season of soil, when everything was drawn to the earth. It was the time when the creatures of the forest began their preparations to return to their burrows, and leaves and stalks drifted to the ground, which absorbed their nutrients as they decomposed.

The air bristled with activity and, as the Tree had predicted, the leaves bled their greens. In their place, a spectrum of colour was revealed. It was hard to believe that the summer had concealed such a fury of yellows, reds, oranges and burgundies beneath its calm exterior. To the child the forest looked incensed and wild, as though one of the ancient fire gods had trailed its magic through the foliage. But the Tree assured him that it was simply the nature of things to change. Without this transformation the forest could not survive. It was the most natural thing in the world, it insisted.

Smells deepened and darkened and hinted at secrets in the earth and a life beneath the soil. Leaves withered and tumbled in great gusts from the trees in sudden winds that seemed to rise from nowhere and meekly retire, surprised by their own bold outbursts.

The child wondered if he too should start building a nest in the earth, so that he might partake of the world beneath the epidermis of the forest. He watched the squirrels gather their stores, and set aside some of his own treats, in anticipation of a colder time when he might need their sugary comforts. The Tree laughed, however, and told him that it was not in his nature to sleep through the months of darkness. The boy sucked thoughtfully on a toffee and agreed that the Tree was probably right.

The day came when the boy was almost able to count the leaves left trembling on the branches, though he preferred to kick the bundles that cluttered the forest floor, sending flurries scuttering into the air. He whirled through the clearing, arms outstretched, inviting the trees to break free of their roots and join him.

∞

It was, perhaps, that very same day, while he spun like a dervish, that a terse voice interrupted his twirling. "Come closer, child." There was an urgency to its tone that the boy had not heard before. Without question he ran towards the Tree, as a wild breeze rose and spun behind him, snapping at his heels and drawing everything it could grasp into its vortex.

"What is it?" the boy gasped, as he clung to the sturdy trunk and watched the whorling spiral bend and weave, spinning leaves and twigs in its widening gyres.

"Hold on," the Tree warned. The boy felt the wind sharpen its edges as it cut through the clearing. "What's happening?" The wind caught and tossed his voice and tore tears from his eyes. He clung to the branches. The vortex came closer, growing in strength. His scarf stood out stiff from his neck and his bones felt chilled and the child feared that it would pull him into its core. It was almost upon him. The boy was lifted off his feet, but his fingers still gripped the trunk. "I'm slipping, Tree," he cried.

"Lies!"

The world stopped spinning. His feet fell to the flat earth and he landed in a thump on top of them.

The wind died and the child regained his breath and his balance, which he lost a moment later when he looked up to see an old woman with wild dark hair, eight arms, and unblinking eyes staring down upon him.

∞

She trapped him in her gaze a moment longer, before dismissing him from her sight.

"Weaver," said the Tree, "you are welcome."

She looked the Tree up and down, appraising its height and judging its strength. A broad smile stretched her face, but it was still not wide enough to reach her eyes, which protruded from a head far too small for its round body. As she assessed the Tree, two hands rested on her hips, a large square handbag hung from the crook of an arm, a hand patted her hair behind her ears, another smoothed the front of her dark hemp dress which covered her frame from neck to knee, two hands crooked a steeple underneath her chin, while another twitched and snatched at the air, as if reaching for something just beyond its grasp.

Her thick legs were hidden by dense wool tights that gathered at her ankles above wide, laced-up shoes.

With little preamble and less ado, she creaked to her knees and implored the Tree,

"Lovely Tree
Timeless Tree
Sprinkle leaves
And shower me

With long life, luck
And lots of seeds
That will produce
A greenback yield."

"I'm not sure that I understand," a bemused Tree responded as she rose to her feet, rooted in her handbag and produced a roll of ribbon and a jar of saffron, one of which she proceeded to daub on its trunk, and the other which she wrapped around its waist.

She painfully lowered herself back to her knees and, with no little drama, she raised her eight hands in supplication:

"*I beseech thee,*
Dear Tree, I pray
You'll answer me
This very day."

"I don't know what the question is," the Tree prompted her to speak clearly. She blew out sharply and then dragged herself up once again, before she gave it another go. This time she spoke very, very slowly, deliberately stressing each word.

"*In truth it's loot*
I beg of thee
To help me feed
My family.

A greedy pack
A feckless lot
Who live to fill
Their belly-pots.

I'll gladly stir
If you can line
My bag with cash
And grubby coin."

"Weaver, surely you know that money does not grow on trees?"
She ignored the interruption and continued, as though she were speaking to an idiot king.

"As I cannot
Compete with thee
In wealth and pomp
And majesty

I call upon
Your lofty heart
To heap our plates
With sweets and tarts."

When the Weaver had rattled off her rhymes, she hung brightly coloured yarn from the lower boughs of the Tree, like garlands. It was as fine as spider silk, and it glinted in the sun.

The boy was dazzled by the finery, but a little frightened of the Weaver. The colours she draped spread the warmth of winter fires, but her eyes were as cold as a frostbitten morning. Her smile was loaded with bullet white teeth and, like her hands, it never rested for a moment. The boy suspected that she put it on in the morning with her garments, and wrapped it up again at night before she went to bed.

All the while she worked, she mumbled. Fetid words, churned by a frenzied mind, breached her defenses and crawled into the forest. She shook her head to clear the clatter, but the creatures that clawed her walls scrawled their demands on her every waking moment.

The boy just caught odd snatches that hung in the air. Jagged lines of thought that tripped and snared the ones that followed.

'Snakes in our dreams, winding tight,' a voice shrieked in the darkness. She tried to ignore it.

'Chokes our throat,' another gasped.

A stronger voice stifled the moans. 'Hearts and minds bound and bowed,' it said. But this was rapidly displaced by a sharp intake of breath.

'Torn dress.' The Weaver startled and patted the folds of her frock. 'Flesh devours flesh.'

'Starve them, then feed them their deepest fears,' a creature instructed. The boy, who was watching her work, thought he heard a snarl, but the Weaver's lips quickly covered her sharp teeth and a sliver of breath escaped as a whimper.

'Where am I? I want to go home.'

'Beg,' another demanded.

'Dredge up the smile.'

'We're slipping.'

The Weaver smiled at the Tree as she hung another garland.

'There's nowhere to hide,' they told her.

"Lies!" The accusation rose as a scream that the Weaver hastened to stifle.

The startled boy stepped back to watch from the safety of the foliage.

'It's too bright.' A hand covered her eyes for a moment.

He was fascinated by what she might do, but loathe to be caught in her gaze.

'Lights. It's time. We're on.'

Arms and legs swiveled in the boy's direction and, before he knew it, her face was inches from his own.

∞

He could smell her stale breath.

"*Little fly.*
Aghem,
I mean, boy."

She corrected, then collected herself, sidled backward and studied the child closely. She hummed, as fingers drummed her chin.

"A trifle thin
Around the rim

But I like him
Just the same.

I could tame
His wide-eyed wonder

Tape his mind shut
Cull his brain."

The boy started at her words, but she put out a reassuring hand, loaded her smile and patted his arm. Then she rooted in her copious handbag. After some time, she pulled a measuring tape from out of its dark recesses. She stretched it across the boy's chest and his back. She measured his arms, then noted the distance from armpit to hip. Finally, she wrapped the tape, rather tightly the boy thought, around his neck. She jotted each measurement in a small black notebook.

"What is she doing?" the startled boy hissed at the Tree.

"I believe she is measuring you up," the Tree responded.

When she had finished, she sucked thoughtfully on her teeth.

"The boy is clearly wide awake.
I hope I have not come too late."

Then she shook her massive body, ending with her tiny head, out of her despondency, and straightened the barrel of her smile. She declaimed officiously,

"A spark's been lit, the boy's found favour
So I shall knit a lovely jumper
To wrap the little child in winter.

I'll mix the tincture from finest dyes
Colours that tingle and creep up spines
Shivering tints of darkness and night.

Blended just right to bleed through my yarn
Seep through the riot of plain and purl
Weaving a rigorous blend of swirls.

Patterns this world has yet to conceive
Delightful whorls the length of the sleeves
A jumper worthy of lords and kings.

Stitching that sings of knitting supreme
Almost a sin to speak of the seams
Mastery singular to my dreams."

Her voice lurched and rolled, and her hands swatted at the air.
A chaos of thoughts spilled out of her vicious mouth, staining the
peace of the clearing, while the creatures in her mind screeched their
applause. Her audience, forgotten, stood wide-eyed and frightened,
huddled close to the sanctuary of the Tree.

"Thoughts lurch and teem with spinning flurries
Suck at the teats of righteous Furies
Sink in the teeth and chew on stories

Of winter's freeze and wooly designs
Mind given free rein slowly unwinds
Images frieze framed of flies entwined

Caught in a bind of fancy stitches
Stuffed on a binge of lies lie listless
On cold steel bins our pile of riches

Can't stand the itch of Weaver's embrace
Necklines that etch chains wrought to enslave
Worse than death it's a tumble from grace."

She caught the child's horrified gaze, cradled the fear and stroked the loathing. Then counseled herself towards stealth and guile. All the while dripping words that were carried on the wind and lodged, unwanted, in the minds of innocent listeners. Her wintery smile stretched wide.

"More smiles less haste, don't frighten the child
All he's learned has polluted his mind
Our murky haze will reign in good time.

For now, our rhymes will fool and beguile
Beat deadly rhythms and spin with lies
Then find the right moment to douse lives.

Spit out the bile and sweeten the bite
Loosen the bind and release the night
Swarm with a billion flies when time's right.

Don't try to fight until the boy's bound
Must drag this figment of light to ground
Then wrap his figure in our wool shroud.

Not crass or loud but a woven treat
No torn or loose knots to mar the feat
Wasted on louts who dance among leaves.

I dream of sleeves all woven with vines
Hems that are sleek and seams quite divine
Studded with sleep and riddled with sighs."

"It sounds like a jumper to die for," said the Tree.

She cackled. It was a mirthless laugh, stripped of all humour. The creatures retreated to the dark corners of her mind, where they belonged. Their voices stilled, for now.

The boy looked flustered. He nudged the Tree, "She knows we can hear her, doesn't she? Anyway, I don't care what she says. I don't want her jumper." He gathered his courage and stood firm, until the Weaver swiveled her eyes upon him.

He blushed and looked down. She didn't blink. He cleared his throat and shifted his feet. "Erm," he began. "You know, it sounds lovely and all that, but I really don't need a new jumper."

He fidgeted. She held her ground and her hands froze rigid. "I appreciate the thought, but I hardly ever feel the cold. Isn't that right?" the boy appealed to the Tree.

She pointed her smile and lowered her voice. "For now you're young, but the winter's long. I've heard your song, but it too will fade. You will learn, as your blood runs cold, that my jumper is all that keeps death at bay."

"Besides," the boy battled on bravely, struggling against her gaze. "I already have two jumpers exactly like the one you described. They're practically new, as I've hardly ever worn them."

"Hurmph," said the Weaver, greatly affronted. "Other's purl, I'm sure, is fine, but no one's can compare to mine."

She turned her head from the boy and stalked up to the Tree. She fired it a grim grin before she plopped her bag open, hauled out her yarn and needles, settled her back against the trunk and started knitting furiously.

The boy shrugged at the Tree and whispered, "I didn't mean to offend her. I'm sure she knits very well. It's just that I really don't want another lumpy jumper that itches my arms and chokes my neck."

The Tree chuckled, "Don't worry. You can snag the Weaver's yarn, slip past her charms, stay safe from harm."

"How?" asked the boy.

"By staying awake and following your path; by being fearless and by opening your heart."

"Ah, simple really," the boy elbowed the Tree playfully.

As they talked the needles loaded and fired stitches at machine gun speed. In no time at all, the Weaver had completed the hem for the front of the jumper. All the while she mumbled to herself. The boy caught the odd snippet of her muttered snarl.

"Slip one, purl two
churlish child

Guile and lies
Should trap the fly.

Slip one, purl two
Bind him tight

Drop a stitch
Seal his mind.

Slip one, purl two
Draw the line

A little night
To match his eyes."

The Weaver pulled some ink coloured yarn from her bag. The boy shuddered and leaned closer to the Tree.

∞

As she clicked her needles and sucked her teeth, the boy crouched close to the Tree, but as far from the Weaver's determined knitting as he could manage. "Who is she, Tree?" he furtively lowered his voice.

"The Weaver is just one of the names that she is known by," the Tree told him. "Spinner, Spider, Stitcher, Fixer are others that are whispered throughout the land. Her skills are spoken of far and wide; and because she spins in rhymes that no one can understand, she is considered by some to be very wise."

"She scares me," the boy confessed. "She makes me feel really cold." He wrapped his arms around his chest to keep the chill at bay. "But don't tell her that, whatever you do." The clacking of the Weaver's needles could be heard above their whispers.

"She brings the winds from the North with her, where she holds sway," the Tree told him. "That's why your bones shiver."

"Where is that?" the child asked. "Is it further than the forest's edge?"

"The North lies beyond any place you have ever imagined."

"What's it like?"

"It's the cold, cruel point of a knife, without conscience and without remorse. It stretches its fingers around the sun, choking its light and casting a shadow on the world."

"It doesn't sound very nice."

"It was, once. But that time is long past. It has been strip mined of warmth and colour and compassion. It is a place of great darkness and deep sadness. The only lights to pierce the gloom are the few renegade stars that sneak past the clouds on restless nights, and even they are viewed as enemies, though the source of their fire is long dead and their light millions of miles away."

"Why would anyone want to live there, let alone rule it?" the boy asked.

"In the darkness a beast will be believed beautiful, if its voice sounds sweet. Words can weave their own spell and create a fiction that will be repeated as truth, if it is seductive enough. A good story, well told, will keep the listener fixed on the dancing shadows, oblivious to the real drama unfolding behind their back."

The Tree continued, "In the darkness a beast can gorge on blood and marrow and hope and joy. It can take what it wants and discard what it steals. It can rule over the night with fear, and steal and slip through the alleys unchecked and unseen."

The boy shuddered. "Is there no hope there at all?"

"Sparks have been lit, but brutally extinguished. Hope threatens the darkness. If light were to seep into the North, the power the beast hoards would be greatly diminished. Power creates a terrible thirst that must be satisfied by draining the lifeblood of others. It will not easily be denied."

"Is the Weaver the beast that you speak of?" the boy asked, his voice dropping below a whisper.

"She is one of its guises. She has savoured its hunger and dragged many others to her web to sate its need. But what she is has yet to be revealed. There are depths of emptiness in her mind that she has filled with pain and darkness. Her self-loathing spatters over all her thoughts and actions. She would escape, if she could leave herself behind. But everywhere she goes she carries that burden with her. She douses light so that she does not have to look upon what she has become. It is only in the darkness that she can hide from who she is."

"Why did she come here?" the boy asked.

"She believes I am a match struck in the darkness."

The child looked around frantically, as though he were expecting an attack at any moment. "Then we must get rid of her. She will try to blow you out!" The boy was on his feet.

"That would take a mighty blast," the Tree chuckled.

"This isn't funny," the boy's words rattled about in panic. "You must send her away. Leave her to her darkness and her knitting and we can live here in sunshine. I don't like her, Tree. She frightens me. I feel she wants to hurt us."

"Light threatens her darkness. It illuminates what she does not want to be seen. I think she is much more frightened of us."

"She doesn't look too scared to me," the boy countered.

"She is accustomed to living behind masks. The Weaver will not show you her true feelings easily. Every word spoken is aimed to deflect from the truth that lies buried somewhere deep beneath it."

"I don't understand why we have to be nice to her. She reeks of darkness and she tells lies. Can't you just ask her to leave?" the boy pleaded.

"The Weaver is a guest and I will not turn her away. Her path has led her here. I will not be the judge of where next it should take her. She is a soul who has lived in darkness. Perhaps it is her time to breathe a little light."

∞

The light was brighter than she had remembered. It was a long time since she had left the shadows of her lair. She hadn't time to step beyond her borders, there were so many whispers and plucked nerves to be seen to along the lines of her finely woven web.

The Weaver shuddered, even though the sun still held some warmth. She was always cold. She was sure that her marrow contained nothing but ice. Her thoughts drifted back to her web and its woven spirals, in which secrets lay buried along the spokes of its furthest reaches. It had taken her years to perfect its design. It had been breached many times in the past, by enemies who later tasted her venom. But she had never abandoned it. After each assault it was rebuilt. She had improved and strengthened it so that she no longer feared the ravage of time or attack. There was no metal on earth that was stronger than the lines she had woven. A terrible, thrilling thing of beauty, it had become the perfect lair in which to lure and devour her prey.

She worried that it would suffer in her absence. The voices, that never gave her a moment's peace, quarreled amongst themselves. They hinted at tricks and deceptions, worming their fears and insecurities into her thoughts. She needed to get this business with the Tree over, and as quickly as possible. The spiderlings could not be trusted with her fortress for very long. Already she had learned of plots and subterfuge hatching the moment she had turned her back. But she sensed everything, and her eyes never, ever closed. Even here, in the forest, she could feel the vibrations. Those who sought to cross her orb and break trust with her would pay with their lives. Eventually. But first, she'd have her sport.

She almost smiled. It was quickly doused by her reflections. She was tired. The light strained her eyes. The child was an unexpected complication. She longed for meat to sharpen her fangs upon. She thirsted for darkness. A deep space in which to gorge and get fat and blot out the voices in her head that clawed and shrieked.

She had been away too long already. She was weary of simpering around the Tree and playing its sweet, sickly games. Far from the centre of her control she felt anxious and exposed. But she needed more time to fathom its purpose.

The Tree was stronger than she had imagined. The light it had poured into the child was terrifying. It would have to be extinguished, or it would shine into the heart of the North itself.

She imagined the Tree's long arms reaching towards her web, attempting to break through her careful spirals. She shuddered. It was impenetrable, she was sure. Yet still she felt a deep foreboding. She pictured the flies stirring as they thawed beneath the Tree's warmth. It would have to be stopped. There was no other way.

But it was wily. It gave away nothing. It held sway over the light. But where were its minions? Where were the hangers-on that could so easily be corrupted? It did everything in plain sight. There was no darkness, that she could detect, in which to hide. But it had to be there, shielding its riches and its twisted thoughts.

'Hold up the mask,' a voice told her.

'Carry on knitting,' another counseled.

'Learn its secrets,' one insisted.

'Find its weakness,' a voice directed.

'Fix your hair!' another thought interrupted.

'Bleed it slowly,' a creature instructed.

'Less haste, more smiles.'

She turned to the Tree with a wide grin and found that the child was staring at her. Never one to shy from a challenge, she stared back. This might be the Tree's territory, she thought, but I shall win him over yet.

The boy blinked.

∞

The Weaver paused in her knitting and winked at the child. Then she addressed the Tree,

"I've spun my lines
Stated my case
Will my journey
Have been a waste?"

"You have indeed traveled far to speak with us, Weaver, and I have listened carefully to your rhymes, yet still I remain in the dark regarding your true intentions. What is it that you seek? Speak plainly. You will not be judged by the quality of your verse."

"Simply put, a pot of honey
Filled with time and stuffed with money."

"If you had more time," asked the Tree, "how would you use it?"

"That's easy, Tree, I'd make more money."

"If you had more money, how would you spend it?" the Tree probed.

"That's simple, Tree, I would hide it." She continued,

"A rich old age is what I crave
Every penny gained is saved
Beneath my mattress safe at night
Out of reach and out of sight."

"And this would bring you peace?" asked the Tree.

In an unguarded moment she dropped a rhyme and snagged her line. "These days nothing brings me peace. I am very tired, Tree," the Weaver sighed.

"I find my mattress has grown lumpy
My nights are black, my nerves are jumpy."

"What would bring you ease and happiness?" asked the Tree.

She didn't even have to think, "I'd give it all for a good night's sleep."

∞

Alarms clattered through her head. She had spoken the truth. The creatures rose as a unit.

'Shame,' they cried.

'Fool,' they chided.

The voices berated, rising in pitch, tearing her mind, tormenting with their exhortations.

"Aaaggghhh." A woman screamed. Deafening and drowning out the creatures. Not her.

The boy looked aghast. "Are you alright?" he asked.

She shook her head to clear the rabble. Her control was slipping. A soothing voice took over, coaxing, 'We are the ruler of the North. Our words are weapons of mighty power. None other can wield so many and say so little. None other is so often heeded and so seldom understood. Stand up.'

The Weaver grasped the thread thrown and pulled herself upright. Her mind cleared. There was no time to lose. If she stayed here much longer, she was sure that she would unravel.

The boy watched as she nodded in agreement with a creature he could not see.

'If we can talk a fly into culling its wings, surely we can talk a Tree into remaining in a forest,' the same voice calmly argued.

She gathered herself together. Her counselors rallied.

'First, we need to learn its tactics,' they advised.

'It will not easily give away its intentions.'

'We must be very, very clever.' She rubbed her hands together and smiled.

'Once the Tree's plans are in the open, we can spin our schemes,' they told her, then retreated to the shadows as she rallied to face their foe.

"Your name is spoken far and wide.
They say that you are very wise."

The Tree said nothing, and so she continued.

"It's said that you have learned the truth.
And sup of the forbidden fruit."

"Have you come to dine with us?" the Tree asked her. She snorted in ill-concealed derision.

"I've come to see with my own eyes
What stirs beneath your wholesome guise."

"I fear that you will be disappointed. I have little skill in the art of masquerade," said the Tree.

"Hurmph." She continued her examination of the Tree, which didn't blink beneath her scrutiny.

"You welcome all into your shrine
And ask no favours for your time."

"The path is barred to no one. But, as you see, this is no shrine. There is no offering plate, and there is no altar," the Tree gently corrected her.

She bowed her head and contemplated a moment, uncertain what route to follow. It was a slippery one. It kept eluding her grip. The creatures rose as a cast to direct her.

'Pin it down,' one said. She measured its strength and shook her head.

'Prize open its darkness,' another prompted.

'It loves light, so feed it fire,' a nasty cackle escaped, as a hand covered her mouth to catch it.

'Finish it.'

'Play with it first.'

'Feast on its nasty secrets.'

'Kill it.' The creatures stepped back to watch, as she turned her attention to the Tree.

"It makes no sense and breaks all rules.
What hunger lurks beneath this ruse?"

Fingers cupped her chin as she considered the Tree.

"One of your stature needs a space
For supplicants to bow and scrape."

"I am not some lordling that demands bended knees and fear-torn promises," the Tree answered.

Her voice rose in accusation.

"And yet you've claimed the loyalty
Of flies who owe me fealty."

She attempted a smile in a pitch to soften the words. Her eyes glittered, betraying her lurch towards diplomacy, and she struggled to drag her gaze from the child who was pottering along the edge of the clearing, out of earshot but finely tuned to the discussion going on beneath the Tree.

"I'm uncertain of your meaning, Weaver."

"You are the five points of the star
A beacon seen from near and far."

"You mistake me for another who came before me. I am a tree." The response, spoken softly, seemed to incense the Weaver who struggled to maintain her poise. The creatures were on their feet. Words flung themselves at the walls of her mind, splitting open their meanings.

"Lies!" she hissed.

She was toppling. The phrases she had mastered and melted to bend to her forked tongue fought with her. Accusations and threats filled her mouth with spit and bile. She swallowed and choked them down. Her throat was dry.

"You toy with me with modest words
Yet spill your light into my world."

"I know of no world other than this one that we all share," the Tree responded.

"More lies!" A hand hurried to her mouth to veil her outburst. Another tore unheeded at her hair. Her voice softened.

"I too am known for sugared words
That slay the truth like sharpened swords."

"Poor fare for an empty belly," the Tree observed.

Her voice rose sharply, and fingers pointed and poked at unyielding bark.

"Feast elsewhere, Tree, I own the night.
Your radiance befouls my sky."

"The sky cares nothing for your claim," the Tree reasonably pointed out.

She calmed, took back control and nodded in begrudging assent, holding up her palms in a gesture of acquiescence.

"But we can reach a compromise,
Join our wits and combine our guile."

"What are you suggesting, Weaver?"

"We both are creatures of the world.
We make the rules and hoard the gold."

"The forest is rich in all the bounty I will ever need," the Tree assured her.

"I'll leave you to your rain and shine
If you respect what's clearly mine."

The Tree asked, "What is it that you believe I have designs upon?"

Now that it was upon her she paused, savouring the moment. For once she would say what she thought. No space for ambiguity. She needed to be very, very clear if she had a chance at quelling the attack before her troops were fully gathered. She spoke deliberately,

"You claim the South, the East and West,
We'll draw the lines; I'll rule the rest."

"The world is not for carving into slivers to be served to gluttons at a feast," the Tree retorted sharply, smashing her moment of optimism.

Eight hands formed eight angry little fists. The creatures stormed with one rabid voice.

"The North is ours. We will not share.
We'll crush all those who breach our lair."

"A compass does not waver at the point of seeking North." The Tree's voice carried a note of steel that the boy had not heard before.

"So, I was right, your mask has slipped,
You want it all within your grip."

She cackled a mirthless little laugh.

"Tree, you and I are much alike,
As similar as day and night."

She waggled her head from side to side and looked mockingly at the Tree.

"The pendulum of wrong and right,
The exact same coin on different sides."

"We are similar in many respects, Weaver," the Tree agreed, "but not in the ways that you think."

The Weaver stepped back a little from the Tree, muttering all the while to herself.

"A wily one, I'll need more time
To find its flaw and make it mine.
Tread with caution, then seize the chance
To lead it on a deathly dance."

She was weary. It hadn't worked. But at least she knew now what it was after. The voices were right. The Tree would have to be destroyed before it led an incursion of light into her realm. She cleared her throat and faced the Tree once again.

"The North is mine, I won't be swayed.
But for now, I'll rest and ease these legs."

With that, she plonked down onto her ample bottom, her feet splayed before her at right angles, leaned back against the Tree, straightened her dress over her knees, and resumed her knitting.

∞

As her hands spun her mind relaxed and the voices came to order. The jumper started to take shape. The clutter cleared a little, allowing her to think through their problem. The Tree, it seemed, was not for bargaining. However, there were other ways to make it bend to their will. Before she could succeed in their task, she needed to know more about what it was and what it wanted.

'Everything wants something.' There was agreement amongst the creatures.

'Desire creates thirst.'

'Stoke the desire.'

'Sate the thirst.'

'Or withhold the beloved.'

It was simple.

'Learn the Tree's weakness.'

'Then command it.'

'Or destroy it.'

She flinched from neither thought.

But first, she needed to burrow to root out the Tree's desires. Her rabble of counselors flattened dissent as a plan was formed. In the quiet of consensus, the margins between her mind and the forest blurred and plots were hatched aloud.

"Perhaps a wild shot in the dark,
But vanity might hit the mark."

The boy was jolted from his thoughts. "Sorry, what's that, Weaver?" A hand brushed off his question.

'Flatter it.'

'Tease it.'

'Learn its squalid secrets.'

"I should have worn my pretty dress."

"The one you have on is fine," the boy gallantly offered, believing some response was required.

"Lies!" she hissed at the child. Then she tucked her hair behind her ears, straightened her smile, flexed her rhymes and set to work, as the creatures cheered and fed her lines.

"I've noted, Tree, your leaves are fine.
How do you ever get that shine?"

"Why, thank you, Weaver, the sun is kind. But I think they've reached their end of line."

Several fingers twirled wisps of wanton hair. She lowered her head and raised her glittering eyes to the Tree.

"Tales of your feats have traveled far.
Your enemies still bear their scars."

"I never meant to mar another. I live in peace deep in the forest," the Tree said.

"Compared to your sweet flowing lines
All other poets' rhymes are dry."

"I try to speak plainly and dust words of lies. I'll sacrifice rhymes to the truth every time."

"Birds plot to nest within your eaves.
No other boughs give them such ease."

"The forest is dotted with nests amongst leaves. Providing safe limbs is the nature of trees."

"Blown by the wind I've watched you dance,
Elegance ripples through every branch."

"Rooted in earth, I can't rightly prance. The wind lifts my leaves, I just sway in its arms."

"Such silky bark and arms so long,
I've never seen a Tree so strong."

"Limbs do not contain my brawn. The heart's the key to all I am," the Tree unguardedly answered.

"I think she likes you," the boy sniggered.

"I think she's trying to find my weak spot."

"You don't have one," said the boy.

"Of course I do," the Tree responded.

'It's the heart!' the creatures exulted, dragging the Weaver's smile behind a mouthful of teeth, before it gave her away.

'Pierce the heart and we'll fell the Tree.' A pair of hands carefully hugged her in delight as the others created a distraction on the chance that someone might be watching.

'We have found the Tree's weakness,' they gloated.

It had been there all along. Hidden in plain sight.

∞

'Out of sight out of mind,' a voice niggled.

'Get back to the web,' another prodded.

'No time to squander,' a creature admonished.

'Lines need tending,' a counselor reminded.

"Just a little rest and we'll be on our way," she promised.

Her mind quieted. She couldn't remember the last time she'd had a holiday.

'You deserve a little sunshine.' This came from a new voice that whispered in soft tones and encouraged her to loosen the laces of her shoes and drag her hair back off her face.

She raised her blue veins and pale skin to the sun, stretched her eight arms and yawned widely, showing off rows of glittering, pointed teeth.

'Close your eyes. Sleep now.' It was that same strange voice.

She might find a little peace here, in the forest, she thought. Far from the interminable twangs and trembling of her web, with its constant scurrying and plotting and designs upon her time and patience.

The Tree suggested that she stretch out on a bed of leaves that the child had piled under its eaves.

It was an odd one, alright. She responded rather tartly,

"Of course, I don't have time to sleep.
I weave my webs and counsel keep
With fools who gather at my feet."

"You need not fear. The only thing beneath your feet is forest floor," the Tree told her. "You could take this time to ease your mind, and to thaw your bones. There's still some warmth left in the autumn sun."

'That sounds nice.' The voice burrowed comfortably into her mind.

'It's a trick.' A screech dragged her to her senses.

'The Tree is not to be trusted.' She put up her guard and rearranged her defenses. She always had to keep the shields up. She could not afford to forget that, even for a moment.

'Let it see us,' a creature instructed.

'Let it fear us,' a voice commanded.

'Let it know that we are not to be toyed with.'

'Teach its shiny little disciple a lesson it won't forget.'

'We are the enemy,' a voice roared, goading her to her feet.

She raised her clenched fists, declaiming sovereignty in the centre of the clearing. "In the North we reign supreme, over flies and spiderlings." Her mind crowed. Eighty fingers flexed and coiled.

"That sounds very important," said the boy.

She spun to face him.

"How did you get to be the leader?" he asked.

"*The stupid flies they call me wise*
Because I flatter and beguile
With sugared words and layers of rhymes
That blind them to my snares and guise."

She watched the Tree carefully. Its expression never changed. Whether it was impressed with her skill at manipulation and her intricate ploys, she could not be certain. So, she continued,

"*They love the words and yarns I spin*
That dim their wit and tame their brain.
I rain false promises and feign
To care about their loss, their gains."

The boy listened to the words, but his eyes followed her hands as they stretched and plucked thoughts, seemingly out of the air.

"*It's all part of my little game*
Their vanity dictates they play.
I reign over their petty days
Their wasted lives spun out in vain."

The boy, who had seated himself on a low branch of the Tree, looked aghast. Not a poker player that one, she surmised. Every thought and emotion ran naked across his face. His eyes were saucers of disbelief. She shouldn't mind, but she didn't like the way he looked at her. Judging her. She snapped,

"Don't look at me, I'm not to blame.
I rule the land of the insane."

"Doesn't anyone in the North ever say what they think, or smile when they mean it?" the boy asked. "Don't people comfort each other when they're sad, and laugh together when they're happy?" He shook his head, troubled by questions that he knew the answers to. "Why does everyone hide from everyone else? Why do they listen to you, when they know you do not speak the truth? Why do they lie to themselves?"

"They crave my tongue because it hides
The truth behind a web of lies."

"But why?" the boy pressed.

The Tree tried to answer the boy's question, but directed his response to the Weaver.

"Your unhappy mind conjures words like weapons. You have the skill to attract souls to you, but you misuse this gift by setting traps into which they fall. As much as they fear your syrup tongue, they crave its drippings because you tell them what they know to be false, but what they want to hear. In this way you drag them into your web of deceit, and bind them so tight that they pass lives of perfect apathy, wrapped in yarn of the highest quality. They never live to see the light, nor battle through their fears of night."

She nodded her head in agreement, unperturbed by the Tree's assessment.

"I wrap them in the finest thread
I lay them on a woven bed.

I whisper what they want to hear
The truth is banished from their ears.

Held deep in sleep they need not fear
The death of smiles, the pit of tears.

They never stir except to scream
Of course, I know not what they dream."

"Why can't they wake up?" the boy asked, horrified at the scene the Weaver spun.

"Fool child, it is no mystery
Sleep shields them from life's misery."

The Tree sounded weary. "Life is a balance of joy and misery. People need to expect and experience both, with the knowledge that each will pass, in time. That life will change. That is the nature of living well and living freely. Accepting this is the first step on the path to knowledge, and the acceptance of self and one's place in the world.

"Each person must learn that they have within themselves the strength to be who they truly are, and to live in peace and harmony with the world. Weaver, even you cannot weave a bed so soft that souls bask in their joys and sleep through their miseries."

The Tree continued, "The wise person delights in the truth and remains wide awake at all times, knowing that neither time, money, nor sweet words will ease their passage through life. It is only the fool who sleeps, as if they were already dead."

"Well, did I not say I was surrounded by fools?" the Weaver demanded. "So, why not give up the North and leave me to rule?" She pushed her advantage.

"The world is unsettled when the balance of light and dark is not maintained. Souls cannot be sacrificed to starve so that others can feast." The Tree finished the discussion, unwilling to barter fates like poker chips.

The Weaver laughed loudly at the Tree's words, a rounded belly laugh that made her hands tremble and her toes twitch. It had played right into her clutch.

"You need my kind to tip the scale.
Without my dark, light would prevail.
Then how could balance be maintained?
Without an Abel, there's no Cain.

"We play our parts in equal measure," she mused. "For Libra's sake we need each other." She continued,

"You speak the truth
I weave in rhymes.

You wake them up
I close their eyes.

You live in peace
I fester bile.

You rest at night
I toss and fight."

∞

"I don't understand the half of what she says," the boy confessed to the Tree in a low whisper.

"How could you understand, you simple child," snapped the Weaver who, while a little short-sighted, had excellent hearing. "The Tree has polluted you with purity."

At which point, she poked the boy in the arm with a needle dangling inky yarn. He jumped back smartly. "Ouch," he said. "What was that for?"

"Tree wants to keep you wide awake
Can't have you snoozing for my sake.

You don't know what foe lies in wait
Keep on your toes, don't trust to fate."

She cackled, phlegm bubbling and frothing in her throat, as she poked him one more time to emphasize her point. Sure enough, the boy leapt sprightly.

He again appealed to the Tree, "Why do you let her stay here? She speaks of honey, but her words are poison."

"Be at ease and open your heart," the Tree spoke softly to the boy. "You should pay less attention to the Weaver's words and give more thought to the mind that formed them.

"We are what we think. Speak or act with an impure mind and trouble will pursue you as your shadow, unshakable. Speak or act with a pure mind and happiness will follow you as surely as dawn follows night. Once you control your mind, you control your actions and your impact on the world."

The Weaver settled down with her knitting. Fours hands teased yarn into large balls, while others fed wool to provide for the jumper that was growing at an alarming rate. The boy sat out of arm's reach of her needles, and listened to the Tree's teachings.

"There are three types of actions, child. A physical action, what you do, can convey love or it may raise its arm in anger. A verbal action, what you say, can cradle the truth or it may spew vile words that damage another's reputation, hurt their feelings or lead them to think or act in a way that is harmful to themselves or others. The third action is a mental action, what you think. This is the most important one of all, because it is in our minds that we form thoughts that we then turn into words or deeds.

"It is easy to like someone whose impact on the world is loving, truthful and kind. It takes much more effort to look beyond sharp edged, damaging actions and words to the thoughts that formed them.

"A mind that is peaceful, happy and in harmony will speak the truth, and its actions will be compassionate. An unhappy mind, which is full of demons, will speak and act in a way that will lead others into darkness, and which will devour itself from within.

"Such a mind wields anger, envy and insecurity like frenzied weapons. Its greatest fury it unleashes upon itself. It slashes and shreds at everything within its reach. It strangles sleep and peace and chokes all that is good in life. However, no one need live in such a manner."

The Tree focused on the Weaver. "The path to peace, happiness and harmony is open to every single soul."

Her knitting lay forgotten on her lap, her hands, for once, were idle, her face seemed deeply troubled and lined with pain.

"Nightly I'm attacked by demons.
I fight back with knitting needles.

I don't know how to find some rest.
My mind's a filthy garbled nest."

She would have closed her eyes, if she could. The compassion emanating from the Tree was more than she could bear. She was the most feared ruler of the North. How dare it pity her.

"You have a mighty heart, Tree. But even it is not strong enough to love a wretch like me."

'What are you doing?' a voice rose in dismay.

'Test it. Yes. Find its limits.' Hands were rubbed together.

'Weigh its heart.'

'Measure its dimensions.'

'Could it find me in all this darkness?' a rogue question formed, tinged with hope.

'Judge its strength.'

'Retreat to the lair to hatch the attack.'

'Return in winter when the sap is low and its heartbeat tremors.'

'Then crush it.'

Another question twitched at another corner of her mind, worrying its prey, refusing to give up its quarry. 'Could it love me?'

The question needed to be answered.

Defying the warnings and rebuffs, in a soft, strangled voice, she painfully drew back the curtains to her mind and laid herself bare before the Tree.

"Jingle Jangle
Words a tangle

Days off kilter
Nights a splinter

Sleep's a jagged
Knife that pins the

Pitted corners
Of my mind.

I can't rest there's
No escaping

Knitting does not
Ease my aching

There's nowhere in
My bed to hide

Guilt snores loudly
By my side.

...

Jingle jangle
Memories rankle

Squandered days and
Nights all mangled

Take a knife and
Tear my heart out

Burn the lump and
Pin my mouth shut.

Doubt curls fingers
Around my neck

It licks my ears
And chokes my breath

Fear pokes daggers
Into my eyes

My thoughts are foes
That stalk my mind.

...

Jingle jangle
Screaming bedlam

Nails on blackboards
No asylum

Shrieking Khaos
Shreds my brain

Slowly driving
Me insane.

My mind's a swamp
In which I'm sinking

I weave yarn to
Stop from thinking

One dropped stitch I
Feel I'm slipping

Hold on tight must
Keep on knitting.

...

Jingle jangle
Madness dangles

Voices wrangle
Nights unravel

By morning light
Webs are woven

Flies are frozen
And bound up tight.

They cannot fight
A foe that feeds

Their need to hide
From truth and life

In silk ties they
Shudder softly

Death comes slowly
With Weaver's bite."

The silence after a scream descended. Her mind fell quiet, for a moment, before thoughts rushed back in.

She averted her eyes from the Tree. Shamed. She did not see the boy move towards her. Her body stiffened in horror. It felt like an attack. She gasped, then relaxed as it finally dawned on her what was happening. The child had wrapped his thin arms around her neck and was holding her tight. If he let go, she might fly apart. She smiled in wonder at what had come to pass. It was the first real smile the Tree had ever seen upon her face.

The moment passed, and in the next the peace was shattered by the passing of Time.

∞

The Weaver pushed the boy aside, shot to her feet, patted her dress and straightened her collar. "Lordy lordy, it's Time," she gasped in an almost girlish voice. "I didn't know that he would be coming at this hour.

"I would have worn my better dress.
My hair is tangled, it's a mess."

She fretted as she worried the wild mop into shape and tried to tame the stray strands that were plastered to her face.

She was as presentable as she was going to get when Time stumbled into the clearing. He wobbled a moment before he toppled onto the flat of his back, his legs and arms flailing in the air like a huge beetle.

"It is time," he gulped, and gasped for air. "It is time," he tried once more.

The Shadow, which was some steps behind, weighted under the load of suitcases, dropped its burdens and stumbled to his assistance. It took hold of one of Time's arms and started to pull. To no avail. The boy hurried over to help and took hold of the other arm. Then, on the count of three, encouraged by the panting, rasping and struggling of Time, the boy and the Shadow heaved with all their might.

As they pulled, a beam sputtered and fired across the Weaver's face, which she leveled at the prostrate Time.

The Tree held its breath to stop from laughing out loud.

It was a great effort, but the Tree held its composure, the Weaver held her smile, and the Shadow and the boy held on tight to Time, who was finally levered to his feet. He tottered like a new foal, tripping over the few steps it took to reach the refuge of the Tree. Then he flopped back onto his bottom and rested his back against the trunk.

"It is time," he finally managed, "for lunch."

"Actually," the boy clarified, "you're a little late." Time lumbered to his feet, his face a mask of horror, and looked down at his belly. Sure enough, his short arm pointed to twelve and the long arm pointed to one.

He turned on the Shadow, "How could you have left me struggling like that for so long, wretch? It is five past noon and I have not yet eaten. You are a sorry shadow of a slave." He shook his jowls, greatly unsettled at the loss of face. The Shadow hung its head, its body wrapped around the failure. The Weaver, who had retrieved her knitting, poked it in the arm with her needle, and tutted loudly as the Shadow let out a soft yelp of pain. It fled back into the trees to retrieve the suitcases it had dropped when Time had tripped over his feet.

Time swiveled his body and squinted at the Weaver. "Ah, Ms. Spinner, what a pleasure. And how well you're looking. Indeed, you don't look a day over 70."

"Oh, Time," she blushed, "I have not yet reached 65."

"Madame Spinster, no Spinner," he hastily corrected, "your youthful bloom betrays your age." He attempted to cover his gaffe.

The Weaver gushed, "Call me Weaver, my dearest Time. It's such a joy to hear your chime."

"And I have greatly missed your rhymes," he gallantly replied. "She's very wise," he added as an aside to the Tree. "Though I seldom understand a word she speaks. It's probably her foreign accent. She's from the North, you know," he confided in a whisper that ricocheted around the clearing.

"Oh, Time, you old devil." She coyly leveled her bulbous eyes at him.

"Always one
To trick and tease me

Cast your line
Catch and release me."

She sidled a little closer.

"Dear old friend
You always lead me

By the nose
You coax then cleave me."

"Ms. Weaver, whatever do you mean?" mumbled Time, in as offhand a tone as he could muster. He hoped, for all he was worth, that the question would be brushed under the carpet with a firing squad grin and a very large broom.

Instead, the Weaver sighed as she reflected,

"*The times we had*
We cut a dash

Talk of the town
You spared no cash.

Money squandered
At the races

Living large on
Champagne chasers.

Chasing nags that
Ran like demons

High on dreams and
Drunk on freedom.

Feckless fools
We lost the lot

Our friendship and
The winning pot.

Nothing left you
Had to borrow

To keep betting
On Tomorrow.

That stupid nag
It ruled our days

And ruined my life
Along the way."

"I remember once you grasped its tail." She paused, allowing Time's thoughts to drift back to that glorious afternoon. "Then it slipped away again." Her voice clipped the reverie.

"Then you said you'd
Call tomorrow.

Hopes once raised were
Crushed by sorrow.

I waited days
Beside the phone.

I spent the nights
Curled up alone.

Was it something
That I had said?"

Her voice dropped like the weight of lead.

"You led me on
A merry dance.

Then tossed me when
You had the chance."

She looked at Time, her eyes softened by painful memories.

"Smitten by your
Ticking tock

You broke my heart
And sealed the lock."

"Madam, I never knew," Time bumbled. "Of course, I meant to call, but tomorrow kept slipping through my fingers." The Weaver hardly seemed to hear his words, so he continued, "You know, I never seem to find the time to see old friends, relax, unwind. Why, it's been a whole season since I last visited Tree."

"It's been 20 years since you said that you'd call me!" the Weaver exploded.

"Goodness, where has the time gone?" mustered Time.

"It has passed in a fruitless dance chasing *Tomorrow Never Comes*," she accused.

"How fast that nag can run," he marveled.

A thunderous silence burst through the clearing. In an effort to fend it off, the boy cleared his throat. The silence grew louder. So, he raised his voice.

"Maybe," the boy said, "he's just not into you." The silence faltered, then fled in terror.

The Weaver picked up her needles and swiveled her body towards Time. Her mouth narrowed to a thin, bloodless line.

"It's not you," Time hurriedly assured her. "It's me." He patted his portly belly. The Weaver advanced on Time in slow-motion steps. The boy felt the air turn to treacle. "I've just never had a good way with the ladies." Time looked around him, frantically searching for allies as he took a sticky step backward, and another.

The needles slashed the air, cutting through the sludge, ominously weaving towards Time.

"That lovely jumper that I knit thee
Never worn, it…"

"Didn't fit me." Time hastily finished her line, desperately casting around for a defense.

The needles dragged the Weaver forward, divining rods in their search for vengeance.

"A masterpiece of plain and purl
A rain-soaked flag not once unfurled
Across your portly belly-pot
Cast in your closet left to rot."

"Absolutely not!" protested Time. "I've lived the high life, put on weight. It simply didn't suit my shape."
The Weaver did not appear to hear him.

"I chose the yarn to match your eyes
Finest stitching, mineral dyes."

Her voice dropped a notch,

"That sweater was my opus magnum
A woven thread cast as a lifeline.

"That you never once deigned to pick up," she forlornly trailed off, before her eyes clouded once again in fury.
Time leapt smartly behind the Shadow as the Weaver came hurdling in his direction, needles poised to plunge.

$$\infty$$

"Enough," commanded the Tree.
Weaver, thrown off balance, faltered mid-thrust. It wasn't much of an opening, but it was enough for Time to fling the Shadow to the ground and dash for the cover of the Tree.
Her arms seemed frozen, the haze of fury still rimming her eyes, words vomiting out of her mouth.
"You would all plot against us!" she thundered.

Her cold, blue blood felt red heat spill through her veins. The world shimmered before her. She tried to grasp hold of it to still the madness.

Words slowed, then dried and with great effort the Weaver let her arms fall slowly to her sides and the needles drop softly to the ground. Time watched her struggle from behind the trunk of the Tree, which he clung to as though he were drowning in a sea of forest. The Shadow remained prostrate at her feet, where it had been hurled by Time. The boy had climbed to a higher branch, frightened of getting too close to so much anger.

"Well now," it was the Weaver who finally broke the silence, "things have a habit of heating up when old friends get together to share a cup."

"What an excellent idea, Weaver." Time let out a huge sigh of relief. "I knew there was a reason I had missed you all these years. Fool, you heard the lady, bring us wine. Be quick about it." Time poked his head a little farther from behind the Tree. His head remained unmolested, so it was gingerly followed by his body.

The Weaver, for her part, in an attempt to regain her composure, gave the Shadow a sharp kick in the ribs before it had the chance to rise and respond to its master's commands. Order, it seemed, had been restored and was soon to be toasted.

Time raised his glass to his lips as the Tree confronted the Weaver, "Your salvation does not reside with Time. This, I believe, you already know. Before you can bestow love, or receive it from another, you must first look to yourself."

'Salvation?' a voice choked, then spattered her mind with derision.

The Tree held the Weaver's gaze, "You have taken your gifts and shaped them into knives with which you stab and peel your tortured mind. You need to heal these wounds before you start to poke at the hearts of others."

The Weaver's eyes bulged at the Tree. She was not accustomed to being spoken to in this way.

Time breathed a sigh of relief. He took a deep gulp of the wine the Shadow had poured for him before he chimed, "Tree's right, you know. It's not my fault. And it's way past lunch time. My head is awry and my schedule's astray."

Weaver looked at the needles, which still lay where she had let them fall. They were made of bone. They had been shaped with skill, and polished until they shone. They had served her for many, many years. It would be such a little thing to pick them up and plunge them into Time's belly.

She accepted the wine from the cringing creature and downed a draught. It was very good. She sank back into her memories. It was a different slave to the one they had tormented together, all those years ago. Those were good times. This beast was fouler, more broken, emptier, if that were even possible. But her skills had improved with honing over time. As she had become a mistress in her art, she must presume that Time, too, had perfected his particular persecutions. She felt a twinge of the old feelings stirring. Her stomach growled. Maybe she was just hungry.

"Time," the Tree interrupted her musings and Time's self-pity-ing whines, "of course you are not free from blame. Your words shape promises that your actions do not fulfill."

"Now, Tree, do you not think that I'm getting a little old for one of your lectures? It's been an awfully long day already, and I've only just arrived," Time protested.

The Weaver sniggered; a small alliance formed.

"Besides," he sidled over to the Tree, as the Weaver went to issue orders about lunch, "it's not what you think. She's really not my type. I mean, would you look at the state of her. But I can't shake her loose. She follows me everywhere. I give her no encouragement. But you know me, Tree, if I see a hungry dog, I can't stop myself from throwing it a bone."

The Weaver stopped mid-step. Her face turned a deep shade of crimson. She could just hear snippets of the Tree's response through the voices that derided her.

'So, who's a pretty girl then?' they all snorted.

"Mangled opportunities," the Tree said.

'An old fool,' one sniggered.

"When you might have found love and happiness." Time shifted uncomfortably.

'Dried bones and thick ankles.' The Weaver looked at her feet and faltered.

"Leeching the life from today." The Tree didn't sound happy.

'Only fit to be seen in darkness.' She dragged her hair over her face.

"No more substance than a shadow." Time picked at his nails.

She busied herself ordering the slave about.

Time slunk to the picnic table.

Under the Weaver's kicks and prods lunch was set up in no time and a companionable silence descended as she and Time set to their meal, tearing flesh from bone and slurping down their drinks. It reminded her of the good old days.

Time, sucking thoughtfully on the marrow of a bone, broke the silence of the glade. "You know, you may well be right, Tree. For all my hurry, I never seem to get anywhere."

He absent-mindedly held out his empty wine glass, which the Shadow scurried to refill. He drank deeply and thoughtlessly, his mind focused elsewhere. The boy watched his eyes tense in concentration as he waded inwards. But, in a short time, the feather of a smile tickled the edge of his mouth.

"Perhaps if I just lose a little weight, shed a few loads, and run a little faster, I can make it. Tomorrow is bound to slip one of these days and, when it does, I'll catch it."

He was sufficiently moved by the thought to spill the remains of his wine, scatter the shards of the bones, and rise unsteadily to his feet.

"Just think of it, Tree," he panted in his pleasure. "Can you imagine what it would be like to hold Tomorrow in your arms?"

"Hurmph," the Weaver gargled her throat. "I imagine that it would be as tired and wizened as today."

Time recoiled at the thought, before he set it aside. "With Tomorrow by my side, I could sit back at my ease. We would play chess together. Learn archery. Study botany. We would travel the world.

"I've always wanted to wander lazily down ancient alleyways. Spin yarns at sunset at Jaws Corner; dip my toes into all the oceans of the earth; compare sky blues from the 14 highest peaks." His voice strained with yearning.

"What on earth are you waiting for?" probed the Tree.

"Tomorrow. It all hinges on Tomorrow."

"And in the meantime?"

"In the meantime, I shall run like the Furies in pursuit of the prize."

$$\infty$$

Time slipped into a blissful reverie, clearly going nowhere for the time being. The Weaver held him fixed in her stare, as intently as though he were prey, unwilling to let him slink from her sight.

"What are you thinking?" she asked.

"Nothing," he replied.

"You must have been thinking of something. You're not some empty-headed bumpkin."

Time acknowledged the compliment with a raised eyebrow and slanted smile, throwing his face off balance.

"I was musing on the beauty of a set of bejeweled eyes."

The Weaver dropped her head coyly, without lowering her gaze. A slight smile twitched at the corners of her mouth.

"And considering my reflection in Tomorrow's pupils," he finished.

The Weaver spat a huge glob of phlegm, which landed close to Time's feet. Time pointedly brought his handkerchief to his face and fastidiously wiped a couple of stray crumbs off his mouth.

The Tree interrupted the silent warfare that was beginning to simmer and looked set to boil over, "Tell me, Time, are you running towards tomorrow, or trying to escape from today?"

He thought seriously about the question, examining his thoughts carefully. "All I know for sure is that I'm running." Time settled more comfortably, "At least it gives me something to do to escape the dreariness of never getting anywhere.

"I'm bored, Tree. I run to give myself the impression that I exist. Otherwise nothing changes and everything remains the same."

"The one thing that is constant in life," the Tree responded, "is change."

"Well, if everything changes, how come it looks so god-awful the same?" He looked around the clearing, noticing for the first time the explosion of autumn colour.

He brushed off the distraction, and continued to explain, "At least when I chase that old nag, Tomorrow, I give people the hope of a better future. That no matter how dreary and grey their lives might seem, they just might score big on the next race. It's a slim chance, I grant you, but it's better than staring down the maw of a loaded barrel."

"Time, you are like the man who stands on the bank of a river and sees nothing but his reflection," the Tree admonished. "You could shatter the mirror by simply stepping into the water. Sometimes, embracing the mysteries of life just involves getting your feet a little wet."

Time, who had discarded his shoes for greater comfort, wiggled his toes thoughtfully. "Maybe I should go in for a dip," he said. "What do you think, eh, Weaver?" He winked.

"Oh, Time, I'm not really all that keen on swimming." She flashed a disturbing smile. "Besides, it would ruin my yarn and frizz my hair." She stared at Time. "Best we just sit on the bank and watch from there."

He looked at her critically, and then smartly conceded.

A quietness descended on the glade. The boy breathed in, the Tree breathed out, each aware of the changes taking place around them.

Another leaf fell from the Tree, thwacking Time, who had drifted off to sleep, on the forehead.

"What? What? Is it time? Are we late?" he startled up. The Shadow, which had curled at his feet, immediately raised an insubstantial hand and brushed his face, making a soft crooning hum in the back of its throat. With the other hand it plucked at Time's sleeve.

"Let us go, Master. We must hurry. We cannot be late."

"Yes of course, yes of course, you're a fool to let me sleep so long." Time picked up one of his shoes that was idling by his side and fired it at the Shadow's face. The Shadow ducked in time, so that it just brushed its ear as it sailed past, clunking the Weaver soundly on the head. She rounded on the Shadow,

"You stretch my patience
With your courageous

Display of tenacious
And audacious thought.

Ducking and weaving
Avoiding a beating

Is most displeasing
And quite unseemly.

Your master's intent
Was honestly meant

To make you repent
Your indolent bent.

To punish tardiness
Guard against laziness

Hazy-eyed fickleness
Lateness and insolence.

Your master's best shod
Of a slave who displays

A crass act of thought
At the hurl of a rock.

Dogs that are shackled
Enthrall to their master

Invite disaster
When impudence festers.

Your owner's so kind
To waste precious time

On one who declines
To acknowledge its crimes.

If you were my slave
I'd spill your entrails

Not waste precious salve
In curing your ails."

She wiped her hands on her skirt, as though she had just disposed of unsavory garbage.

The Shadow slowly slithered with downcast head to where the awkward stone lay forgotten on the grass. It gingerly picked it up and, with both hands, started banging it against its temples with increasing ferocity. Kneeling in supplication, its assault was accompanied by its pleas for forgiveness.

"Merciful master," the Shadow begged, "forgive your slave." The parchment skin above its eye broke and bled. "Wretched fool will do better. Will run faster." Blood poured down its face.

"Stop it. Please, stop!" the boy yelled, his voice breaking into sobs.

"Crave your beating. Sorry fool." The attack continued. The boy buried his face in the Tree. The Shadow's voice eventually petered out as its arms gave up, its energy spent, and red welts plotted its face. The stone spilled from its trembling hands onto the bloodied grass.

Time gazed upon it with the stern eyes of a benign father who was satisfied that an important lesson had been learned.

"I accept your apology, though you have indeed behaved abominably. You have the Weaver to thank for my generosity. She brings out my softer side, you know." The Weaver glowered at the Shadow and simpered at Time.

"That killed a few minutes nicely, though," Time added. "With all this shoe business, I hardly felt the time pass. But what shall we do now?" he asked of no one in particular.

He looked at his belly, "The day is still young, and we have hours to kill before dinner time."

∞

"We could sing," suggested the boy.

"Oh, what a wonderful idea!" Time clapped his hands, delighted as a seal. "I have been told that I have a very fine voice indeed. It was once described as a brutal baritone that could knock the sense out of any note.

"Weaver may have furnished that remark," he added as an aside, "as I'm not really sure what it means."

"Agh-erm," he cleared his throat loudly. "So, who would like to begin?"

Before anyone had a chance to respond, he bustled, "Well, in that case, I don't mind taking the show by the throat and shaking it into life."

He strode to the centre of the clearing with the aplomb of a ring-master, and surveyed his audience, who were in various states of antic-ipation. The boy sat on the lowest branch of the Tree, swinging his legs idly. The Weaver had resumed her knitting, and was engrossed in counting stitches and talking in asides. The Shadow was audibly panting and practicing its adulation under its breath, "Masterful Mae-stro. We want more." The wind was whispering softly to the Tree. The birds had fallen silent and had tucked their heads under their wings, hidden amongst the highest branches. A cricket bravely beat a rhythm and, after a suitable pause, Time took up the beat.

"*Tick tock, tick tock,*
Hickory dickory dock
The...

"Lord, what is it? My memory is not what it once was."

"Mouse," prompted the Shadow.

"What?" yelped Time. "There's a mouse! Where is it?" He hopped from foot to foot.

"The mouse ran up the clock," the Shadow whispered from the wings.

"Get it off me," squealed Time who, in his panic, was running in circles and brushing at his belly. The cricket had stopped its percussion support, and the birds had popped their heads out to see what was causing all the commotion.

"There's no fool like an old fool," cackled the Weaver, pausing in her knitting to heckle Time. "It's part of the song. 'The mouse ran up the clock. Hickory dickory dock.' So, stop your pansying and get on with the show."

Time bowed low to cover the flow of blood to his reddening cheeks. "Well spoken, Madam. Nothing must stop the show. I will throw caution to the corners of the clearing and defy a beast, even a mouse, to interrupt my singing."

He faced his audience who were, as a group, now caught in the grip of the drama.

"*Tick tock, tick tock,*" he sang,
"*Hickory dickory dock*
The minutes attacked the clock."

There was an audible sigh from the Shadow, and a giggle escaped the boy. Time acknowledged their appreciation and continued,

"*They scaled the tower*
And broke the lock
Tied up the arms
And ran off with the tock.

The tick was demented
And swore to the stars
It would hunt down the minutes
And tear out their hearts.

It called on the seconds
And rallied the hours

Who chimed in the battle
And wielded their arms.

Alarmed by the frenzy
The minutes fell back
They gave up their prize
While under attack.

The tock was restored
To uproarious delight
The mouse was beheaded
Its tail set alight.

They captured the minutes
Who were in mid-flight
Made them slaves to the clock
For the rest of their lives.

All together now…"

"Tick tock, tick tock
Hickory dickory dock," the audience bellowed. Some more in tune than others.

"Wonderful!" beamed Time.

"Not bad for an old fool, eh, Weaver?" he grinned rakishly.

"I've heard worse," conceded the Weaver with great reluctance. "If you like that sort of thing," she added. "I'm more of an opera aficionado, myself." She announced to the clearing,

"The pop art of the masses
Doesn't interest me at all

Any fool can hold a high note
But an artist scales the skies."

"Will you sing for us, Weaver?" asked the boy, somewhat awed, expectations soaring.

She delayed just long enough. "Please," he entreated.

With the professionalism of the consummate performer, the Weaver set aside her knitting with a flourish, and outstretched a hand to be escorted to centre stage. She walked with deliberation on Time's arm, as though wishing to avoid treading on the flowers she imagined preceded her every step. She melted with ease into the spotlight and gazed benignly upon the upturned faces of her fans. "Water," she demanded, and the boy rushed off to fill a mug from the brook.

She gargled her throat as though the acts of hawking and spiting were an appetizer to prime the audience for the main course. She cleared the detritus and warbled up and down the scales. "La, la, la, la, la, la, la, la." Each note stepped on the back of the one before, flattening heads, clamouring and straining to reach ever higher. Eight arms stretched to give the notes a final shove. The clearing trembled. Her bosom heaved and her eyes strained from their loose sockets.

The performance began.

"One, two, three, four, five, six, seven, eight, nine." She stomped up the steps of the scale in hobnailed boots.

The boy felt his teeth grinding and cradled his mouth.

She pitched her voice to a shriek, threatening to rip the sun from its orbit as she pierced the final note.

"A stitch in time
A stitch in time
Will tame the tear
That threatens time.

A stitch in time
A stitch in time

Waste not thread
Nor squander time.

A stitch in time
A stitch in time
A stitch well placed
Will save you nine.

One, two, three, four, five, six, seven, eight, nine."

As the final note trailed off and fizzled out, Silence, who had been wandering in the forest, hurried into the clearing and went directly to Time to still the ringing in his ears that was threatening to throw him onto his back again. In the distance, a beast wailed.

The Weaver swiveled her mighty body at the hips and bent low. Her audience gave her a stupefied round of limp applause. Even the creatures in her mind had been reduced to stunned spectators.

"Thank you, thank you," the Weaver bobbled her little head. "But I am afraid you cannot convince me to sing another aria today. I must take care of my voice. It must not be over-strained. I have shown you this precious jewel. But now I must lock it away."

"Indeed, you must, Madam. For its own safety. Such a gem must not be worn with any old frock."

The Weaver straightened her hemp skirt a little self-consciously.

"Put it away. Put it away this very instant," Time urged. "And now, who is next?" he added, eager to move things along.

"I know a song," said the boy a little shyly.

"What's it called?" Time asked.

The boy pondered a moment before he replied, "*My Heart.*"

"I don't know that one," said the Weaver.

He moved a little closer to the centre of the clearing, but he was unable to persuade himself to claim the stage.

Silence settled more comfortably, then stretched out. The boy did not begin. His cheeks flushed pink as he looked steadily at the ground. Silence started to fidget. Then, from high in the shelter of the Tree, a soft bird song trembled in the air. The boy looked up and caught the tail of the note. He started a little unsteadily, unsure of himself, but as he gathered confidence the note grew, blossomed and filled the clearing.

It seeped into the grass and the air, and the heart and the bones of his listeners. As it swelled, it filled all those who received it with abundant joy. Light spilled into their smiles and lit up their eyes.

The boy was a small boy and was unable to carry this single, pure note for very long, but those who heard it never, ever forgot it.

The Tree picked up the note from where the boy set it down and followed it with another and another and another. They swirled like leaves on an autumn breeze, and fell like raindrops on the soft earth.

The birds carried the high notes to the roof of the forest, while the wind blew through the boughs, creating a softer base. The Tree thrummed with the rhythm of the season. As the music faded to a close, the audience rose to its feet as a unit and cheered until their voices were hoarse.

"My boy, my friend, that was wonderful." Time, who was a little choked up, wiped his eyes discreetly. "I believe I am quite overcome. For a time, all thoughts of Tomorrow were banished from my mind and I felt," he paused as he searched for the word, "happy."

He smiled, "It would be impossible to top that one, so I believe it is the perfect way to close."

"Thank you, Time," said the boy, while the Tree gracefully bowed. The boy added, "But not all have had their chance to sing."

Time looked around at those present in the clearing and counted on his fingers: "Time - check; Weaver - check; boy - check; Tree

- check; and, of course, Silence has already wandered off. No, I am afraid you are mistaken, my boy, that's everyone."

"But what about, you know, your friend?"

"Weaver? Again? You can't be serious!"

"No, no," the boy hastily corrected his error before the misunderstanding secured a toehold.

"Who are you talking about?" asked a puzzled Time. The boy nodded towards the Shadow. "You mean that?" asked Time, incredulous at the boy's foolishness. "That's not my friend, that's my slave," he patiently explained. "The only thing that dog can do is howl."

The Shadow drew its head deeper into the folds of its darkness. The boy stood his ground. "Time, it's not right. We have all sung. This creature too has a life, and therefore music. You cannot take that away."

Time good-naturedly chuckled and ruffled the boy's hair. "You're quite determined, aren't you, for a quiet one. I shall indulge you, this once." He waved his hand at the Shadow. "You heard the boy, give us a tune."

The Shadow did not move. Time's temper rose. "Bash your teeth for all I care, but get out there and batter a note."

The Weaver tutted, raking Time's failure to control his charge with her contempt. She shook her head. "I can look after this for you," she offered, happy to take matters into her own, many capable, hands.

She grimly advanced on the Shadow, which was trembling like a whipped dog. She balanced her needles, slightly tightening her grip.

"I don't want to hear it sing," the boy shouted, fear causing his voice to falter.

"The time for song is long past," the Weaver agreed, barely throwing the remark over her shoulder. She focused on her target. "All it's good for now is bleeding."

"No." She couldn't tell if the voice came from Time, or from the boy. It was always so hard to pin down the source.

"You take too much upon yourself, Madam," Time's fists were clenched, and his face had turned deep red. She did not know if he was angry with her or with the Fool. Perhaps she had over-stepped the mark. It didn't matter. This was the figure she had fallen for all those years ago. She stepped aside, "The stage, Maestro, is yours."

Time turned welts of eyes onto the Shadow.

It almost imperceptibly shook its head. The boy interceded, "Please don't," he pleaded. "It's okay. Honestly."

"It's not okay," barked Time, reaching for his whip. "It must do as I command. Now sing, Fool. Sing."

The boy gulped back tears. The Weaver smiled contently. The hour chimed.

∞

The Shadow hurried to the centre, as time echoed through the clearing. Without raising its head to look at anyone, it began in a soft, and surprisingly sweet, voice.

"There will be time
There will be time
To seal my lips
Erase my mind.

There will be time
There will be time
To stop my heart
And close my eyes.

There will be time
There will be time
To lose my soul
And vanquish joy.

There will be time
There will be time
To kill my peace
And slowly die."

Leaves, which had held onto the Tree throughout autumn, were torn from the branches by a sudden, violent gust. They were caught in a vortex and spun towards the centre of the clearing, where they fell upon the Shadow in a maelstrom of tears. Before the Shadow dissolved towards the wings, it picked one up and pressed it against its forehead, its mouth and its heart.

"Not bad. Indeed, it was almost nice," the Weaver approved. "I think I may teach my flies that one, if I can rouse them long enough to learn the words," she added.

A nip of winter seeped into the clearing. "It's time we got a move on," said Time a little sourly. "Still, that shoved things along nicely. Time passes so slowly that sometimes I think I could die of the tedium."

As Time bustled and the Shadow packed up its bags, the Weaver sidled over to the boy.

"No one needs to stay awake.
No one needs to face their fate.
Come with me, child, leave this Tree.
I'll shield you from life's misery."

The boy looked her full in the eye as he replied,

"I think instead
I'll stay awake
Discard the fake
And face my fate."

He started as her head darted forward to within just an inch of his own. Her eyes narrowed and turned darker as she hissed,

> *"I leave you to*
> *Your cursèd life.*
> *I wish you ill*
> *Long days of strife."*

To his great relief, she swiveled her back on him, then threw one last dart over her shoulder, "You can forget the jumper. I deem you unworthy."

He shouldered the blow with a delighted grin, which she willfully misunderstood as a shattered grimace. All the voices in her mind agreed on the delusion.

She carefully packed up her needles, stored her knitting, then set about de-festooning the Tree of the ribbons and yarn she had draped over its branches. When she was finished, all that remained was a smudge of saffron that would soon be cleansed by a shower of rain.

'You offered a compromise,' a voice reasonably argued.

'Every option chewed.'

'Better to spit it out.'

'The Tree is beyond reasoning.'

'The light must be destroyed.'

'It might have loved me.'

'Shut your mouth.'

'There will be no pleading.'

'There will be no mercy.'

'It will be given nothing.'

'Except what it deserves.' Voices laughed raucously, drowning out the scream that almost escaped her lips.

"You will rot in your mind, unless you open it up to a shaft of light," the Tree said, softly shattering the Weaver's thoughts. "I will help you."

'Another trick,' they whispered.

"Maybe not," she rallied back. "It has a big heart. Perhaps it can anchor the wreck of my nights."

'Fool,' they hissed. 'It would drag us beneath an ocean of tears and bury us screaming amidst all our fears.'

"I would not harm you," the Tree told her.

"You would fog up my reason with all your lies; have me dance like dry dust in your arrow of light," she spat back.

"I would not lie to you," the Tree assured her.

"Lies!" a voice screamed.

'It would destroy us.'

'It would give us hope.'

'Make us weak.'

'Then wreck us from within.'

'Reduce us to motes in its beam of light.'

'Fight back!' she was instructed.

She rounded on the Tree.

"You're stealing flies
That should be mine.

My ire is stoked
My patience choked."

"It does not have to be this way, Weaver. You have the power within yourself to change."

She closed all the doors to her mind and drew across the blinds. It was dark. It was safe. She could hide there. And, in the darkness, she could plot and plan and rally her flies.

"Pay heed, this is not over, Tree
I will be back to settle thee."

"Come in peace and the path will not be closed to you, Weaver," the Tree promised.

The words lost their meaning on her and she turned away.

"Time and tide wait for no man," intoned the Shadow, as Time was making his rounds of the clearing to get a good running start.

"Or woman," Time added with pompous good humour. "Let's not forget the ladies. It's simply not sporting."

Weaver was sufficiently distracted from her ill-temper to pick up her skirts and traipse after Time, whose tick was already starting to fade as he gained distance.

"Time, I'm coming," she gasped in a choked breath as she ran to catch up, splintering piles of dried leaves.

"Do you think she's coming back?" the boy asked.

"The Weaver's final story is not yet spun. The threads are dark and hard to decipher, but my heart tells me that it is not an ending that will bring us joy."

"What should we do?" the boy asked. "I would help her if I could. Though she scares me, and I fear that she would do you harm."

"That chance may yet be yours. There are many possible fates awaiting each of us. You are on your path, but the choices you make along the way will decide your destiny."

"The path is long and has many turns. What if I get lost?" the boy asked.

"No matter how dark the road, if you look within yourself to find the light you will not go astray."

The boy relaxed against the Tree.

"You have grown, child," the Tree remarked, as Silence returned to the clearing. The boy stood as tall as he could stretch himself and made a notch on the trunk at the top of his head. He stepped back to compare his height from when he had last measured himself against the Tree. "At least an inch," he excitedly pointed.

"Indeed," said the Tree.

Silence drifted off as the boy and the Tree closed their eyes and softly breathed in and breathed out, at peace and in harmony with their world.

∞

As the days shortened, the boy watched leaves tumble and tousle like dancing butterflies on the current of spurious winds. They coated the ark of the Tree's shadow with the colours of sunshine and embers.

As the forest bared itself for winter, the sun dipped its head to peer into the misty recesses where toadstools kept their fiery secrets and pleated flesh hid rainbow hues.

The darkness deepened to the sound of urgent bird calls and anxious squirrels that sprinted from tree to tree gathering nuts to store for the winter. The air was rich with the scents of moss and magic. In the tempest winds that tore asunder the webs that spiders patiently rebuilt, the boy sensed expectantly that anything might happen. And, as the last leaf plunged from the Tree, winter quietly covered the clearing.

WINTER

now coated the arms of the Tree and the sky dropped so low that the clouds grazed its boughs. Spider webs froze and squirrels snored loudly in their nests. Winter squalls and wild winds spun the forest in an exuberant dance. Breathless and sweating, trees churned and whirled their limbs in joyous abandon.

"Aren't you cold?" the boy anxiously pressed the Tree again and again. "Not at all," the Tree repeatedly reassured him.

"My roots are deep. I warm my toes at the earth's core where winter cannot quell the fire. My bark is solid, and my spirit is strong. I am a tree. Winter is part of my cycle of loss and renewal."

The boy set aside his worries and, wrapped in his warmest down-filled jacket, traced the ice whorls on the frozen stream. In the silence of the snow he could hear the water flow beneath its diamond-cut surface. His nose turned red and his eyes glittered as the wind sharpened its blade and stoked the winter fires.

He busied himself gathering fallen logs and kindling, which he piled just beyond the clearing. He enjoyed tramping through the forest, gathering his stores, his blood pumping faster as he wandered along familiar paths that had been transformed by the season. Then, later, sitting by the fire, picking out the driest kindling to get the sparks crackling, smoke swirling in the air and his fingers tingling as the flames lapped the wood and his hands thawed.

Everything looked different in the firelight. Shadows coiled and sprung where none had been before. As the boy drew closer to the heat, the forest cast off all its trappings and flung itself headlong into the season. Naked and exposed, it danced recklessly with impunity. It did not attempt to cover itself, or offer apology for its shorn nudity. It was a primal, untamed thing, unashamed of its beauties and secrets, engaged in a ritual that stretched right back to the beginning of trees and time.

The Tree reveled in the heavy snows that coated its limbs before unpredictable winds sent drifts spinning about in dervish flurries. It laughed joyously as fierce tempests tore through its eaves and tossed the fire's flames. It tried to explain to the boy the pleasure that it took in these short days and deep silences. "We are born naked and free of burdens," it said. "Our spirits have not been trapped and made timid. The wheel turns and we get older. The axle creaks and our souls tremble. Then we discover that in the end is the beginning. Another crank and we are naked once again. Winter lies on the cusp of endings. In death we feel the stirrings of new life."

The boy drew his chin into the folds of his coat and tossed another log onto the fire as the wind rose and the sky sank lower. Creatures that dreamed the winter long whimpered softly into curled tails and shuddered until the howling eased.

∞

While half the forest slept, those that kept watch became more fully alive, keen to the changes in the air, the earth. The world's edges sharpened beneath ice that held subtle curves and soft wisps in hard vices, revealing winter's cruel beauty. Everything seemed more clearly defined; the world set in relief.

The boy felt it too. His nerves tingled and the hairs in his nose twitched in the cold. He became more aware of the hidden parts of his body, awakening to the rhythm of his limbs and the flow of his blood to his toes and fingertips. Even his breath made crisp loops in the air, leaving trails of vapour plumes that he could reach out and brush with mittened hands.

Everything was deeply familiar, yet utterly different. Scents were sharper. Shadows were deeper. Groans and tremors, hidden by the life of day, took on substance and shape. Walking through the forest felt like creeping through the house at night while all the family slept. It was exciting and strange, and the boy treaded its paths and trails, alert and alive, keen to every creak and whisper. He had never felt so fully awake.

He could hear the flames singing, as his blood warmed and surged when he returned to the comfort of the fireside. The Tree hummed its own strange tune, tossing wild notes to the wind, as light loitered a moment longer before heading off with the night. Snow began to fall in soft drifts, muffling the world, pushing everything deeper beneath the surface. The boy's head began to droop. He stirred and threw another log on the fire. The night was quiet. Dreams came and took him.

∞

In this space, where the familiar and the strange overlapped, the boy woke to the cracking of a twig in the forest. The sound snapped the snow-laden silence of the glade. The noise startled a bird, which launched a raucous warning. This was picked up by other birds across the forest. Dreams were splintered. Someone was coming.

Time evaporated as the boy wiped his sleepy eyes and waited. A tendril of light crept into the clearing. Night edged towards the exit. Embers sputtered and faded. Shadows blurred and a figure stepped out of the darkness, trailed by a draught of blue seas and warm skies. Hints of spices drifted on the air. The boy took a deep breath. His first thoughts shaped by a glimpse of a well-worn travel cloak and a hat pulled low.

"Welcome, Wanderer," said the Tree. "You have traveled many paths to get here."

The stranger came closer so the boy could see more clearly. A tumble of dark hair flowed down her back as she pulled off her hat and looked around her. "The road has many forks and turns, and Fate seldom takes the direct route," she responded.

"Take rest for a while," said the Tree. "Lay down your burdens and share our warmth."

The Wanderer nodded her head in thanks as she shrugged off the pack, which was strapped to her back, then she stowed her gloves and loosened her walking boots. As she peeled her traveling skin, the boy set about carefully re-kindling the fire. It did not take long for the flames to lap at the dried wood. In very little time, a circle of warmth enclosed the boy, the Tree and the Wanderer. A comfortable silence settled in which no explanations were needed, for a time.

∞

The hour toppled and the boy burned with curiosity. As he poked the flames, he furtively watched the Wanderer, who had stretched out on the forest floor beside the fire, using her pack as a pillow and her cloak as a bed. Her eyes were closed, and her breathing was steady, but he sensed that she was not asleep. He also guessed that she was not unused to making a bed where her boots happened to rest.

He wasn't sure where his assumptions came from. She gave nothing away. Not a word of introduction, or a reason for her coming. Of course, the Tree would know, but it was always encouraging him to be patient. People shared what they wanted you to know when trust was earned, and the time was right.

He didn't wish to pry, but she was different to the others who had come before her. He wasn't sure how he knew this. If pressed, he would have described it as a feeling, no more. For now, he had nothing else to go on. Other than the pack she had carried on her back, she had no other burdens that he could see. From her clothing there was no telling where she had come from, or where she was heading to. Yet he knew she had seen things he had not yet imagined, and suddenly the forest seemed terribly small and he yearned to know what lay beyond its boundaries.

"Are you asleep?" he whispered loudly. The Wanderer opened her eyes a fraction. He took that as an invitation to continue. "It's starting to snow again."

She shifted the hat that was shading her face and grunted assent. He caught a glimpse of her eyes, as they flickered across him and briefly scanned the clearing, coming to rest at the Tree. He searched them for whatever they might tell him. They were woody green, tinged with moss and veiled with thick lashes. He looked away. She had caught him staring, but she didn't seem to mind.

He shifted, sat on his hands, and then fidgeted again. It was morning, even if it wasn't very bright. Surely it was time to talk and start the day? If he didn't get answers soon to some of his questions, he thought he just might burst. She seemed oblivious to his discomfort.

"Where have you come from?" he eventually blurted.

"I came from the West," responded the Wanderer.

"Is that further than the forest's edge?" he probed, alight with interest.

"It is," she said.

A hole of unanswered questions loomed. The boy lurched forward. "Why did you come here?" he asked.

"I am a wanderer. I have traveled to the North, the South, the East and the West. My path led me here because it is said that the Tree is the kernel of the compass."

She looked at the boy, as though noticing him for the first time. "You are just a child, and yet you found your way."

The boy grinned, pleased to have finally caught her attention, then confessed, "I havn't gone anywhere. Though," he continued, "each season I go a little farther into the forest. By myself," he added, with proud emphasis. "I can show you my favourite places," he offered, "if you're not too tired. There are lots and lots of paths, and it is easy to get lost if you do not know the way."

"The Tree is spoken of in many lands, both in this world and across the seas. I have heard it said that it is the path from which all journeys begin and end. As my wanderings draw to a close, it would seem that yours are just starting." She sighed. But it didn't sound like a sad sigh, or a weary one. The boy could not fathom her. She was a secret that he wanted to spill, but he didn't know how to upend her thoughts.

In the silence that followed, the boy studied the Wanderer in the light of the fire. Her face carried lines that hinted at laughter and sunshine, but there were shadows beneath her eyes. She wore a single green gem around her neck and, as she warmed her hands, stones glimmered on her fingers. But he was most taken by the hilt of a dagger that sat snuggly against her hip. It was a fine thing, as beautiful and as dangerous as a snake.

The boy pointed at it. "Can I see it?" he asked.

"Maybe later," she deflected. Her hand, unbidden, hovered protectively over the hilt. She sat up, legs crossed, the cloak falling off a shoulder.

The boy probed again. "How did you get here?" he asked.

"By chance," she replied.

Catching his disappointment, she settled more comfortably. She had traveled many paths and seen many sights. But there was only one story that mattered. It was time it was told.

∞

The boy's plans for the day fell like petals off a flower. Caught in the grip of her story he leaned forward, his entire body intent on catching every single word.

"There was a time, once. And upon that time there lived a girl. She was a lot like other girls her age. She was good. And kind. And she was wise enough to know that it was better to try to understand the world, than force the world to understand her. But, for all her smiles and gentle words, she knew that she was different. Beneath her skin. It was just a feeling. But it had the surety of knowledge.

"She did not dream of puddings and white dresses. Nor did she picture dimpled fingers clinging to her hands. These were all good dreams. But they were not hers.

"Her dreams were feral things. Yearnings she could not put a shape on. Mountains echoed in her mind. Winds twisted and lifted her aloft. These were not things that she could speak of, for she did not know the words to name them. They left her with a sour taste for all that she did not want, and with a hunger for all she had not yet eaten. But she was young and believed that the future would deliver her destiny. And so, she waited and, as she waited, she got older.

"Routines reared up to fill her days and deaden her dreams. The time came when she could no longer hear the mountains or feel the wind. The din of schedules and doing the right thing doused every other sound as she put her head down and diligently followed the only path she knew to a dead end.

"Faced with the prospect of marching in step and going nowhere, she sought another route. Open to possibilities, it was then that she heard it again. The sound of longing carried on the smell of an ocean breeze. Her soul listened cautiously, as her mind made lists.

"Wild imaginings, long submerged, drifted towards the surface. They serenaded her gut and ransacked her dreams. Their voices wrapped around her heart like tendrils; sounds so sweet that they filled her mind with desire and choked her breath.

"She finally flung aside her fears so that she might claw for air. An uncertain space opened and shifted beneath her feet; a place without plans or a clear destination. This other path flickered and faltered before her. The horizon stretched in directions she had never before conceived. She took a hesitant step onto this phantom road. It held fast and she gained courage. So, she followed the first step with another. And another.

"She wandered deeper into this unfamiliar realm, eyes straining ahead, neck craning behind. Cherished hands reached for her from the world she was departing. Yet the voices that called to her could not be unheard.

"She forged ahead, until she reached the point of no return. The road divided into two paths. One continued forward, the other circled back. The world pulsed. Her eyes swam. She curled upon herself, containing the moment. She quavered. The decision evaporated. She crumbled, and I emerged from her chrysalis," the Wanderer ended with a slight bow and a flourish of her hand.

"What happened then?" asked the boy, eyes wide.

$$\infty$$

"Then we have breakfast," the Wanderer sat up and busied herself with her pack, while the boy reluctantly set off to gather firewood. His disappointment at the story's wane dissipated as his hunger swelled.

When he returned, the Wanderer was softly humming as she flipped an omelet on a hot pan. Water simmered in a can and warmth seeped through the clearing. She nodded to him when he placed his stash on the pile. He smiled, accepting it as approval. He wanted her to like him.

They ate in silence, the Wanderer at ease in her thoughts; the boy straining against the world to be seen. He felt timid, and unsure of how to hold a fork without it clattering against the side of his plate. Her hands were steady, assured. He watched them glide smoothly from dish to mouth. Hands that could hold another's, or wield a dagger. Fingers that could wrap around a spoon could as easily curl around a hilt, or a throat.

"I'll clean up," he offered.

Again, that smile. "I'll help you."

Dishes and pans were washed and stowed. This time he felt her eyes on him, appraising. He carried his back stiffly. His arms seemed to drag in their sockets. Hands needed to be told more than once what to do. He hardly trusted himself to walk, fearful of stepping on feet and laces.

She had offered her story. But still he knew nothing of where she had come from, or what she had seen. The dagger, dull ache in the firelight, might have revealed a little more if it had a mouth, as well as teeth. He hoped she would let him see it, later.

Eventually, gear stowed and chores completed, she lifted up the tale where she had left it trailing. The boy came scampering from behind, trying to catch up.

"In a roar, my destiny slipped into the world, spilling onto the road, soaking it with its blood and mucus and potential to begin again. It opened its eyes, shiny and glittering in the glare of first light. The cord was severed, and a new life took shape.

"I was reborn." The Wanderer said simply.

"The road stretched before me, hinting at adventures. This time, I vowed, I would do better. I would learn the world and my place in it.

I would live freely, without artifice or lies. I would love boldly, without fear or boundaries. I would pursue knowledge as a huntress, and seek happiness as a quest. Everything seemed clear as I cradled my destiny, feeling the new life fluttering against my breast."

The boy quivered with charged delight. "Weren't you frightened?" he asked, thrilling with the tremor of fear felt from the safety of the fireside.

"I was more afraid of what I would have become had I chosen differently. I had been careless once. I had let my happiness slip away from me. It was I who had marched that girl to a dead end, when there were so many other roads she could have taken.

"I wasn't torn with regret, for I had learned my lesson; but I was determined that once I caught up with my happiness, I would never be foolish enough to let it go again."

"Did you find it?" the boy asked.

The Wanderer's eyes glinted in the firelight. "I found more than I bargained for," she replied. She reached for a log and tossed it onto the fire, causing an uproar of sparks. They cackled and spat like angry old men, before settling back down to their smoke.

The Wanderer eased back into her story. She spoke slowly, with unhurried gestures, long thoughts stretching the length of the road she followed. "In my search for happiness I had no guide, other than my instincts. No compass, other than my heart," she said.

"I had many false starts and wrong turnings, yet I never deviated from my path. My quest led me across continents over many, many seasons. I traveled the ancient world, and the new. I met countless souls upon the road and listened to more stories than I can recall. Some seeped into my skin, lingering, while others faded as soon as the teller had drifted from the fireside."

"Where did you go? What did you see? Who did you meet?" asked the boy, tripping over his questions.

She shook her head at his hurry, and then she settled on a tale.

"One adventure drew me to the New World, where night outdid the day for its glitter and brightness. Everything moved faster than I had thought possible. Even the people ran from one point of rest to the next. It was bewildering, and wonderful, and utterly strange to me.

"One evening, I came across a raucous group of tailored folk in smart suits. White teeth glimmered; while restive hands possessively clutched bleating phones, which were given the same attention as small children crossing a busy road. They laughed so loudly that I lingered on their verge. Straining to see if happiness was lurking in their midst, I stepped a little closer and was gathered into their fold.

"Up close it seemed that clothes and smiles were worn like coats of armour. Everyone kept their guards up, and eyed each other with deep suspicion. Yet my road had led me here, so I attempted to disarm them and listened carefully to what they had to say.

"'Are you happy?' I asked of each, naive in my directness, yet unwilling to dissemble.

"One man declaimed loudly that power was the master of happiness and that he worked its strings. He brooded over the company, his voice flattening all others' words, his eyes seeking only his own reflection.

"Another boasted of his holdings, claiming pleasure in lording over the chattels of his neighbours. Photographs of his possessions were herded on his phone and paraded one by one in front of disinterested viewers. Beneath his brashness was the gnawing fear that another mobile might be drawn, and a shot of a bigger house discharged to shatter his image.

"A woman offered to sell me some happiness, but I could not meet her demands. Another wanted to buy my happiness, but by this time I had none to sell.

"As the night wore on, and cups were refilled, faces melted and dripped bitterness, and hoarse confessions sputtered of unfulfilled desires.

"'I have everything I thought I wanted,' one confided, 'but when I stand on my balcony surveying the city beneath me, all I can think about is jumping off the ledge.'

"I tried to slip out into the clean air, but found myself trapped in their stale misery. During the night gold coins had been stacked high, barring all of the exits. I circled our prison, looking for an escape route, and eventually spotted our gaoler. A dull figure hovered on the edge of the gloom, with head bent and eyes downcast, intent on its task and diligent in its designs. It cradled a bulging sack from which long bony fingers drew bright shiny coins. I flung myself against the bars and called out to it until my voice was ragged and my fists torn, but it buried its face in the darkness of a cowl and ignored my imprecations.

"I attempted to rouse my companions and alert them to our peril, but their bodies lay draped across tables, where bleary heads lolled on well-cut sleeves.

"I realized that if I were to get back to my path, I would need to act alone. So, with soft words and glittering promises, I eventually drew the creature within my arm's reach. As it leaned forward, hand outstretched, I saw points of light glimmer in the well of its dark hood. I had just one chance. I lurched and grabbed its neck and, in the struggle, it dropped its sack of loot. Amidst the havoc of tumbling gold, I managed to make my escape."

"What of the others?" the boy asked.

The Wanderer sighed, "A small few grabbed the chance I had seized and scrambled through the opening. Others lurched through the gap, but stumbled on the coins. A few more made a start, but faltered and filled their pockets. Then there were those who joined the creature in rebuilding the columns of their cage."

"What did you do then?" he prodded.

"I returned to the road, turned my back to the lights, and continued on my journey."

"The road sounds really scary," the boy whispered to the flames. He drew his knees more tightly to his chest. "I don't believe that I would have the courage to leave behind me everything that I know and face into the world alone."

"We are all ultimately alone," said the Wanderer, "though Fear loves company. I found it to be a total chatterbox, and an utter bore. It has nothing of interest to say, and even less to teach. I shook it loose by ignoring it. In time it gave up on me and left me for another, who huddled under their blankets at night and clattered their teeth in response to its jabbering."

She gathered her thoughts as she gazed at the fire. "The road has its perils. But every quest comes with a cost, and it's through such hardships that knowledge is won, and wisdom earned.

"The road also has its wonders," she smiled.

The boy leaned a little closer.

∞

"Maps were of little use to me, as I ended up in places which had not yet been defined. I traveled through jungles where blue butterflies swarmed, and I returned to a time when the world was first created."

The boy's eyes swam with the marvels she described, and he felt a dull ache of longing in his heart.

She spoke in a low voice, tones falling in smoky drifts. "It was beautiful. Unsullied colours gloried in their newness. Blue was given meaning by skies that knew no sadness. Trees, fully formed, shaded the landscape. Their giant minds shielded memories of the time before creation. The earth hummed with life, and happiness inhabited the land."

When she fell silent, the Tree continued, "It was a world full of hope and love. Everything existed in its pure form, and everything understood its place in the world. The time of darkness had not yet come when trees were slaughtered in great numbers, when the waters were sullied with sludge, when memories were forgotten, and when people lost their happiness."

"How did this happen?" asked the boy.

"Because happiness, for some, was not enough. They traded their light for false promises, and, in the end, they lost everything."

The Wanderer, the boy and the Tree drifted along the stream of their thoughts to the sound of the keening wind.

∞

The sharp yelp of a tormented animal rose above the wails, shredding their thoughts and shattering the peace of the forest. The boy and the Wanderer immediately jumped to their feet, trying to divine which direction the sound had come from.

"You're a fool!" a voice they recognized berated his companion. "You should have brought the compass."

"We are not lost, Master."

"I shall die in this foul forest, and it will be your fault." The hiss of a whip slashed the air and landed with venom. They stiffened as they heard the sharp intake of a chilled breath.

Words, spat in anger, were unleashed like blows.

Low, long whimpers cut the air, and slowly faded.

"You should have packed the compass."

"Follow me, Master."

Another whistle, snap, and sizzling flesh rent the curtain, giving the companions a brief glimpse of pain imagined.

"You presume too much. You are a fool. And I'm a bigger one for trusting you. It will be dark soon, and I will be done for."

"Even in darkness, my heart would know the way."

"You have no heart, dog."

The voices came closer. The Wanderer, alert, with hand on the hilt of her dagger, stood lightly on her toes, poised as a cat.

"Easy, Wanderer," the Tree spoke softly. "Everyone is welcome to this clearing." The Wanderer relaxed her stance, a very little, just as the Shadow gently parted the foliage. It gazed at the Tree with the trust of a child.

"You are welcome home, my friend. But you have suffered much on this journey." The Shadow seemed somehow frailer than when the boy had last seen it in autumn. There were fresh bloody welts across its shoulders, and it shivered uncontrollably in the cold air. It dropped its heavy bags in a heap and spoke falteringly to the Tree, as though searching for unfamiliar words. "I am happy to see you. I have ached in my bones to return."

"And my heart is full now that you have rejoined me," responded the Tree. "Be at peace."

The Shadow moved painfully slowly to the Tree. It bent its head and leaned its forehead against the trunk, where it rested a moment before it slid down to the earth in an exhausted heap, and immediately slipped into unconsciousness.

"Fool, Fool, where are you?" bellowed a frightened voice. "Time is running ahead of me. It shall soon be nightfall." The words were grabbed and stretched by the wind. "I need you."

The Shadow did not stir. Tree turned to the boy, "Fetch our guest, child, before he murders peace."

The boy ran off, and returned, a few moments later, with Time in tow.

"Don't worry, there's still many hours of light," the boy could be heard reassuring him. Time clutched the child's arm as he staggered towards the fire. His brilliant fur coat brushed the snow at his feet.

"Is that you, Time?" asked the Wanderer, sizing up his bulk and bulging eyes, which peered above a thick wool muffler. As Time settled his gaze on the blaze, the fear slunk from his face. He loosened the scarf around his throat and pulled open his coat.

"It is three o'clock," he informed the clearing.

"Ahem," the boy nudged him in the ribs and jerked his head towards his belly.

"Quiet, boy, I'm working," Time hissed.

"But, Time," the boy persisted.

"Shut it!" Time spat. "It's three o'clock," he repeated, glaring at his audience.

"It's not," the disgruntled child countered.

"It is," Time insisted, unaccustomed to self-doubt.

"It is not," the boy stubbornly refused to back down, legs rooted, finger pointed accusingly at Time's belly.

Time looked down and let out a yelp, which he quickly camouflaged as a cough. "It is two o'clock," announced Time.

"Really?" the boy pushed his advantage.

"Yes, yes, you were right. Are you happy now? I have been wandering lost and alone in the forest and finally stumble to the hearth of friends to find myself subjected to interrogation like some common criminal. I might have died out there in the cold, but instead of offering to share your fire you drag me over the coals on a technicality."

The child shuffled, embarrassed, cheeks reddening and head hanging low.

"I have been discombobulated, wandering in this cursèd wasteland, and somehow seem to have been lumbered with an extra hour," Time added as an explanation. "If you know who it belongs to, do tell. I'm sure I've plenty of my own," he sniffed.

The boy nodded his head vigorously, anxious to be redeemed.

"No matter, Time," said the Tree. "Settle yourself by the fire."

Time dropped by the warmth, his legs spread before him. "My bones are getting older," he complained. "The cold seeps deeper every year.

"Tree, you look a fright," he added. "I hardly recognized you without your leaves." The Tree chuckled, "I've seen a few winters in my time. None of us are getting any younger, but I have no complaints. The winter has been kind."

Time pulled off his furry hat, which had large earflaps and baubles dangling from the ties. "That's better," he said, dabbing at the sweat that was pooling down his neck. As he twisted his head his eyes fell on the Shadow, which was slumbering in a heap, half hidden by the Tree's trunk.

"Would you look at that." Stunned disbelief flattened his voice. "While I was lost and foundered in the forest, that wretch was sleeping comfortably all this time." His face deepened a crimson red and his eyes narrowed in anger.

"Wake up, Fool," he roared, causing chaos amongst the birds of the forest. His hand went to the handle of the whip he had tucked into his belt. As he smoothly rose to his feet, his body fueled by fury, he hissed through clenched teeth. "I will teach that wretch a lesson it will not forget in a hurry."

The boy's eyes widened in horror. The Tree breathed out and grew in stature. "Time, sit down," it instructed in a voice filled with authority. "This soul is under my protection and will come to no harm."

"You have no right, Tree," he mewled. "The slave is mine and is not for the taking."

"You lay claim to that which is not yours. A life is inviolably its own. It is never for the taking." The Tree weighed its words and poured them out slowly.

Time's feet wavered, but his hands did not loosen their grip on his whip.

The Wanderer, who had not moved from her place by the fire, raised her eyes to Time and lowered her voice. "I stand with the Tree," she said, "and to reach that creature you must first pass me."

Time's gaze drifted to the dagger which glinted on her belt. Deflated by the opposition he shifted uncertainly, frightened to move forward and loathe to back down.

"Why don't you sit, Time," suggested the boy.

"Why don't you listen to the boy," the Wanderer prompted.

"I'm not unreasonable," Time whined, drifting towards the earth. "But it's sleeping on my time. Would you look at it, lying there comfortably without a care in the world or a thought for its poor master."

All eyes settled on the Shadow which, even in its sleep, was wracked by tremors. The red welts on its back stood out in sharp relief to the snow, on which it lay curled in a heap of bones, rags and blood.

The Wanderer grimly strode to where it had fallen. She crouched over the broken form, murmuring soft words. Then she carefully scooped it up in her arms. It stirred and cried out, but she whispered something the boy could not hear, and it settled back into its dark dreams.

"What are you doing?" sputtered Time. She ignored him. She carried the creature, which weighed no more than a shadow, over to the fire, where she settled it gently in the circle of warmth. She draped her cloak over its shrunken body. A whisper of a smile softened the bruised face, which was partly hidden beneath its wisps of hair. The boy knelt by its side and brushed back the tangled mess with gentle fingers. He traced the line of the cheekbones and its jaw. It was the first time he had ever touched the Shadow. He was shocked. It felt human.

It felt the touch. Fingers probing. Tender. It did not hurt. Perhaps it was someone else's face.

"You go too far, Wanderer," Time fumed. The Wanderer faced Time. Green eyes devoured by black anger. Time nervously shifted his hand to the comfort of his whip. She might have laughed at his stink of fear, if the time for gaiety had not long since passed.

As so many others had considered before, she thought how easy it would be to kill Time. She could have her knife at his throat before he could muster another bleat. The scene played before her mind. His cruelties, judgments and his yearnings bled onto the snow at her feet. She savoured the image. Time gulped. She breathed slowly in and out, and claimed control of the anger that would have her do its bidding. The Tree murmured. She felt its force. It knew her thoughts, and it waited. Steady, calm and frosted, she flexed her fist and released the taut muscles. "There's room for all," she said with finality.

"Indeed, indeed," Time agreed, whistling through his teeth, a long-drawn note of relief.

"I can see that I am outnumbered, but I will have you know that it is many hours since I have eaten." He thought for a moment, "At the very least two, and I'm heartily hungry. But of course, no one cares about that. No one cares that I am wasting away in the cold grip of winter."

"Don't worry, Time," the Wanderer found the heart to laugh. "I may have a few marshmallows in my pack that will tide you over till dinner." Time brightened immediately. "They might be a little deflated," she added, "but I think we can risk it."

In no time at all, squashed marshmallows were puckered on the ends of sticks and the mood in the clearing mellowed as they melted stickily, and fingers were licked.

∞

Flames lapped at pools of sugar as the companions settled comfortably into their thoughts. Time drummed his fingers on his belly contentedly, eventually breaking the silence, "I don't suppose you came across a sprightly nag named Tomorrow on your travels?" he asked.

"The name doesn't ring a bell. What does it look like?"

Time thought for a while. "I'm not really sure," he admitted. "I've never actually had a good look at it myself. But it sounds like thunder in the distance and smells like summer grass on your skin. I nearly caught it once, you know. For just a moment I had a clasp of its tail. But then it got away from me."

"What did it feel like?" asked the Wanderer.

"It felt weightless. For a moment time stood still."

"It sounds a lot like happiness to me," mused the Wanderer.

"I've been looking for it ever since," Time sighed.

"I wish you well in your quest," she said.

"Where has the road led you since last we met?" he asked.

"It has been scores of years since we crossed paths. I have traveled a long road since then. As you see, it has led me here."

"Has it really been that long?" Time asked, a little shocked. "It seems just like yesterday."

"I have stopped counting years as I have stopped counting minutes, but I was young then and you filled my head with promises," she recalled.

Time scratched his brow in an effort to spark his memory. "I remember you asked if I knew the path to happiness." He beamed delightedly at his victory in cornering the thought.

"And you invited me to join you," she looked across at the Shadow, and shuddered.

"That's right, that's right," he nodded, still buoyed by his successful snare. His eyes clouded a little, so he scratched some more.

"You talked of traveling without fear or burdens," he reminisced. She nodded, smiling at the memory. "I wanted to look at the world with fresh eyes every morning, free of routines, guided by my instincts."

"Sounds like a dog's life to me," Time snorted.

The Wanderer laughed, "I remember that you talked of coming with me."

"Certainly not. I had responsibilities. I couldn't simply drop everything and walk away from them. Though," he added, "it wouldn't be the first time that I had my head turned by a pretty lady." He almost winked at her, but thought better of it.

"What an odd pair of traveling companions we would have made," she mused. "As I faced towards the sun, you would have measured my footsteps."

"But of course I would. Otherwise, how would we have known how to calculate your distance to the horizon?" Time countered.

The Wanderer leaned forward to cast another log on the fire. A sliver of white wrist was lit by the flames. Time drew in a short, sharp breath. "The watch I gave you is gone," he gasped.

"It was a very fine gift, Time. I simply didn't need it." She spoke gently.

"What are you talking about? Of course you needed it. Otherwise, how could you know when to eat or when to sleep?"

"My belly tells me when it is hungry. The stars tell me when it is night."

"You have an answer for everything," he harrumphed.

He wanted to berate her, but feared to risk more than a grumble. "Traveling without a watch is like wandering without a compass," he muttered. "Look, I never leave home without mine." He drew up his sleeves to display thick arms encircled with watches to his elbows.

The boy leaned forward to take a closer look. "They all tell different times," he said.

"And that, my boy, is why you always need to carry more than one. The heart's pulse," he tapped the inside of the boy's wrist, "can easily lead you astray." He stroked the face of the largest watch that sat like a weight on his arm. "I wouldn't be without it, but I never fully trust it."

"Time, you worry too much. You should face life a little less burdened. For every missed bus another surely follows. It arrives when it's ready and leaves when it's full."

"Spare a thought to all that wasted time," Time pounded his point.

"Some of my happiest moments were spent waiting by the roadside. As my mind loitered, all kinds of quare thoughts wandered by. Some quare hawks too," she added.

"Don't talk nonsense," snorted Time.

"I believe that's where I first encountered you," she said. "Everyone I met was on a journey, and everyone had something to teach me, if I kept my ears and mind open. Even you, Time."

"Well you clearly didn't listen to a word I said. If you had, you wouldn't talk such balderdash. But don't worry," he visibly brightened, "I believe I may have just what you need."

He ambled to the heap of strewn suitcases and selected a small brown leather case, which he brought back to the fire. He undid its claps and, with the flourish of a magician, revealed its contents. In the absence of any other response, Time let out a voluntary gasp.

The satin-trimmed case was draped with every conceivable style of watch. Chrome finishes glinted dully in the firelight; glass faces stretched Time's reflected grin; leather straps rested comfortably in soft, supple folds.

"Ladies and gentlemen, I have a watch for every wrist and every pocket." They gathered around as Time lowered his voice to a conspiratorial whisper. "For one day only I'm selling them at a knockdown rate. Everything has to go. Don't ask me where I got them, 'cause you will not want to know. But that is not why I'm practically giving them away. I woke up feeling generous, and I wanted to make your day. Don't be shy. Come a little closer. I'll tell you this once, and I won't say it again, I'm not going to sell you one watch; I'm going to practically give you two. They're red hot and they're yours for a steal."

As the boy leaned in, his hand stretched out, Time jerked his head up, ears alert, and snapped the case closed.

"What's that, what's that? There's someone coming. Not a word now," he winked at the boy as he hid the case beneath the pile of luggage.

"I didn't hear a thing," the boy said. "Can't be too careful," Time responded. The Wanderer laughed, "You always had a flair for drama, Time."

"Wanderer," the boy spoke up shyly, "you never did tell us what happened to your happiness."

"A story!" Time clapped his hands. "How marvelous. Nothing passes the time quite so well as a good story."

∞

The Wanderer smiled at the boy and pulled a few more marshmallows from her pack. "Toast those, child, and I'll see what I can cook up for you."

The boy's heart melted another drop.

"My quest became my obsession and my delight. I met priests and lawyers, mothers and adventurers, stalwarts of propriety, and black sheep of society. I met people who claimed that happiness was a myth. And I met souls who overflowed with joy, soaking all around them.

"Some told me that if I lived a good life, I would find happiness in the next. Others agreed that happiness rested on the whim of God, Mohammad, Buddha, Jesus, Krishna, the Messiah, Death and the Dollar.

"I had already looked for happiness in the New World, so I decided to change my tack and seek it in the old.

"I visited an ancient land, where I wandered labyrinthine alleys behind old city walls."

"Oh, I love cities," said Time. "I'm appreciated there. Everyone knows me. My chime is admired and my tock desired." He slipped into reverie and the Wanderer continued.

"Happiness lurked around every corner. It dodged and weaved between mysterious shadows. It hid behind bread-sellers' stalls, and slunk along worn cobblestones.

"I chased it down and finally cornered it against a great wall as the sun was setting, casting a warm glow."

The Wanderer's eyes shone. The boy held his breath and Time bit into another marshmallow, rolling his tongue around its soft centre.

"The low light suffused the huge blocks of coarse stone. Swarms of worshippers bowed their heads before the wall and swayed in demented rhythm. I pressed forward. Happiness was in my sight, but not yet in my reach. I placed my right palm against the wall. Energy swelled. I felt the stones breathing as they wrapped me in its memories."

The Wanderer's voice filled with an old ache. "Then a wail rose above the prayers. At first, I thought it was the wind. But it was older, harsher. Voices ascended in pain and anger. 'Mine,' they roared, spattering my mind with their blood and fury.

"In the chaos that followed, happiness slipped through the stones and I could not follow."

The boy let out his breath as Time let out a groan and shifted his ample bottom to find a more comfortable cushion.

"As I turned to leave, a small scrap of paper, wedged tightly between the blocks, caught my eye. I prized it out and smoothed its creases. It was covered in faded script. I was able to make out just one word: Salvation."

Time rolled his eyes, "That old chestnut."

∞

The Wanderer shrugged, "I had nothing else to go on, so I set out on the road to salvation."

"I'm surprised that it hadn't been worn away by bloodied feet marching in time to matins," Time snorted.

The boy gave Time, who was filing his nails, as brutal a look as he could muster. "Go on, Wanderer," he urged.

She ignored the child's open face and looked more intently at Time's, "You've become a cynic. Don't you believe in anything?"

"Tomorrow's my mantra. Time's my missal," he chanted dryly.

"And yet, you are here." She considered him a moment longer, then continued, "The road led to a church filled with solemn heads bent in serious prayer. It was cool and peaceful and smelled of dust and incense. Light sifted through stained glass windows, and candles burned low to the drone of petitions.

"I made my way deeper into its secret recesses, running my fingers over old stone. The candles sputtered and the shadows lengthened.

"'What are you searching for, my child?' A low voice spread over the darkness like butter. 'I'm over here,' it said. I moved slowly, carefully, as my skin crept over my bones. I came to an upright wooden box, which had a window in its centre over which a red curtain was drawn. The voice floated from behind this covering. A door opened. 'Please come in,' the voice invited. 'There is nothing to fear.' I sheathed my knife and entered the darkness. 'Close the door.' A shaft of light filtered through, and a face belonging to an old man appeared behind a metal grill. He had kind eyes.

"Once again he asked me, 'What are you looking for, my child?'

"'I'm looking for salvation,' I said. 'Then I think I can help you,' he replied. He conjured a huge bundle, which he instructed I carry with me at all times. We stepped together outside of the box, and he handed me my burden. I tried to pick it up, but stumbled beneath its weight.

"'What is it?' I asked. 'It is guilt,' he replied. He told me that it was my passage to salvation and, if I carried it faithfully, I would find what I was looking for at journey's end. He helped me to attach it to my pack. I staggered under its cruel weight. 'I will never make it,' I confessed. He counseled me, 'My child, the road may be long and the passage hard, but think of the reward.' I did and I left, placing one slow foot in front of the other."

The boy eyed her pack and tested its weight. "It's heavy alright, but I think I could manage it."

"Don't talk nonsense, boy," Time interrupted. "Why would you even try? That's what Fools are for. I wouldn't dream of lifting my own bag. It's simply not dignified. And I don't mind saying it, Wanderer, I have told you this more than once."

"Indeed you have, Time. But each must carry their own burdens."

She turned to the boy. "No matter how hard I tried, I never got far. My knees sagged and my back buckled. Walking with a bowed head I lost sight of the stars and saw nothing but the muck beneath my feet."

Time tutted, "I've never laboured under guilt myself, but I have been told that it's dreadful heavy stuff."

She nodded in agreement. "After days of getting nowhere, I dropped my load by the side of the road, dug a hole, buried my guilt, then raised my face to the sun and continued on my journey."

"Hurray," clapped Time. "That's the spirit."

∞

"My spirit was diminished. I was no closer to fulfilling my quest, but at least I was on the move again.

"In time the road brought me to a dry town, surrounded by low hills. As fate would have it, I came to a book shop. The smell of happiness drifted through the open windows. I followed the waft and encountered a woman pulling books from the shelves. She put down her bundle and sized me up. 'I am a wanderer too,' she told me, 'but I have finally come home.'

"'And what shall you do now?' I asked her.

"'I shall wait,' she said.

"'Wait for what?'

"'I'm waiting for the Messiah.'

"'What shall you do while you're waiting?' I probed.

"'I shall eat,' she said. 'These books are my food.' She stepped back from me so that I could survey her ample figure. 'And I have a big appetite!' she laughed.

"She seemed to have plenty, so I asked if I could join her. 'Of course not,' she jumped back defensively, 'there's not enough here for everyone.' She scooped up her books and placed them back on the shelves and showed me to the door. The road was empty, and I was starving."

∞

"My dear, Wanderer," Time commiserated, "that's simply dreadful. There's nothing worse than walking on an empty belly. Did you find a bite to keep the dogs at heel?" he asked with uncommon concern.

"Disenchanted and weary I returned to the road where I met another traveler draped in white, unhemmed cloth. He carried no weapon and, defiant of the sun, his head was bare. He traveled much lighter than I, and he offered to share my load."

"It would have been much better if he'd offered to share a sandwich," Time interjected.

"Shush!" the boy hissed.

"We walked the road in silence. I had not eaten for such a long time that I felt empty inside, with little to offer and nothing to share, other than my burdens."

"Which, of course, you had to carry yourself," Time sniped.

153

"As darkness settled my companion rolled out a mat by the side of the road and knelt upon it, his back towards the setting sun. As he chanted, I went in search of a campsite. My hunger padded beside me, startling and growling at every shadow."

"I can't bear it," Time yielded to a delighted shudder. "Did you have to resort to devouring each other?"

She shook her head, smiling, "It didn't quite come to that. I found a quiet, sheltered spot, protected by boulders from the sandstorms that rose like demons in the night. It was wintertime and, though the days were hot, the nights were often bitterly cold. I lit a small fire and wrapped myself around my hunger."

"Enough of the hunger," Time importuned. "Give me a marshmallow, boy, quickly." He waggled his empty hands at the child, who pretended not to notice.

"As the moon rose in the sky, my companion returned, brilliant in white and radiant in his happiness. 'The time of denial is over,' he declared, and burst into a smile. 'Now we shall eat.'"

"Wonderful," Time clapped. "Spare me no detail."

"He spread out a feast before me."

"Go on," Time prompted her.

"Foods I had never before tasted."

"How exciting!"

"I must have looked ravenous, for he said, 'I have been fasting for many days, but you have more need of nourishment than I.'"

"You know nothing of hunger," Time told her. His voice rose in anguish, "Would that I had met that gentle soul, for I have suffered such pangs of emptiness." The boy flung a marshmallow at him, which Time promptly stuffed into his mouth, corking his words.

∞

"Words flowed easily that night," the Wanderer said. "Ripe and mature they sweetened tales with their telling. We talked long into the darkness, arriving at the understanding that we were both on a pilgrimage, following the same path.

"So, we set out together at sunrise."

The Wanderer smiled in reflection. "The moon waxed and waned, and still we journeyed, our faces turned every evening from the setting sun. Our companionship eased the passage of the days as we traveled miles in sparse, rocky landscapes under the hot sun. The desert is the quietest place I have ever been," her thoughts meandered as she recalled their wanderings. "It's as silent as freshly fallen snow."

For the first time the boy noticed that their footprints had been covered and soft flakes fell in quiet drifts.

"I had never before seen such stars. The Milky Way arced across the sky, and the constellations plotted our route. It was a time of friendship and light. Until the darkness fell."

"What happened?" asked Time, who had stretched out comfortably by the fire.

"A gleaming city appeared on the horizon like a star, heralding the end of our journey. As each day brought us closer, its walls loomed larger and we were joined by many other pilgrims along the road. Men and women, with a common purpose and intent of mind, divested of wealth and status.

"Then, when we were within sight of the gates, our path converged with many others. The flood of people swelled and broke its boundaries. They poured over us. Our excitement and anticipation, which had been building for days, was submerged beneath the deluge, and I was separated from my friend. I searched for him amongst the throng, but every man wore the same simple white cloth. Women sought my eye, solicitude in their gaze, then turned away as my desperate glance raked past them.

"So, I carried on alone to the imposing gates, hopeful that I would find my friend within the city's walls. But, as they reared before me, a great shadow loomed to fill the intervening space. I strained my neck to look up at the face of the mighty Goliath that had come forward to block my path. He had a long, dark beard and cold, black eyes. His legs, which seemed planted in the earth, were muscular and knotted like a tree. A cruel blade, cared for, gleamed. He announced himself as the Guardian of the Gate, and he would not let me pass.

"Over his shoulder, the city poured welcome on the heads of other pilgrims who entered beneath its eaves. I alone stood challenged. I reasoned and pleaded, but my words fell on stone ears. His eyes never saw me, yet he deemed me unworthy and refused to grant me passage.

"My anger spat and writhed around me, hissing its venom and fury. I burned to kill him on the spot. To make those leaden eyes look into mine and know that I had found him wanting."

"Well, why didn't you?" demanded Time. "It would clearly have been the easiest way to get around him. He sounds like a rather large fellow."

"He was and, as my mind cooled, I knew I couldn't best him in a fight, which is why I left my knife in its scabbard and turned my back on the city. Cowardice is a great counselor for keeping you alive, but not always for pointing you in the right direction," she sighed.

"Did you ever get to see your friend again?" asked the boy.

"I never did, though I often think of him as I last saw him, his face alight as the city rose before us. I think that if he found his destiny, then I can forgive the gatekeeper for withholding mine."

∞

The fire burned low. The boy and the Wanderer gazed into the embers. Time fidgeted incessantly. "What's bothering you, Time?" the Tree queried.

"It's all this sitting around. I can't stand it."

"What would you rather be doing?"

"Oh, I don't know." He looked accusingly at the Wanderer, giving fright to her thoughts. "It's these feet of mine. They're itching like demons and I can't reach the soles.

"You wouldn't, you know, give them a little scratch for me?" He glanced at her again with, what he considered to be, a beguiling look.

"Of course, Time," she readily agreed. "I'll happily scratch them for you." She drew her dagger, and playfully tested its point on her fingertip.

"You could try hopping," the boy suggested.

"Now that's not as easy as it sounds," Time countered. "First, I would have to stand up, and we all remember the problems that can pose. Then, there's the hopping business. That requires balance and poise. Neither of which, I think we'll agree, are my strong suits. It needs to be timed just right and the knee bent just so, the ball of the foot curled at an angle like this," he demonstrated.

"Usually the Fool hops with me, so that we can get a rhythm going. It's quite good at hopping, you know." A hint of pride slipped into Time's voice. "But that wasn't always the case. You wouldn't believe the trouble I had with it in the beginning. My hands were blue, belting out the beat. Though no sooner had it cottoned on when I realized that the simplest thing was to get it to rub my feet. In fact, I have a lovely foot scratcher for that very reason in one of those bags.

"Fool," Time roared.

"Shush," hissed the Wanderer.

"Why on earth?" demanded Time.

"You'll wake it."

"That's the point."

"You've stop fidgeting, Time," the boy pointed out.

"You're right, boy. Perhaps my feet were not itchy at all. Maybe I was just bored."

"You'd better continue your story, Wanderer," the Tree advised, "to keep Time's itch at heel."

"Capital idea, Tree," Time grinned. "And perhaps a few more of those marshmallows."

The Wanderer leaned forward, her eyes fixed on the ember's heart. "When I was refused entry to the city, I felt the absence of light more keenly than ever before. The darkness was deeper, and I shuffled and stumbled, uncertain of what direction I was going in.

"In time, my eyes readjusted to the gloom. I almost stopped mourning my loss, content with edges and outlines. Until, once again, a shaft sent the shadows scuttling for cover.

"The road led to me to a river, where I sat on the bank listening to the soft murmur of nighttime voices.

"As the darkness softened, I watched long-nosed boats lazily drift past, parting the heat, while silhouetted figures leaned over the sterns to feed the river offerings of light. Candles, encircled by flowers, drifted on the ebb and flow.

"As dawn approached the air ripened and changed colour. The dogs woke from their heat stupor in snarling bad humour, giving fright to all the young boys who crossed their paths. Shadows silently joined me on the steps, each wrapped in their thoughts, some brighter than others. Men carefully folded up their clothing and entered the water. The women stood waist deep, resplendent in silks that vied with the sunrise.

"The sun rose as it must have that very first morning of creation. The bathers lifted their arms and their faces to the light. They shone with joy and gratitude for this blessing, as they cleansed their souls in the sacred river.

"As I watched, the sun tightened its grip and the air thickened with heat and the smells of bodies, both putrid and pure. My skin prickled, and the water beckoned. I tossed off my sandals, skipped towards the edge, and stopped in my tracks. The river, which lapped my feet, was so dirty that I dared not enter.

"I clambered onto the higher embankment, ashamed of my weakness. In refusing the mortification of my body, I was left with the more searing humiliation of the mind.

"In the face of my shame, I didn't know where to turn. Eventually, the heat chased me from the river and I headed towards the mountains, to a place that had called to me since my very first memories."

∞

"The mountains sang to me and I followed their music, steadily making my way towards their peaks. Along the road I came across temples devoted to more gods than I had names for. I saw a figure haloed by a wheel of arms, and a lofty elephant dancing burlesque, elevated by its lightness of being."

The Wanderer continued, "In each temple, I rang the bell when I entered to awaken the god. I watched priests dress doll-sized figurines in the finest silks, and daub their cold bodies with rose water. I heard devotees whisper with the gods as coins were dropped on plates and transactions sealed.

"Then, in the folds of the mountains, I found peace. Capped with ice, crowned with terraces, and canopied by willful skies, no place of worship could have competed in magnificence. The wind carried smells of alpine mint, and wild flowers dotted trails that had been forged by goats and their herders.

"Walking in the mountains, I crossed paths one day with an Elder. I had heard tales of her ilk, but it was my first time to encounter a mage. I did not recognize her at first for what she was. My eyes were closed to her magic. But I noted that she had a gentle face and a regal bearing. She introduced herself as Krishna. 'Ah,' I said knowingly. 'You are a devotee of Lord Krishna.' I had learned little for the length of time I had spent in this land.

"She spread her arms wide, as though to embrace the entire universe. 'I am a devotee of creation,' she said.

"And so, my apprenticeship began.

"I visited her every day in her hut in the mountains and drank of her tea and her wisdom. The darkness was banished in my awakened awareness of the rise and fall of my breath in rhythm with the ever turning cycle of the seasons.

"My eyes were not big enough to see the whole of creation, so I opened my thoughts, my heart and my instincts. My nerves tingled in response to the beauty of a world of which, I understood, I was a part.

"I listened to the song of the mountains, and my soul echoed its response.

"Then, one day, standing at the edge of everything I had ever known, a condor rose and soared before me. Its throbbing wing-beat and keen, cold eyes erased all time and space. Forgetting all I had ever learned about my limitations, I reached towards faith and leaped off the mountain ledge."

∞

Time whooped, "Did faith cushion your fall?"

"I wasn't crushed," she replied.

"When I realized that the earth hadn't swallowed me, I cautiously opened my eyes. My mind lurched and I thought that I might be ill. I spun out of all control, uncertain where the sky began and the world ended. Wind pounded my ears. Flight dizzied my brain. My senses could not name the barrage of scents and sights that battered my consciousness. Finally, I stopped fighting for control and allowed the currents to carry me.

"I soared high above the landscape, which seemed scraped of dirt and human detritus. Muscles contracted and beat a rhythm that I knew was not mine; keen eyes spied movement below that I knew I could not see.

"But I abandoned myself and, in the first frenzied freedom of flight, I was a child reborn. Blue hurt my lungs. Green filled my nostrils. Red fired my brain. The sun grazed my mind."

Time rolled a marshmallow luxuriantly over his tongue as the Shadow slipped deeper into its troubled sleep. The boy peered into the fire where the Wanderer's eyes rested to see if he could pluck the images from her sight.

"Do you think I might fly some day?" he timidly asked her.

"I'm sure of it."

"I think I would be a little scared," the boy admitted.

"Only the fearful are truly brave," replied the Wanderer. "The Warrior is one who makes the leap with sinking boots and a fluttering heart. Fools walk with their eyes closed, never fearing the hole that gapes to greet them."

"So, it's alright to be scared then?" the boy asked.

"It's highly advisable.

"Since that joyous flight, my world is created each and every day. I view it with new eyes and give thanks for having been born."

"Your quest is a noble one," the Tree remarked. "It is the duty of every living being to be happy. It is our ultimate achievement, for without happiness there is only darkness, and without the light the true fullness of being can never be realized."

"Do you really think I could fly?" the child harried the question, refusing to let it go.

"You shall soar."

"When?"

"When it is time."

∞

"What does that even mean?" the boy asked, a little petulantly. "I do not understand time."

"Perhaps you'll allow me," Time held up his hand to forestall the Tree and the Wanderer. "I am a complex individual. Desired by many, but loved by few. My needs are paltry, but my wants are great. I inspire wild envy, and prick wanton lust. My appetites are rampant, and I concede to every whim. I am the chicken and I am the egg. Devoured by hunger, I smash what I create to batter omelets. I rule by the hours, and I'll die by the clock. I am an enigma, doomed to be misunderstood. Even by myself. Any questions?"

"That's not what I meant," the boy grumbled.

"Can I be any clearer?" Time asked.

"It's a riddle indeed," the Wanderer accepted. "The road doesn't come with a guide and a counter. We each must walk at our own pace and overcome the obstacles we meet in our own way. We must make our own decisions, and live our own lives. That is the nature of being a unique part of the world we inhabit. You will fly," she told the child, "in your own time."

The boy nodded his head thoughtfully.

"Now that your path has led you here, what adventures await?" Time asked. "Your quest, it appears, is done."

The Wanderer rose from the comfort of the fireside and walked to the centre of the clearing. The boy thought that perhaps she had not heard Time's question and almost repeated it, a little louder, for he too was anxious to know what she would do next. She dropped her shoulders and raised her face, seemingly oblivious to the cold. Snow clustered on her eyelashes and she stood very still. Energy gathered and poised as she breathed in and she breathed out. She faced the Tree.

"I have learned so much, but I know so little," she began.

"I am neither a sage nor a hermit, a priest nor a tree.

"I live amongst people, not in a cave.

"The mountains are my refuge, yet the road is my home.

"The world is seldom beautiful, but its ugliness is also part of me.

"I cherish happiness, but I battle anger.

"How can I live well, being who I am?

"I am a Wanderer."

"You are a Warrior," the Tree amended.

She acknowledged the Tree's revision with a nod, and continued, "I do not wish to shut myself off from the world. It astonishes me every day with its capacity for beauty. It also burdens me with its filth, stupidity, thoughtlessness and greed. People trample on the weak, tumble into strangers' arms, trade in lies and inanities, trapped in minds that look no further than a billboard to tell them what to think and what to dream. Words lose all meaning as they are used as wallpaper to cover cracks in the silence. Thoughtless words, rote conversations, empty lives that bore through life and bore to death.

"If I am to embrace the world, I must accept all of it with equanimity - the ugliness as well as the beauty. This, Tree, is my quest, and I am in great need of your guidance."

"Lord, yes," Time chimed in. "Is there anything duller than conversation?"

∞

Conversation petered out as the Tree gathered its words carefully.

"It is easy to be a tree in the forest.

"Supplant it, and the sun may no longer dapple its leaves; electricity wires may rustle through its eaves; its roots may crackle along concrete paths; and noxious fumes may seep into its seams. Yet still it will reach for water and light. Birds will continue to nest in its branches. It will strive to grow and be what it is. Beyond the forest, it is still a tree.

"It is easy to be happy in the mountains.

"Live in the world of people and your spirit may encounter darkness; noise and confusion may splinter your nerves; anger may seethe through your veins; and disappointments may wrack your dreams. Yet your spirit will still struggle for light and love. Others will continue to seek your protection and guidance. You will fight to fill your skin and be who you are. Beyond the mountains, you are still a Warrior."

The Wanderer carefully considered the Tree's words.

"I am beauty and I am pain. I am the celebration and I am the stale room the morning after the party. Knowing who I am, how can I be a Warrior?" she pressed.

"The Warrior must embrace their capacity for love and command their propensity for anger. Love is the Warrior's greatest strength; anger is the sword they wield. This weapon should be controlled by the mind and only unleashed by the heart.

"The Warrior must slash a path through the fears and the failings of the spirit that whisper of disillusionment and disappointment. They must fight to control their response to the world, so that the darkness is met with their light.

"They must stand strong in the face of those who nettle their will and speak with fools' tongues. They must seek to understand before they stand on judgment. They must protect those who are weak, and offer guidance to the lost.

"Life is a war. In battle the old ways are destroyed, and a space is cleared for the new. Destruction is the fertile soil of growth. The Warrior has the potential to be an instrument of great change on the battlefield of the spirit."

"Sounds dangerous to me," Time commented. "You'd be much better staying at home and minding your own business."

∞

"Life is a dangerous business, if left unchecked," the Tree responded. "To live well and fully requires work and commitment.

"Interaction with the world often leads down alleyways of discontent, as we test ourselves and find ourselves wanting, and trust others who let us down."

Time looked pointedly at the prone Shadow, "I hear you, Tree. But sing it louder."

"You cannot control how the world will treat you," the Tree continued, "but you can control your response to those with whom you engage, and circumstances in which you become involved.

"For example, wealth, prestige and power need not be negative trappings, once they're treated as tools to sow goodness and grow wisdom. If they become a substitute for joy, then lives of great misery follow.

"Neither can poverty, loss or disappointment be excuses for living meanly.

"Nothing is gained by blaming the world for the absence of happiness. The light is always within, waiting for the Warrior to rise up and release it.

"No matter the hole in which you fall, get up. Fail again. Strive harder. Do better.

"Mistakes may occur. Temptations indulged. Anger unleashed, directed unchecked. Light may be doused; a rug over a flame. Darkness embraced, head lowered in shame. But do not give up; the war's not won. Forgive yourself. Start again.

"And afford the same kindness to others." The Wanderer nodded her head slowly, thinking on the words.

"It is easy to be happy in the mountains," the Tree said again. "But happiness does not reside there. It can be found on the battlefield of the spirit. The Warrior's task is to fight in the muck as well as in the clouds, against the darkness and against the odds, with the certainty that happiness is worth fighting for."

"Happiness is within," the Warrior said softly, the question answered.

"Always," the Tree responded.

Time burst into laughter, "To think that you traveled all those miles to discover that you were dragging your quest with you all along." The mirth seeped from his eyes and fell down his face in tears. "It's got to be the funniest thing I have ever heard! Sure, you might as well have been lying in your warm bed, rather than running the roads, tormenting fools with your damnably stupid crusade." He gulped, as his merriment got the better of him. "Wanderer, I'll tell you one thing for sure, you've helped me find my happiness this day!" He laughed and laughed until his face turned red and it was clear that he was either going to break into hives or into hiccups.

His mirth became a live thing that tore around the clearing, barking wildly. The Wanderer and the child joined in Time's infectious glee.

When the laughter had subsided, and the Wanderer had sobered, she bowed her head. "Thank you, Tree."

"What shall you do, now that your quest has come to its end?" asked the boy.

"It has just begun," she said. "I am a Wanderer who must learn to be a Warrior." She thought for a short time, "I believe I shall continue to roam. I will bring the Tree's teaching to the road. I will share it with other travelers who have lost their way. And I will fight," she added.

∞

"Where's the fun in that?" Time prodded. "Why on earth would you continue to live the life of a vagabond when you could curl up safely in your own bed and never need to leave the house again? You've found what you're looking for. You can stop this nonsense and get a clock, like a normal person," Time challenged her.

"I don't want to be manacled to a timetable," she replied. "To continue to live a life where every day is different is, for me, a joy beyond measure. I will not worry about what lies around the bend; nor shall I have care for where I lay my head this night, or the next. Unburdened, I shall be free to be happy and revel in my light, while the song of the road hums contentedly within me."

It seemed to the boy that the Wanderer shone. Her eyes sparkled and her smile came easy. He looked carefully and decided that it was not simply the fire that lit her face that was the source of the light. For Time was huddled by the flames and, while his cheeks were brightly flushed, there was a dampness about his spirit.

Time wrinkled his nose in disgust. "It's a sickness, this wanderlust. It will spin you a merry dance and make your head a dizzy whorl. If you're not careful, Wanderer, you'll end up on your hands and knees examining your dinner. Tree, you know about the importance of roots. Talk some sense into her," he appealed.

"I'll play the music, Time, and I'll dance with my happiness. Aye, my head will spin. But we shall be a merry pair, and none shall still our feet. And if they do," she grinned dangerously and patted her sheathed dagger, "they'll hop fairly lively to my tune."

A worry flitted across her face and she twirled to the Tree. "I want to live as you have instructed, but can I love myself and others honestly with a blade on my hip? Should I leave this with you?" she asked.

"I have no need of it," the Tree responded. "Set upon the road with the noble intent of doing no harm to another. Give and receive love freely, without self-consciousness, and without fear. However, remember that with love comes responsibility. Protect yourself and those who are weaker than you. And ensure that your actions are always motivated by love, not by anger. If you can live according to this instruction, then keep your dagger, Wanderer. Follow your path, and guide others to their happiness."

"I make my promise to you, Tree, that I shall never pull a blade in anger. I will use my strength as an instrument of love, and I will not breach the trust you have placed in me," she responded.

As the low winter sun brushed past a cloud, the companions gathered by the fire, faces lifted to the light.

"Feel the warmth," the Tree instructed. "Allow your happiness to course through every atom of your body. Breathe in and out."

Eyes closed, they experienced moments pass as subtle changes were wrought in each of them. The Wanderer sharpened her will to a point in preparation for the road, and the battles that lay ahead. The boy passed beyond the boundaries of foreign shores and scented spices to a limitless space within himself. Time stopped fidgeting for a while, and toppled over in a heap of soft snores. The Shadow, curled beneath the cloak, was warmed by the soft light that washed over its face, giving a semblance of peace to its wracked form.

Then, as Time rolled over onto his tummy, he set off a blaring alarm call.

∞

Sleepy head get out of bed, a mechanical voice commanded.

You're late for a date, it admonished in a metal whine.

Time's up, your goose is cooked, it threatened in a tinny hiss.

"Turn it off!" yelled the boy over the ruckus.

Time rested on his side, head propped on his hand, as his metal cap jangled up and down, beating out irate reprimands.

Listen honey, time is money! it angrily prodded.

The Shadow, wrenched from sleep, rose unsteadily, swaying painfully on its feet. It hesitated, baffled. It touched the cloak and looked at the dent that its frame had made in the earth. It took a cautious step towards Time, who had settled into a comfortable smile, eyes half closed, as though listening to music only he could hear.

The first step was followed by an even more reluctant second. Time held up his hand to prevent it coming closer. The Shadow halted, mid-slink, foot half raised as the alarm barked its orders.

Idle fool, it's time to move.

The Shadow crept forward.

"Not an inch!" Time hissed, his apparent good humour flustered.

The Shadow lowered its shoulders and brushed at the mat of hair that covered its face. It looked to Time for further instruction, uncertain whether to move, terrified to put a foot wrong.

Tyrant Time demands you rise! The alarm let loose a metallic roar.

The Wanderer shouted at Time, barely scraping the din, as she scooped up a snowball.

She drew her arm back,

Hurry up, you lazy runt.

took aim, and hurled the missile at Time's metal cap.

It flew off his head, clanked off the Tree, and sent Time hurdling onto the flat of his back.

"Terrific stuff!" Time kicked his legs in the air in childish delight. "But, seriously now, I want your candid opinion." He propped himself back onto his elbow and surveyed his disgruntled companions. "Which one did you like the best?"

He looked from one to the next. Silence ensued. The Wanderer cleared her throat.

"Come now, come now. This is your chance to influence Time."

"What do you mean?" the boy asked.

"Couldn't be clearer. I need a new ringtone. The classic alarm is done. If you want to get people's attention you have to keep up with the times.

"I've been testing this selection for the past six months and I can't make up my mind. Each has its charms. But as soon as I settle on one, I immediately start to miss the others I'm choosing to discard."

"It hardly matters which you pick, they're equally hideous," the Wanderer voiced what the others were thinking.

"No need to flatter me." Time squirmed in a horrible display of delight. "Give it to me straight."

"Give over, Time. If you want to annoy the sleeper into wakefulness, then simply ring your own empty bellows. I promise they'll be on their feet faster than any of the idle taunts you just flaunted."

"Magnificent!" Time gazed at the Wanderer in unguarded admiration.

"Why didn't you think of that?" He turned on the Shadow, "You useless lump of maggot meat. Perhaps if I yell at you loud enough, I might eventually manage to drag your good for nothing head out of your filthy, blackened dreams and back to the task of serving your long-suffering, starving master."

It suddenly got very cold as a gust of northerly wind raked through the clearing. The Shadow shivered and shrank into the cloak that hung in folds over its thin shoulders.

"As you slept, do you know what I've been doing?" Time screwed up his face, crushing his round eyes into pinholes of anger.

The Shadow stood frozen, as though it was coated in a film of ice.

"Eating marshmallows!" Time exploded. "Marshmallows," he repeated through a clenched jaw. "As though marshmallows could possibly hold me to dinner. The indignities I've put up with. I've suffered the most appalling stomach cramps and general agonies, while you," he spluttered, "slept." He kicked his legs, as though in a death throe, and groaned alarmingly.

"Agonies indeed," The Wanderer rolled her eyes. "If you stood on your own two feet you might feel significantly stronger. You could start by getting up."

"How can I?" Time demanded indignantly. "I'm weak with hunger and stung by betrayal." He flung a look at the Shadow, which remained rigid.

"Surely we won't have to ring that hideous alarm to get you up and moving?" she teased.

"A fantastic idea, Wanderer!" He positively beamed as he reached for his cap, felt the empty space and spat spleen into the snow."

"My cap, Fool." Nothing moved. "Now!" he bellowed as the Shadow startled into life, as though emerging for a breath from the bottom of a very deep pool.

The boy looked with great concern at the Shadow, who was advancing on the metal cap. Then he hurried to Time with his hand extended. "I'm sure it won't come to that," he gasped. "With the Wanderer's help I can get you to your feet. We won't need the alarm at all, will we?" he beseeched the laughing Wanderer, who had grabbed Time by the collar of his coat and was hoisting him to his feet as though she were landing a large carp.

"That won't be necessary at all, boy."

She strode over to the Shadow, which had stopped by the Tree, the cap in its hands apparently forgotten.

She took it gently from its slack grip and returned to Time. "There you go," she settled it on his head, then stood back to examine her work. She tilted it a little to the right. "Very rakish indeed, Time," she smiled. Time discreetly whipped a pocket mirror from his coat and peered at his reflection from behind his shoulder. Satisfied, he wiped the blush from his cheeks and whirled back to the Wanderer.

"Am I presentable?" he coyly queried.

"You'll do," she answered dryly.

"Now, it is time that I made my sweet adieu of you all. But first, my mittens."

The boy placed them in Time's meaty palm.

"My hat, my hat, where is my hat?" The Wanderer rummaged around until she spotted a furry pommel peeking out from under the heap of suitcases. She rescued it and wedged it over Time's metal cap.

"My ears, I beg you. Be sure that my ears are covered from the tempests. I have such sensitive, delicate ears," he added as an aside to no one in particular.

Then, just as all was in order and all extremities muffled and bound, he hesitated.

"For some reason," he spoke slowly, as if struggling with a thought, "I seem unable to move."

"Perhaps your scarf's too tight?" suggested the boy. Time considered this a moment, "No, I believe that it is something quite different.

"It's this place," he shook his head furiously, sending a flurry of bobbles swinging across his face. "It has bewitched me, and I am loathe to leave.

"This won't do. This won't do at all!

"I have places to be, people to badger. Night will soon be upon us, and I have not yet stepped into the dark forest."

The Tree spoke gently, "You don't have to leave, Time. The winter is long. There is time aplenty to reach your destination. Stave off the darkness and stay a while by the fire."

The Shadow raised its head. A small glimmer of light reached its eyes.

Time shuddered. "It is getting darker. I can feel it creeping."

Then he pulled himself together and straightened his shoulders as he peered at the group from a fur-framed face.

"I know my duty, Tree. You shall not seduce me into lingering. We move out. This very afternoon."

Still he didn't budge.

"Why don't you rest here, just for tonight?" the boy suggested. He looked towards the Shadow, whose momentary hope lay heaped in ashes.

"Don't be ridiculous, boy. Sleep here? Like a common tramp? Wrapped around a fire? Have you no sense of the dignity of my person?" He drew himself up another centimeter, so that he almost touched the Wanderer's shoulder.

"I shall find lodgings more suited to my position in life."

"But it is getting dark, and that Fool forgot to bring a compass." His shoulders sank.

"There's all manner of things hidden behind the shield of darkness." He shuddered, "Who knows what we might encounter," he nodded towards the forest, "out there." Limbs seemed to point at him, mocking him. Or so he imagined.

"Have no fear, Time. You shall come to no harm in the forest. But you are indeed welcome to stay the night. You are both most welcome to stay," the Tree offered.

But then another thought flittered across Time's consciousness. He reached out and grabbed it before it could escape him.

"Madam, you can certainly handle yourself in a corner." He nodded approvingly towards the Wanderer's knife.

"But a lady, such as yourself, should not be wandering these paths alone." He gallantly presented his arm, "Time at your service, ma'am. Perhaps I might accompany you to the edge of the forest? It will be dark soon and I'm sure you could use my protection." He shuffled nervously.

Wanderer glanced towards the Tree, who nodded slightly. "I am happy to travel to the forest's edge with you, Time."

"Wonderful, smashing," Time clapped his hands and jiggled in glee. "Then there's not a second to be lost. Let us move out this instant.

"Stick close to me, Wanderer. Don't leave my side for a moment. For how else shall I be able to," he cleared his throat self-consciously, "protect you."

"Don't worry, Time," she laughed. "I'm not going anywhere."

"Fool!" Time roared. "Get a move on."

The Shadow shuddered and backed slowly from the Tree as though it were pulling against an invisible force.

"Tick tock, we're on the clock.

Cannot dally,

Time is money."

Time fidgeted with his watches and anxiously surveyed the second hand's unceasing progress around his stomach.

The Shadow shrugged off the cloak and carefully folded it up before creeping over to the Wanderer. It shivered as it raised its eyes to shyly look at her from behind its veil of hair as it held out the cloak with its two hands, like an offering.

The Wanderer smiled and shook her head. "It was a gift." Taking the cloak, she shook it out and placed it, once again, around the Shadow's shoulders.

"Oh, enough of all this nonsense," Time snarled. "Next I suppose you'll be looking at yourself in a mirror and expecting us to tell you how pretty you are. You're a beast, Fool. Nothing more. Now, carry my burdens." He spoke deliberately, beating out every word.

"If you want my companionship, Time, you'll mind your tongue," the Wanderer warned.

Time immediately shrank. "Don't be cross with me, Wanderer. I'm just worried we'll be late. The forest is a maze and we don't have a compass." At the last words he looked spitefully at the Shadow, which was bent under the weight of Time's baggage.

"Don't worry, Time. We can use the stars as our compass," the Wanderer reassured him.

"Good lord, surely it won't come to that." His face registered shock. "By nightfall I intend to be tucked up warmly in a goose-down bed, having fed on roast beef and gravy."

"Then it's best we get moving, Time." The Wanderer turned towards the Tree. "I shall return to your light. If you will have me."

"You know the way, Warrior. Simply follow the path and you will find us changed as we ever were."

"Thank you, Tree."

"My friend, my friend," blustered Time, "we would love to stay, but duty calls us elsewhere. Adieu, farewell, till next we meet."

Time blundered at full speed out of the clearing at the helm of the small group.

"The other way, Time," the Wanderer's voice followed.

The Shadow lingered for a long moment at the edge of the clearing, before disappearing into the grey mist.

∞

The boy rested his chin on his knees as he curled by the fire. "Do you think that we will see her again?" he asked the Tree.

"I believe we will."

"How can you be so sure?" his voice sounded small, even to his own ears. "The world is so big and we fill such a tiny part of it. I fear that the road will take her away from us."

"The road does not sever the binds of love. Like my roots, they get stronger and deeper."

"I would have liked if she could have stayed a little longer."

"She must follow her path, as you must follow yours."

"I want to be a Warrior when I grow up," the boy declared. He jumped up, grabbed a stick, and brandished it in the air like a sword, whooping and thrusting at the shadows flung at him by the flames. When he had worn himself out, he threw himself to the ground. "Can I get a knife?" the boy looked hopefully at the Tree.

"What would you do with it?" the Tree asked.

The boy thought, "I would wear it in my belt and use it to peel my apples." He added, almost as an afterthought, "And if anyone tried to hurt you, I would cut open their stomachs."

"I love you, Tree."

"I love you too."

"Can I get a knife?"

"For now you can eat your apple skins."

The boy sighed. "I would give them to the Shadow, if you let me have a knife."

The snow had covered his companions' tracks, almost as if they had never been. "I thought it would disappear," the boy said. "But it didn't. It seemed more. Maybe it was the cloak. I thought that it might stay with us. Why didn't it stay, Tree? Why didn't you make it stay?"

"It is not my place to force my will upon others."

"So, you wanted it to stay too. Didn't you?"

"It doesn't matter what I wish for. Every creature must make their own choices and find their own destiny. It is only in this way that they can be masters of themselves."

"Still and all, Tree, I think if you had pressed a little more it would have stayed with us."

"Perhaps."

"Are you sure you're not cold?" the boy asked for the thousandth time, as he snuggled closer to the fire.

The Tree shook its branches and smiled at the boy, who was lit in a sleepy glow. The embers cast a soft light in the clearing as silence settled over the forest and the night deepened.

∞

"Be quiet! It will hear you," a voiced hissed above a curse as ice snapped beneath the weight of stumbling boots.

"Get back on your feet. We don't have all night."

"Don't tell me what to do. You're not the master of me."

"Oh fine, lie like a beetle, but you can explain to Mistress just why it is that you failed her this night."

More grumbling was followed by the sound of heavy steps and splintering branches, carving a trail to the clearing.

Muscled shoulders brushed aside the undergrowth, battering or obliterating all that lay in their path. Destruction trailed their wake, and beauty lay bleeding beneath the weight of their madness.

"I didn't come all this way to fail."

"My axe knows no mercy."

"I'm tired of your talk."

"Show me the field of battle and you will hear my axe sing."

"As if it wasn't bad enough in this stinking hole of winter, now he wants to sing."

"Keep this up and I'll hear you squeal!"

"You first, pig."

They fell upon each other. Pummeling blows, right hooks, fingers stretched towards bulging necks. Insults dropped like anchors as the blood filled their sails. The mist descended, clouding eyes and minds.

They tore onward, aware only of splintering wood and shredding skin. Snarling and clawing they fell into the clearing, staining the snow with their sweat and their fury. A tangle of bodies, dismembered from themselves. No sense of whose leg belonged to whom, whose fingers curled around whose neck, whose grunts, whose blood.

"Welcome, Woodcutters." The Tree spoke softly, so as not to wake the boy.

They quickly fell apart and scrambled to their feet, as if seared by the whispered greeting.

"Don't come any closer," one hissed at the Tree. He stood taller by a head than his opponent. His jaw was clenched, and his eyes lined. A scar, old and untended, scrawled down the left side of his face.

"I'm not going anywhere; it is you who have come to me," the Tree responded.

"Don't listen to it. She warned us not to listen to its lying words. We're here to do a job. Now let's get on with it," the other urged. He was slight. A wisp of air grounded by solid muscle.

The Woodcutters stood shoulder to shoulder, animosity forgotten, axes balanced in their strong hands.

"It's nothing personal, Tree. It's just business."

"And what business do you have with me this night?" asked the Tree.

One of the Woodcutters stepped a little closer. He tested his blade on the tip of his finger, drawing a drop of blood, which fell unheeded onto the white snow. "Your time is over, Tree. Our mistress wills you dead."

"Wants your heart, she does," the large one added for clarity.

"Whose bidding do you follow?" the Tree asked.

"She who speak in rhymes."

"Why does she burden you with such a task?"

"She does not share her thoughts with us. We do as we are commanded."

"You stole what is hers," his accomplice snarled.

"So it has come to this," murmured the Tree.

The Woodcutter took another step and tightened his grip on his axe. Those same hands could as easily have held a paint brush. Or caressed a lover's face.

"I shall be swift. My blade is sharp. I do not wish you ill."

"It eases my heart to hear it. But if that is the case, why do you carry this weapon and threaten with dark looks."

"He has indeed a dirty, mangy grimace. I always said as much," interrupted the second Woodcutter. "I could never understand why the women looked at him as they did. Tongues hanging out, ready to lap up his drippings."

"I simply do my job," he addressed the Tree, ignoring his companion.

"Ah, your job. And what do you receive in return for your efforts?"

"Our mistress has promised us great stacks of firewood to warm our hearths for the winter. It is terribly cold in the Northern realms. The nights are long, and we live in darkness.

"I ache for the light."

"Your mistress promises you what she cannot give."

"I warn you, Tree. Do not dare to speak ill of our mistress. Her word is not to be questioned. She is all powerful and would be most displeased if she heard you talk so. She might prefer it if I carve you slowly."

"You talk far too much," his companion growled. "Let's get this over with and claim our reward. Or would you rather bring it to its knees by idle chatter?"

"My arm is not wanting. Take care, fly, that I do not unleash its might on you," he warned, swinging his axe in an arc above his head.

"Futile threats and girlish banter. I recall a time when you could hardly yield a pen, let alone an axe. You were a sorry excuse for a scholar with your sniffling rhymes and blunt allusions. Posting your poems on the doors of the homes of anyone you thought might read them. Craving attention, but never good enough to raise yourself beyond the ordinary. Despite your every effort, you could not beat back mediocrity. The worst, of course, was failing after having tried, burdened with the knowledge that you just weren't good enough." He sniggered.

"Shut your filthy mouth, or I'll carve a grin on the other side of your face."

"And that's when she found you. In a heap of self-loathing, scratching cuts with your pen. She took it from you and gave you an axe. And look at you now, all empty wind and grand flourishes, still trying to prove that you're something you're not. She should never have wasted her time on such a worthless creature. She should have left you with the other flies. It would have been a fitting punishment for such dreadful lines."

"Your tongue is as sharp as your companion's axe," remarked the Tree. "I venture it has left some wounds. Careful, friend, words can sear as deep as any weapon and, when laced with poison, heal even slower."

"This I have already learned from my mistress."

The Woodcutters shivered as a sharp wind cut through the clearing, passing cold fingers over all it touched, coating arms and legs and hands that held axes in a film of ice. "There is nothing that you have to offer me, Tree," one breathed through chattering teeth.

"She has taught you well. Well enough to know cold and fear. You tremble like a child in the snare of a nightmare."

"Don't doubt my valour, Tree. It is but the cold. The swing of my axe arm will soon get my blood moving and bring life back to these petrified fingers."

"Or you could simply thaw by the fire," the Tree suggested.

"You are as wily as she said."

"Fear not. I neither question your nerve nor tempt you from your path. That decision is yours alone to make. I simply offer to share my fire on a winter's night, for the cold has clearly seeped into your heart, and you are in great need of warmth and light."

The Woodcutters moved cautiously towards the glow, walking stiffly as though their very joints were frozen by the chill.

They eased themselves slowly to the ground. "Place more wood upon the fire," the Tree urged. "Old limbs have fallen in the forest, according to the natural order of the earth. There are more than enough logs to keep the fire blazing and melt the ice that burns you."

In a short time, the Woodcutters were hunched comfortably over the flames. As they slowly thawed, words came in breaths, wavered in the air in front of them, then disappeared.

Their axes rested idly on the ground, the blades catching the dancing light. Still the boy slept, innocent to the men's intent.

They whispered amongst themselves. "We'll just sit a moment. Loosen up the limbs. Keep an eye on it, yeah? Make sure it doesn't pull a fast one while our backs are turned."

"It's a tree. What's it going to do? Where's it going to go?"

"Under the head of my axe." A grim chuckle lilted to the crackling of the sticks.

"I'll give you the first blow."

"Very decent of you."

"It doesn't seem a bad sort."

"It has a fine stock of wood."

"Can't remember the last time I was warm."

"I can almost move my toes."

"There's no rush."

"We've got all night."

"Do trees scream?"

"How would I know?"

"Ask it."

"What difference does it make?"

"I just wanted to know. I've never killed a live one before."

One of the men coughed as the wind changed direction, causing a tremble in the clearing.

"It bleeds. It dies. What does it matter if it screams?"

"It will come to an end one way or another, I suppose."

"Death at our hands is just speeding up the inevitable."

"It should be thanking us for sparing it crumbling old age."

"Withering senility."

"Forgotten sentences and stories that ramble on and on in spirals, going nowhere."

"All told a hundred times before about the good old days when music was in tune and bread a fraction of the price it is now."

"Shields held before the body to fight off the axe."

"That always falls."

"One way or another."

"Let's get this over with."

The boy stirred softly in his dreams.

"He might have been my son," one of the men murmured.

"She would never allow that."

"Human frailty, she'd call it."

"There's no space for humanity in our line of work."

"There's no space for anything save the cool eye and the sharp edge."

"The empty heart and the cold bones."

"You're just putting it off, with all this talk."

"If it screams it will wake him. And then what will we do?" He nodded towards the boy, "It would be a shame to wake him."

"We'll do what we have to do."

"What do you mean?"

"We'll slice his dreams."

"Stuff his mouth with cotton."

"We could bring him back to her."

"Another fly for her web."

"Might keep us out of her snare for another while."

"We mean you no harm, Tree."

"And yet you speak of endings."

"Are you frightened?"

"Every creature fears its death."

"We have nothing against you personally. It's just business."

"You already said that."

"Another five minutes by the fire, yeah?"

"It wouldn't hurt."

"It's the first time I've felt warm since the start of this long winter."

"Is there any other season?"

"Not where we come from."

"Then it's the first time I've been warm."

"It feels nice."

"Almost human."

"Thank you, Tree."

"You're welcome to my light."

"I don't want to kill you."

"What do you want?"

"I want to sleep as he does."

"What stops you?"

"The numbness."

"I feel it too."

"It aches. Everywhere."

"The pain of emptiness."

"There's no escaping."

"It seeps into the very bones."

"The blood."

"Every atom crying out."

"For what?"

"For warmth."

"For light."

"To feel."

"Anything."

"And this you cannot find in the North?" the Tree asked.

"There's nothing there."

"Aeons of emptiness."

"Wrapped in a web."

The men seemed to shrink within their skins.

"It covers everything."

"It haunts my dreams."

"Millions of flies."

"Lie supine, enmeshed in her twine."

"Row upon row."

"Layer upon layer."

"Like files in a cabinet."

"Like bunks in a boat."

"Shadows and footsteps."

"As she haunts her lair."

"A flickering candle."

"Screams rent the air."

"She paces the floor."

"Scurries up cots."

"Stuffs their mouths with cotton."

"To muffle their dreams."

"She never rests."

"She's always knitting."

"Jumpers that cling."

"Like film round your mouth."

"That's how she traps you."

"She promises warmth."

"Something to keep the chill out."

"She promises light."

"Colours to push the dark back."

"But the wool chafes."

"The weave's too fine."

"The dyes fade."

"The pattern mocks."

"The neck's too tight."

"Like a noose around your throat."

"And you can't get it off."

"The stitches never give."

"Even my axe can't shred her knots."

Flimsy threads, which had withered to grey, stretched across the men's backs, providing poor shelter from the winter chill.

"I can't stand it."

"It scratches day and night."

"Like she's wrapped around my throat."

"Clinging to my back."

"No escaping."

"A shadow over the night."

"A burden to be borne."

"Bent double under the weight."

"Communing with the worms."

"A life lived looking at dirt."

"I want to see the sun."

"You only need to snag one thread," said the Tree.

"It can't be done."

"The rest will easily come undone."

"I tell you, it can't be done." The Woodcutter was almost shouting.

"Why torment us with hope, when there is none to be had?"

"We should have killed you the moment we arrived."

"This promise is worse than anything she can serve up."

"I do not lie to you. You can choose a different path. Become your own masters. But it is a choice, and only you can decide."

"It's a trick!"

"Think of what we're risking. She promised us piles of wood."

"We can drag its carcass to the North and feed it to the fire."

"There are fallen limbs aplenty. Enough to feed your hearth. There is no need to slaughter that which lives and breathes."

"We have to do what she commands."

"You have to do what your heart demands," the Tree responded.

"We are slaves to her desires."

"You are masters of your destinies."

"It's not that simple."

"It never is."

"Help us, Tree."

"You must first help yourselves."

"Show us the way."

"I am the way."

"Forgive us."

"Free us."

"You are already free, but I can help unbind your cords.

"Step a little closer."

The men swayed to their feet, drunk in the moment of choice.

The Tree stretched out its limbs. They stumbled forward, collapsing into a tangled embrace. Arms and branches intertwined with no sense of where one ended and the other began.

Their jumpers snagged on the twigs and the bark. Stitches were torn.

The men stepped back. Frightened at what had come to pass.

"Is this really possible?" one whispered.

"You have a lot to unravel, but a start has been made. A choice lies before you. You can repair the tear and finish what you came here to do; or you can pull apart the threads that have bound you in darkness."

A woodcutter grabbed for his axe.

The other immediately flung himself upon him. "I've made my choice and I won't let you harm it."

"Easy, easy, my friend." He looked past the fist aimed at his face to the eyes behind it. "I too have made my choice. And I plan to get this cursèd jumper off me as fast as axe and teeth can tear it."

The Tree counseled the men, "There are many knots and you have much work to do. Return to the fire and, in the warmth, you can release them one by one. It will be dawn soon, and it will be easier to work in the light."

Peace descended over the clearing after the long night. The men worked patiently at their jumpers, feeding piles of thread to the sizzling flames.

∞

The sun rose and the boy stretched. He opened his eyes slowly, chasing after dreams that lingered at corners before disappearing into the morning rush of yawns and bird calls and twisted blankets.

Eventually he sat up, caught tousled and sleepy in the sun's net.

"Good morning," he calmly greeted the men.

"Morning, Tree," he hollered.

"Good morning," the Tree responded. "We have guests."

"What brings you to these parts?" the boy politely enquired.

The men shuffled uncomfortably.

He looked towards the axes, which were resting against the tree trunk, and he returned his gaze to the men. All signs of sleep were gone.

"What business do you have with us?" he enquired again, this time a little louder and, he hoped, a little braver.

One of the men cleared his throat. "Boy, we mean you no harm. We came in darkness, but we will leave with the light."

The boy looked at their jumpers, which they were unraveling slowly up their arms and their waists. Their goose pimpled flesh shone pale beneath them.

"I like what you've done with your jumpers," he nodded approvingly at the shards that were crackling in the fire. "But you must be cold. Here, wrap these around you." He handed a blanket to each of the men, who gratefully draped them over their shoulders. "I'm off to collect more firewood," he told the Tree, before disappearing into the forest.

"It is a long time since I have seen the sun," one commented, as he stood and leaned his back against the Tree, wrapped in his blanket, face towards the light.

The rays danced around the branches, spilled over the clearing and rested on the Woodcutter's jagged brow and tightly drawn mouth.

"I had forgotten the feel of morning's first light." The sun seeped beneath his eyelids, forming an orb of light. It sank into his mind, pulsing around dark corners, chasing out the shadows. It caressed his face, smoothing lines and relaxing his jaw. It thrummed in his ear and his heart picked up the rhythm.

"I am born anew," he murmured. "My life is yours, Tree. If you'll have it."

"It is a fine offering, but I do not want it. This life is yours alone to live as you choose. Serve yourself. Live well and fully. For only in this way can we be of any use to another."

"What will we do now? Where will we go?"

"Those are questions only you can answer. You are welcome here for as long as you wish to remain. Your axes will serve you well in the forest, as there's plenty of wood to be chopped. But you must decide how you wish to live. You are your own masters now."

"I am frightened. What if I am not good enough? You heard what he said," he nodded towards the scarred man hunched over the flames.

"I tried once before. I was a fraud. What if I fail to deserve the gift you have given to us? I know I am weak. I know I am ordinary. I am ashamed of what I have done, and fearful of who I might become."

"To be alive is to be extraordinary.

"Most people forget the miracle of their being. They wake up in the morning and pay no heed to the movement of their limbs, the flow of their thoughts, the air that they breathe, the heat in the sun and the rhythm of the earth of which they form a part. Remember who you are, and you will have nothing to fear," said the Tree.

$$\infty$$

The men spent the morning pulling at yarn that fought their fingers and bundled in knots as they tried to unravel its hold on them. Despite their strength and their efforts, it was slow, painstaking work. The neck seam was the most stubborn piece of all. It clung like a collar around their throats, refusing to give up a single stitch.

The boy wandered in the forest amongst dried fallen branches, collecting kindling and logs for the fire. He didn't go very far; just the distance of a voice's reach.

The Tree did whatever it is that trees do.

The air shimmered clear and bright.

Nocturnal creatures slept.

The sun shone.

All was as it should be.

Until Time burst into the clearing.

"Tree, Tree," his voice was ragged and his coat was torn. He was immediately followed by the Shadow, which had filled out its cloak with apprehension and dread.

"You're okay!" Time practically wept.

"Where's the boy?" The Wanderer snapped into the sunlit space, dagger in hand and taut as a wire on a finely tuned night.

"What have you done with the boy?" fast as a whip, she grabbed the nearest Woodcutter and held her blade to his throat. The blanket fell from his shoulders and drifted slowly to the snow, where it lay like a shroud.

"I'm coming," a well-known voice sang out from the forest.

The Wanderer let out her breath and relaxed her stance. "Tell us what happened here this dark night. The Shadow had a great foreboding, and the forest itself seemed to scream of evil tidings."

"The danger has passed, my friends," offered the Tree. "The night is over and the light has returned."

"I, who have so much time on my hands, feared that this night I would not have enough. If I could have stopped time, I would have done it. I would have done it for you." Time stood before the Tree, his hand on the bark. "We came back as fast as we could. We didn't eat. Never rested. I thought I would die from exhaustion, but the Fool carried me." His voice cracked.

"You were wise to fear our hearts," whispered a Woodcutter. "We were sent to kill the Tree."

Time shuddered.

"What happened?" demanded the Wanderer.

The Woodcutter straightened his shoulders where he sat by the fire, then opened his clenched fists to show her the yarn he had spent the morning unraveling. "The Tree saved our lives," he said.

"The Weaver," Time spat. "I'll wring her wizened little neck."

The Wanderer lowered her weapon.

"That woman's spite grows by the day. She must be stopped, Tree."

The Shadow stood rigid, eyes blinded in the glare of an axe. Then, as if a spell had been broken, it tore the blade from the Wanderer's hand and poured across the clearing to where a Woodcutter stood bare in the sun's harsh light.

"You would have done such a thing. You would have killed Tree."
It wasn't a question.

The Shadow thrust at the Woodcutter's throat. The Wanderer leapt forward to grab the knife. Time stood frozen for what seemed a lifetime.

In an instant, it was over.

The boy's delighted laugh filled the clearing. "Wanderer, Time, my friends, you are back! Is it time yet for breakfast?"

∞

Time lowered his head. The clock thundered nine.

The Woodcutter fell to his knees. The dagger fell to the snow without making even the faintest of sounds.

The Shadow stood unmoved, save for a vein that throbbed at its temple. The knitted collar lay limp and lifeless in its grip.

"You have released me," the Woodcutter gasped.

"It is done," the Shadow returned to the shelter of the Tree.

"My boy," Time clapped his hands in glee, "I believe you are right. It is indeed time for breakfast, but as our baggage is strewn across the forest," his face fell, "we must content ourselves with sunshine and good company."

"I'm impressed, Time," the Wanderer nodded.

"Don't be foolish. You can't expect me to go hungry," he interrupted her. "Not on my busy schedule. I have just about enough to keep one body whole and fed." He pulled a side of cooked ham from one of his pockets, recovered a hunk of bread from another, and three uncracked eggs from an inner fold. "It's not much, but it will do until the Fool has restored my belongings."

"Don't fret, Time. There's plenty here for everyone." The Wanderer took the meat from his protesting grip and started carving it into thick slices.

"I'll fetch the water," the boy offered.

"I'll stoke the fire." A Woodcutter set to work.

The Wanderer unlatched a small pot from the side of her pack, humming as she prepared the food.

As she worked, the second Woodcutter continued to scratch and pull at his neck. "Do you want me to take care of that for you?" she offered.

He knelt before her, head bowed as though in prayer, as she cut the final threads that bound him to his past life.

∞

"That will hardly keep me till lunch," Time complained as he regretfully swallowed the last morsel. "Much as we'd love to stay and chat, we can't delay today as we are already miles behind our schedule.

"Not that I blame you, Tree. It was not your fault that we were dragged back on a fool's errand. It was that blasted wretch. Howled like a dog, it did. Nothing would quiet it until we dropped all the baggage and hightailed it back here.

"The Wanderer wouldn't let me lay a finger on it. Foolish sentimentality! I should have shut its mouth with a lash, and we could have continued on our way. But, oh no. These days I'm expected to carry my own weight, pour honey into dense ears, and hand out food to every vagabond we meet on the road. I don't know what will become of me, Tree. I really don't."

"We are sorry to have delayed your journey," the Woodcutters apologized as they brushed crumbs from their knees.

"Oh, I won't hear a word about it! We're all friends now. Besides, I have no one to blame but the dog. This is the last time the master will jump to a bark, I can assure you."

"What will you do, now that you're free of the Weaver?" the Wanderer asked the Woodcutters.

"We have much yet to decide, but for now we will remain in the forest to gather our strength and absorb the light. There is a lot of darkness to wipe from our souls."

"I wish you well in your new found freedom."

"Our debt to you is great. If ever we can be of service."

"Thank you. Should I ever be in need I will certainly call upon you, though I claim nothing more than friendship."

The Wanderer gathered up her belongings and took her leave of the Tree. "If anything should have happened to you," she faltered.

"Be at ease. No harm was done. Though pay heed. The time will come when I will not always be here. Do not rely so heavily on me that you cannot walk unaided."

"I know that, Tree. It is just that you are dear to me and your absence would be keenly felt. You are part of who I am, what I have become. I hear your words in my mind and almost believe them to be my own."

"You, too, are part of everything that nourishes my heart. Even when you are not present, I feel you in all that I am. Travel safely, Warrior."

"You do me great honour, Tree."

"By nightfall I aim to be tucked tightly into a goose-down bed," Time informed the Woodcutters, "having eaten my fill of braised veal shanks and lightly smoked mackerel.

"Hurry on, Fool!" he barked his orders, checking his watches and straightening his time.

Amidst the bluster he whispered to the Tree, "I don't mind telling you that you cost me a day. But, my friend, I am heartily relieved that you are unharmed. We have known each other so long now I would not easily part with you."

Before the Tree had a chance to respond, Time picked up a stick and poked the Shadow hard in the spine. "Keep moving, now. We havn't got all day. Hup now, hup."

"Why does it not fight back?" one of the Woodcutters whispered.

The Shadow raised its head, like a hound on a scent, "Because Time is my master. Where it leads, I follow. There is no escaping Time."

The air lost its lustre as a cloud covered the winter sun.

"Be careful you do not end as we were. Dogs blindly snapping and snarling at death, spurred by fear and self-loathing."

The Shadow shuddered and lowered its hollowed eyes. "Torment it no further," his companion urged. "Can't you see it has lost its will?"

"I see that it had a mind to cut that noose from my throat. I see that it had a heart to forgive me my failings."

The Shadow pulled its head inside the cloak, stole one last glance at the Tree, bent its shoulders as though bracing for a burden, and silently left the clearing.

$$\infty$$

The ice cracked and the rivers swelled, yet still the coldness gripped the forest. The sun barely touched the tree's lowest branches and the earth felt hard beneath the boy's feet.

The Woodcutters visited the glade every day with bundles of logs for the winter fires. They talked with the Tree, but more often they sat in comfortable silence, carving simple wooden furniture and utensils for the cabin they had built amongst the trees. Shavings littered the floor and sparked blue in the flames.

The boy watched as they revealed the lilt and swirls hidden beneath the outer bark. He marveled at the strength of their arms and the skill of their fingers that bent the wood to their designs, transforming a dead block into a joyous carving, flowing with the life of the tree that bore it.

One of the Woodcutters explained his work to the boy. "There's beauty in every piece of wood. I don't attempt to change it. I simply try to find it. Each block is different. I never know what the finished piece will look like until the wood decides to reveal itself to me. Then, once I discover its texture, I can bare its spirit."

He ran a finger along a dark vein which curled into a knot in the folds of the wood. "The joys and the pains are what make it so beautiful. They are the essence of what it once was. It would be wrong of me to try and alter it in any way. I neither add nor take away from it. I celebrate its life by capturing all of it."

As the boy wandered amongst the trees and scrub, the only sounds he heard were the chipping of wood and intermittent rumbles of laughter.

Beneath the silence, he sensed a changing rhythm. The forest's heartbeat, which had slowed to a soft echo as though it were coming from somewhere deep in the earth, grew louder and stronger.

The Tree could feel it too.

"It's waking," it told him. "Though it never, ever sleeps."

When he spotted the first flower, head bowed from the strain of pushing upward through the hard-packed earth, he knew it was over.

Winter had passed. As it always does.

SPRING

It was a very small flower. Its bud was even whiter than the snow that lingered in shadowed spaces.

It seemed like such a delicate, brittle thing. Yet its small stem had forged a passage through the frozen mud, roots, soil and stone.

"I could snap it in my fingers," thought the boy, "but its strength overcame the earth's might.

"How can a flower be stronger than a rock?" he asked.

"Because it is not trying to be a tree."

The boy furrowed his brow.

The Tree gestured towards the modest head, "It fulfilled its potential to become a flower. It did not waste its energy on that which it could never be. In knowing its purpose, there was no obstacle it could not overcome."

"I wonder if it was disappointed."

The Tree, in its turn, looked puzzled.

The boy explained, "It spent all that time in darkness. It must have been terribly cold. It struggled upward. Then, when it finally pulled itself to the top, the world must have seemed even harsher than the one it had worked so hard to leave.

"Last night's frost might have killed it. This morning my boot might have crushed it. The wind, at any time, might have flattened it. The sun might never have found it, half hidden amongst your roots.

"Maybe it would have been better off staying where it was."

"Then it would have remained a pile of unanswered questions.

"It would never have felt air's breath on its petals, or trembled beneath frost's icy touch. It would never have swayed to the wind's crazy music, or felt a droplet slide down its lovely stem. It would never have brought joy to the hearts of those who spied the first flower of spring. It would never have foretold the end of winter. It would never have been beautiful. It would never have been. To live fully is to risk everything. Even death."

"I don't want to die," the boy said.

"Death will come. The trick is to live."

"That sounds like a good trick. Perhaps you'll teach it to me." One of the Woodcutters stepped into the clearing, axe in hand, a smile on his ragged face.

"Did you see the flower?" the boy pointed out the blossom which turned its head, shy of their gaze.

"Careful where you walk now," the boy cautioned.

The Woodcutter set aside his axe and crouched down to get a better look at its innocent face. "So, it's true then. Winter's really over.

"I felt a new surge in the earth. But I have gained so much of late that it almost seemed wrong to hope for more."

"You have suffered enough. You have a right to hopes and dreams. These are the things that urge us to grow, even if the passage is harsh and the struggle great," the Tree counseled. "Yes. Winter's really over."

"You seem sad, Tree," the boy said. "What are you thinking about?"

"I'm not sad, child. My thoughts are of endings."

"But it is spring," the boy countered.

"Every beginning is an ending. The circle always starts and finishes at the same point."

"Like the snake devouring its tail," the Woodcutter supplied.

"Or the mourning wail of the newborn's cry."

"It's the center of the vortex."

"The first note of the unsung song."

"Now you're both just trying to confuse me," the boy grumbled.

"Never, child," the Tree assured him. "Spring has arrived. Winter has passed. The gyre has turned. That is all."

∞

Life flooded the forest. It began as a slow trickle that swelled and gathered and eventually burst its seams. It poured over everything, drenching the earth with colour. Gnarled, grey branches, and wizened, dun stems shrugged off their pallor and astonished even themselves with the newness and delicacy of the petals that sprouted from their once-worn limbs.

The earth hummed and thrummed as bulb after bulb and seed after seed made the slow ascent to the surface, drawn by the light and their will to fulfill their potential.

The little flower danced in sudden gusts and surprise showers that sent the boy and the Woodcutters running for cover, breathless with the infectious gaiety that rippled through the forest.

Somber trees and serious shrubs were transformed into dewy saplings preparing for their first spring. They flittered in the wind and sprouted ribbon-bright blossoms. They twirled till the boy's head spun as he caught the tail of whispers and giggles behind newly sprung leaves. No pink was too flushed, no green too satin. Innocent in their newness, they plunged into colour. They let it trail down their sap-filled limbs, unsure of their beauty and their power to turn heads and catch breaths.

Winter was forgotten.

Its silence was replaced by frivolous, scatter-brained, heart-hammering excitement. It felt as though the whole forest was balanced on the brim of a very great adventure.

The boy had never seen such preparations. Birds flew from earth to tree, gathering twigs and soft leaves for their nests. Small creatures brushed the sleep from their eyes and stumbled into the world, drunk on dreams and kaleidoscope images. Velvet-backed ferns slowly unfurled their whimsy secrets. Tiny buds clenched their wills and pushed with all their might until they finally delivered their blossoms.

Even the Woodcutters seemed to have shed their winter cares. They greeted the sunshine every day as an old friend, and the darkness in their eyes faded. They teased the Tree and played with the boy, hiding behind wood piles as he counted to ten before running off to find them.

A wheel of arms and legs, the boy spun through the forest. Measuring up to the Tree he marked a new notch on the trunk. "Almost a whole inch!" he marveled as he sprinted off to try and uncover where the grey wren was building its nest.

The Woodcutters watched him with soft smiles that easily poured into laughter.

"It's younger we're getting," they told each other. "Another season in the forest and we'll be as sprightly as the boy."

"Dreams don't torment. So much," they confided to the Tree. "I can sleep a night through, and wake refreshed in the morning."

Though there were still times when they were driven from their beds long before the sun had risen. On these nights they walked the forest floor. As always, they ended up at the clearing.

"You never sleep," they chided the Tree.

"I rest and I dream. So, it makes little difference whether I sleep, or not."

"What do you dream?" they asked.

"I dream of sun and wind. Darkness and rain. I smell the damp earth and feel the soft breeze lilt across my mind."

"I wish I had your dreams."

"That's like wishing you had my limbs."

"My legs will do just fine."

"They've gotten you this far."

"I suppose we have come a-ways. Yet I sometimes feel that we've a distance yet to travel."

"Then you will get there. When the time is right. If you trust your heart and listen to your instincts."

"I'm trying, Tree. Of course, it's easier in spring. I can hear them singing."

"Spring has a knack of turning up the music," the Tree agreed.

∞

"Turn it off. I can't bear it anymore."

Neeeeee

Horrible, painful, jarring noise screeched through the forest. It tore and scratched at everything it touched. Innocence shrieked and birds squawked in fright and protest, dropping large twigs from their beaks while just a feather's reach from their nest.

Skreeeeeelll

It came closer, driving beauty into hiding and thoughts from minds. Clawing, bleeding, it slobbered over young trees and fledgling flowers, staining their colour with its black discord.

Skrraaaaaaawww

On and on it went. Jarring sounds with no rhythm, pitched to a point of hopelessness. It felt no joy. It knew no mercy.

Eeeeeeeeeeeeehhhhhh

It jangled and spun out of all control, shaking loose the past, foretelling no future, before it smashed open the moment, and fell into the clearing.

For a heartbeat nothing moved. All seemed frozen in the space created by the din.

Then, like a movie clicked off pause, a Woodcutter reached for his axe and hurdled towards the noise. His battle cry merged with the screeching horror that writhed on the forest floor.

"Treeeeeeeeeeeeeeeeeeeeeeeee

Help me."

"Hold." The Tree hardly raised its voice, yet it carried above the noise.

The Woodcutter had barely covered the distance of a breath, but he stopped in his tracks and looked towards the Tree for instruction.

"Boy," the Tree commanded, "grab the blankets and muffle the sound." The child bundled an armful and flung them over the shrieking chaos, his face distorted by the ugliness of the blasts.

"Good," murmured the Tree. "I can hear myself think."

It looked towards the Woodcutter. "Easy now. You're going to have to knock it off at the head."

A shriek soared above the skrangling screech.

"One good thump should do it."

The Woodcutter sidled up to the noise, the butt of his axe at the ready.

"I can't gauge the exact spot. It's too hard from this angle." A bead of sweat trailed down his face, following the gully of his scar.

The second Woodcutter, alerted by the siren warning, rallied into the clearing. Without preamble he grabbed the noise and hauled it off the ground. "Now!" he yelled.

Jarring noise, thud of wood on metal, then a moment of nothing was followed by buzzing, as Silence rushed in and set about restoring peace to the forest.

The boy couldn't tell if the pinging was in his head, or if it was coming from outside of himself. He held on to the Tree to steady his knees as he wiped his eyes to clear the confusing, scratching fog.

However, in no time at all, Silence had done her work and had magically restored the music of busy birds and soft breezes.

She wiped her hands on her skirt, rolled down her sleeves, lightly kissed the Tree, and disappeared as suddenly as she had arrived.

"That's better," the Woodcutter sighed, as the heap mumbled beneath the blankets and let out a long and hopeless moan.

The boy looked to the Tree. "What will happen if I take off the blankets? It won't start again, will it?"

"Let's find out."

With the swagger and dash of a drunken magician, the boy grabbed a fistful of the covers and tugged them off the painful noise.

The Woodcutter jumped back in fright, losing his grip on the sound he'd been propping.

It plonked down to the forest floor like a dropped stone.

"Time!" he gasped.

"My head," Time moaned.

He rubbed the dent in his metal cap, which was dangling at a precarious angle.

"Where am I? What is this place? Who are you people?"

Time shivered, cringing on the forest floor, a wreck of rags, dried blood, mud and dark shadows. His arms fell uselessly by the side of his belly, while the second hand lurched and stuttered around the dial.

The boy dropped to his knees beside him. "It's me, Time. Don't you know me?"

"I know that once there was day, followed by night. I know that once there were hours, followed by years. But that was a long, long time ago."

He spat at the boy, "Get away from me. I have nothing left that you can take from me." Then he turned his head from the circle of faces as tears fell down his mottled cheeks.

"If you had done your job properly, you might have finished me off," he whispered. "It would have been a mercy."

He suddenly lurched upward and grabbed the Woodcutter's hand. "Do it. Now. Please." He sought the Woodcutter's eyes desperately with his own.

The Woodcutter gently shook his head.

"Then there is no hope left. I am done for." He fell back.

"No, you're not, Time. Don't say that," the boy urged. "There's always hope."

"You're young."

"You're Time. Don't you remember?"

"I don't know what you're talking about."

"You told us that you were all that is past and all that is to come."

Time looked at him with shadowed, vacant eyes.

The boy plodded on. "You're always running around chasing Tomorrow."

Time shook his head.

"You love schedules and timetables and you have a watch for every second of the day."

Time held up his empty arms.

"Breakfast time is your favourite part of the day. Or maybe it was lunchtime."

Time's belly growled.

"You travel with a companion. A Shadow."

Time searched the boy's face as though peering through a lifting fog.

"Why do you torment me?" he moaned. "What are you, that you would say such a thing to me? I have no one. Can't you see that?

"Fool, Fool," he moaned. "I am all alone."

"No, you're not alone. You're with friends. You're in the forest. You're safe now, Time."

"Don't you understand, you stupid child, that without my Fool, there is no Time."

"I can see you," the boy countered.

"You see nothing. I am the word never written. The song never sung."

"I have heard you sing," said the boy.

"The story will go on without me," Time murmured brokenly. "As though I had never been."

"But it's your story."

"Enough of your cursèd kindness," Time roared. "I am nothing."

"Tree?" the boy whispered.

"Help him to his feet."

Time offered no protest or aid as the Woodcutters took a hand each and hauled him up, while the boy pushed from behind.

He was a sorry sight. Springs twanged from his back at painful angles, and his head hung as low as a beaten dog's.

He looked at the Woodcutter. "You hit me." There was no accusation in his voice.

"I'm sorry, Time. I meant you no harm. I can fix the dent in your cap, if you like," the Woodcutter offered.

"It doesn't matter. Nothing matters," Time wheezed, turning his empty eyes away. "Nothing is as it was."

"I am here."

"Tree?"

Time took a few tottering steps towards the Tree. "Help me, boy." He threw out his arm like a blind man stumbling across an unfamiliar room. "I cannot make it on my own."

They covered the distance in short, shuffling breaths.

"I'm done for," he gasped. "My time is over."

However, five steps later they had reached the shade of the Tree.

"So far," Time whispered as he shook off the boy and reached for a limb.

Clinging to the Tree he started crying in long shuddering sobs. "Hold me."

Snot and salt mingled with dew and wood. The Woodcutters turned their heads to allow Time a moment of privacy.

"You don't know what I've suffered." His belly stuttered in rhythm with his gasps as the tears finally slowed and the choking heaves began.

After what seemed a long, long time, his breath evened and he lowered himself to a comfortable position on the forest floor, his cheek resting against the Tree's trunk.

$$\infty$$

"I don't know how it happened, Tree," he began his story.

"We were so happy together, the Fool and I. Wherever I went, it followed like a dog. Meeting my needs was its one and only desire. It would have done anything for me.

"'Time is my master,' it used to say. Oh, you have no idea how happy those words made me.

"I took it in. I treated it as my very own slave. I gave it a purpose in life. I gave it time. I even gave it a watch.

"Of course, that's where I went wrong. I treated it far too well. I gave it bones when I should have given it my boot. But I've always been too soft. You know that better than anyone, Tree.

"We were as happy as a master and slave could be. The world belonged to us. There were tasks to be completed and minutes to fill. We never missed an appointment. You could have set your watch by us. We were inseparable, the Fool and I. People used to point us out. We were the talk of the place.

"How could it do this to me?" Time shook his head and lapsed into silence for a very short time.

"When I think of what we had together. It was the misery to my delight. It was the shadow to my form. I believed we were made for each other. I thought it felt the same way. Did I really read the signs so wrong?

"No. It's not my fault. It was besotted by me. You saw it yourself. You did, didn't you?" He looked towards the group for confirmation.

In the silence, he continued, "Every morning, I'd open its cage and wind its watch. Oh, how it used to shiver. And it was a good Fool, you know. It never missed a second. It was as committed to time as I was myself.

"I gave it every menial task I could think of. Every moment of its time was filled with my presence. It counted seconds better than anyone. Stretched them, even. It had no life. I was its everything.

"Of course, I don't have to tell you that no dog was treated better. I overlooked its faults and fanciful notions. I taught it how to do everything, just the way I like it. My demands could not have been clearer.

"Without me, its life would have had no meaning or purpose. Without me, it had nothing. No one else would have had anything to do with such a sorry wretch. I told it so.

"I told it what a stupid, ugly thing it was. I told it that I was the only one who could even bear to look at it. I told it that it should disappear, become a shadow, so that no one else would be forced to gaze upon its hideous countenance.

"I laughed at its attempts at conversation, and finally managed to shut it up completely. Almost.

"I showed it who was boss, and it respected me for it. It understood that if I was to be the smart one, it needed to be stupid. It took time, but I persevered.

"Of course, there were many disappointments along the way. There were even moments when I thought of giving up on it altogether. I remember it dared to give its opinions. And once it questioned mine. Just once, mind."

A breeze whimpered through the Tree.

"We got past all that. It learned to compromise. On everything. I'm sure I must have made sacrifices too. I put up with it, didn't I?

"There had been other Fools in the past. But this one was special. I used all my skills to twist and break it.

"It lived by my bell. Oiled my springs. Wound me up tight every night. It had just the right touch."

The Woodcutters tightened their grips on the hilts of their axes.

"It was my finest work. It was mine."

The boy's eyes filled with tears.

"Then it betrayed me."

Time took a breath to regain his composure.

"One day it was there, devoted to me. The next it was gone. No note, nothing.

"At first I didn't believe it. I thought it had simply disappeared as I had slept. It had been heading in that direction. To please me, I believed. But when I saw that the watch I had given it was dangling on the hook in its cage, I knew with a steel certainty that it had left me."

The boy clapped, then wiped his eyes on his sleeve.

"I made enquiries, but the trail was cold. I couldn't even begin to guess where to look. It had no one, other than me. It had no thoughts, other than mine. What on earth was it thinking?

"My only comfort was conjuring up the punishments I would inflict on it when it finally came crawling back.

"I waited. It didn't return."

"You're just like her," the Woodcutters recoiled.

"Don't be ridiculous!" Time snorted. "That gnarled spider, for all her tricks, is still trapped in the web of time. Whereas I can no longer tell the days, let alone the hours.

"I'm all astray, Tree. Nothing is as it should be." He buried his face in his hands.

"I'm finished! Done for. Kaput." His voice trailed off.

"Without the Fool, I'm lost. For, how can I be master if I do not have a slave?"

"Aren't you still Time?" the boy asked.

"A ruler without subjects is a balloon without air."

"It's spring," said the boy. "You could turn over a new leaf."

"Do I look like a tree?" Time's patience snapped and another spring twanged in his back as he glared at the child.

The Tree interrupted his hand-wringing and phlegm clearing. "Settle yourself, Time. The boy spoke in sympathy."

Time nodded mutely, almost apologetically. "I have lost my purpose, and with it my senses. I am no longer what I once was. My time, it would seem, is up."

"It's from the maw of endings that beginnings are born."

"I'm hardly some fledgling chick poised to leap from its egg. I'm too old to change, Tree. Look at me. I'm covered in snot and self-pity. I haven't washed in days. My belongings are scattered halfway across the forest. I can hardly tell if its day or night, and I can't remember the last time I had a hot meal. I'm completely spent.

"My alarm has turned on me. My arms berate me. Even my second hand has taken to trading insults with me. It has given me the finger, more than once, I'll have you know.

"I just don't make sense without my Fool to worship me. I, who soared, can hardly breathe at ground level. The stones trip me up and the earth rises to beat me.

"I have absolutely no idea how to exist in this world alone. I need my Fool."

"Maybe you just need to unwind," suggested a Woodcutter, relaxing his grip on his axe.

"That's not funny," Time pointedly waggled a spring. "Not funny at all."

"You're worn out, Time," the Tree told him. "Rest for a while. It will help you to see the world a little differently. A lot has happened here while you were gone. The world is a much kinder place than you give it credit for. There is a lot you might learn from it."

"I am tired, Tree. I've had to carry my own burdens for so long now that I no longer know where my arms end and my load begins. No wonder my hand is affronted with me."

"I'm a sight to sear eyes." He surveyed his tears and tatters. "I'm practically reduced to skin and bone." He took stock of his boulder-sized belly.

"I'm little more than a shadow." He pulled at his sagging jowls.

"It is too much to bear," he moaned. "To remember what I once was is torture. To know what I will become is hell."

"Then perhaps it's best to focus your energy on what you are," the Tree suggested.

"I don't think I can do that."

"I will help you."

"You would waste your time on a shadow?"

"The moment's mine to squander."

Time wiped his nose on his ragged sleeve and brightened perceptibly. "If I had a little something to nibble on, I'm sure it would raise my spirits.

"Fools," he roared at the onlookers, "fetch me roast beef and be quick about it." No one moved.

"No, of course not. I must do everything for myself now. At my time of life, this is how I am to be treated. I should have known it would eventually come to this. That the best years of my life would be used up in selfless service, but when I needed some care and attention in my twilight days, I'd be left by the roadside to fend for myself."

It seemed inevitable that the endless supply of tears would be unleashed upon the Tree once again, when the boy, who had slipped off into the forest, returned with a prize which he dragged with both hands to the center of the clearing.

"I think this belongs to you." He dropped it with a thud.

"I don't believe it," Time beamed as he gazed at the suitcase the boy had located not a quarter of a mile away. "Quick, open it. I think there may well be enough food in there for all of us." He clapped his hands excitedly.

"Sounds like you just cracked the shell," the Tree chuckled.

∞

The boy guided Time to the river to wash off the grime, and the Woodcutters gave him a pair of clean trousers and a checkered shirt. He was pitifully grateful, for about five full minutes, before he started berating the Woodcutters for their taste in clothes.

"I wouldn't normally be seen dead in these. Though I'm hardly living, so it scarcely matters," he grumbled. "It's not as if any of my set will be wandering in these parts anyway."

He flung himself down on the forest floor and closed his eyes. The boy and the Woodcutters slipped into the forest and soon the rise and fall of their voices faded.

"I don't know what to do, Tree," Time breathed unevenly, his eyes fluttering to hold back the flood.

"Talking doesn't help. There are days when words dissolve, and it seems like all that remains is the gap they leave behind. In the empty space, there's nowhere to hide from the pain. My mind whimpers and my body gasps at the thought of what I've lost."

"You lost what you never had a right to own," the Tree said.

"You're talking about the Fool? That's not it at all. The Fool was a catalyst. It helped to create me. But now that it's gone, what I've lost is me. I've splintered, and I don't know how to piece me back together, Tree.

"I cannot stomach it much longer. My heart is caught in a noose and it's strangling my breath. I can barely suck in enough air to stop from drowning. I'm wretched in body and mind, and I can't tell if I want to retch or scream.

"I cannot do this by myself."

"Sit up, Time, and breathe with me," instructed the Tree.

"Close your eyes and open your mind to the sensations in your body. Feel the air pass through your nose. Concentrate your thoughts on this single action. Breathe in and breathe out."

Time sat beneath the Tree, his legs crossed, hands cradled in his lap.

Slanted shafts of hazy sunlight patterned the clearing, lighting up butterflies and insects that filtered through the rays.

A soft breeze carrying scents of spring flowers brushed against the Tree's leaves, causing a fluttering amongst its branches.

The beat of a wing twanged like a plucked wire as a bird soared on the currents high above the forest floor.

The air vibrated with the humming of industrious insects, and a spider web glimmered in the light as a cloud brushed by the sun.

Bird song drifted through the clearing, while a single leaf fluttered on a silent bush, dancing to its own music.

Time leaned back against the Tree, and in no time his soft snoring mingled with the sounds of the forest.

∞

Time awoke with a start and rubbed his neck to ease the stiffness. "You shouldn't have let me sleep for so long, Tree," he groaned, stretching out his arms. "What time is it anyway?"

The Tree shrugged its branches.

"I'm sure it must be lunchtime, at the very least."

"Are you hungry?"

Time thought for a moment, "No, not really. But it's time to eat."

He settled more comfortably. "I suppose I could wait a little while longer."

As the Tree swayed to the breeze, Time watched its movements.

"You look different, Tree. I'm not sure what it is." He studied the Tree more closely. "Did you do something with your bark?"

"It's my leaves."

"That's it. Of course. I hope you don't mind that I didn't mention it before now. You do look rather well. Much better than the last time I saw you, at any rate."

"Thanks, Time. It's spring. Hadn't you noticed?"

"Not really. As you probably gathered, I'm a bit of a mess."

"You haven't been subtle."

"I'm not what I once was."

"Everything's changing, Time," the Tree told him.

"Even you?"

"Always me."

"I count on you always being the same," Time said.

"That would not be possible. It's through change that we grow and renew ourselves in the world. Spring's arrival shakes up the earth and opens our eyes to new things."

"People say that it gives them hope, but it just makes me scared, Tree. I'm too old to change, and I'm not sure that I want to."

"The world is older even than you, yet every year it embraces this renewal with pleasure. Without the capacity for rebirth, it could never have survived this long."

Time looked around him. "It is nice," he granted. He idly dug his fingers into the soft earth.

"It's as though the winter never happened."

"Don't let your eyes deceive you. Without winter, spring could never have come to pass. This moment is the result of all that has ever been."

"Then perhaps my suffering has some meaning," Time mused. "Though if it has led me to this point, it's a poor story in need of a better ending.

"I was great, once. Sages foretold me. Kings worshipped me. They hitched their fates to the hours, and I powered through their veins.

"I pulled philosophers to their knees, and harnessed innocents for my pleasure.

"I emptied minds of thoughts, and watched bodies turn grey as youth was traded for what I offered." Time smiled as he remembered.

"Whole cities fell under my sway, as its inhabitants crawled from their sheets to tarnished street corners, itching to get their hands on what I peddled. I fed them minutes until the seconds finally chased them to their graves, where they clung to the lip with rotten fingernails, still pleading with mouths long drained of their sap for a little more time, just one more day.

"When their time was up, there was nothing more I could take from them."

In the silence that followed, Time turned accusingly on the Tree. "I feel that you're judging me. You think you're better than I am. If you had a little taste of what I had to offer, you might not be so high and mighty.

"You don't think I can change. You think I'm hooked on the ebb and flow. Well, I'll show you. I'll show all of you. I don't need that stuff anymore. I'm on the straight and narrow now. From here on out, it's good old checkered shirts and power breathing for me."

"I'm not judging you, Time. You are the sum of this moment."

"So, what's next?"

∞

Time sat twitching beneath the eaves of the Tree. The boy sat at a little distance, his eyes closed, breathing in and out in harmony with the forest. A distant tinkering could be heard coming from the Wood-cutters' cottage as they toyed with Time's springs.

"Damnable fly!" Time furiously burst out.

"What's wrong?" enquired the boy.

"It's been tormenting me all afternoon."

"Where is it?"

"Of course, it's hiding now. It's trying to make out that I'm the one that can't sit still. As soon as I saw it, I knew it was a crafty one. You couldn't trust a bug with eyes that big."

"I thought you said it was a fly."

"A fly, a bug, a flug. What difference does it make? If it thinks it can outwit me, then it does not know just who it's dealing with."

"Well maybe it's learned its lesson," the boy suggested.

"Humph," Time didn't sound convinced, however he settled once again and closed his eyes.

"There! Did you see it?" he demanded of the clearing. Driven by outrage to his feet, he was practically hopping.

The boy sighed, "I did not, Time. But perhaps if you just ignore it, it will go away."

"How can I be expected to concentrate with all this commotion? Between the buzzing and bird song I'm being driven to distraction. Perhaps we should take a little break and have something to eat?"

"We just had breakfast a short time ago," said the boy.

"I'm wasting away to nothing in this forest. I'm sure I've practically forgotten the taste of crispy fried bacon, its rich aroma mingling with the scent of freshly baked bread, salt smeared and doused in sizzling fat."

The boy dug in his pocket and produced a handful of dried nuts.

"It's alright," Time sighed, and wearily lowered himself to the ground. "In and out," he reminded himself. "How hard can that be?

"I need to discipline my mind," he muttered. 'Focus on my breath. In and out. In and out, in and I wonder where that fly has gotten to,' he thought. 'Plotting under a leaf. A strange shade of green. Citrus? Darkens over time. Mustn't think of time. How long have I been sitting here? Orange juice would be nice. I'm thirsty. There's not enough air. It's impossible to breathe. My throat's raw. Just one sip of water. A little moisture. Swallowing's not working. I'm all dried up. Not a bit of spit left in me. I'll show them. I'll get my figure back. Havn't been eating properly. Just three meals a day. Bacon and eggs would be nice, fried on the griddle. Always tastes better outdoors. Cooked over a fire. What torment! My Fool. Where are you? I need you. It wouldn't even look at me now if it could see me in this stupid shirt. I'll get a burgundy dinner jacket when I get out of here. Satin trim on the lapels. Maybe an eye monocle. Oh, I could see myself in that! A toast for Time, please, ladies and gentlemen. A rich oak aroma to match the colour of my jacket. Swirling in a glass. Candlelight catching the glint of my polished shoes. This little thing, madam? Why I believe it was woven in India. They have the finest silks. Rubbing my arm. A tad too long. Madam! Just a little more gravy. Have to watch the figure. Fill up the glass. Let it trickle slowly. Don't think of drinking. Still, it was nice of them to give me anything at all. Could have turned me away. I've nowhere to go. Couldn't be seen dead looking like this. My cap should be fixed soon. They've been working on it long enough. They did dent it. Wish they'd hurry up. I look foolish without it. Keeps the flies off the head. Not as stupid as the Fool looks. Looked. I can hardly breathe. Where's that buzzing coming from. I'll kill it!'

"This is killing me." Time flailed at the fly and trundled to his feet.

"What's going on here, Tree?" he demanded. "This place is going downhill rapidly. If you don't pick things up, I'll spread the word. Your reputation will be ruined. You'll be finished!"

"What's wrong, Time?"

"It won't leave me be," he complained, his voice petulant. "Here I am, doing my best. I'm focusing my mind, just as you told me. But every time I try to think, that blasted creature ruins everything. How can I be expected to breathe if I am to be besieged by a fly?" he demanded.

"The world is full of discomforts, Time. To live well you have to learn to deal with the unpleasant, as well as the pleasant, and face both with equal calmness of mind."

Time sighed. "It's hard," he moaned.

The fly rubbed its feelers together as Time dropped like a sack, once again, to the forest floor.

Time crossed his legs and wiggled his bottom until he found a comfortable spot. Then he drew in his breath and started again.

$$\infty$$

As Time closed his eyes and focused his mind, the fly closed its wings and flexed its legs before fixing its six padded feet on Time's shoulders. It sat for a time, swiveling its eyes, waving its antennae, plotting.

Then it spotted them. Crumbs from Time's breakfast hemmed in the creases of his shirt.

It swooped. Time swatted, but the fly was fast. It immediately set to work on the remains, liquefying them with its saliva before drinking them in.

Time concentrated on the flow of air as he breathed in and breathed out. The fly concentrated on his food as he spat out then sucked in the messy feast.

'What I wouldn't give for a long drink of cool cola,' Time thought. 'Bubbles fizzing in my mouth, battling my thirst. Resting in a hammock. My legs outstretched. The sea sucking on the soft sand. An umbrella in my drink, served by a waiter in white. I wonder would Tree let me hang a hammock from its branches. I'm sure there's one somewhere in my luggage. The Fool would know. What am I talking about? The Fool's not coming back. You're on your own now, Time. If you want a hammock, you'll have to fix it yourself, that's all there is to it. How hard could it be? That's not the point. It's undignified. I deserve better than that. It's not much to ask for. My throat is savagely dry. I'm drowning for want of water. I never knew the Tree could be so cruel. Why is it putting me through this? It wants me to suffer to prove some stupid point that's not even worth making. All I want is a drink of water. Then get it. You know that this is not the Tree's doing. It's my choice. I could get up and walk away. I won't fail. I just need to get through this moment. Hold on for just a little longer. Start again. Breathe. If I could just scratch my cheek. Lift my hands and tear away that damnable itch. What if it's the fly, crawling all over my face with its filthy feet? It's too much to bear. Tree said it was better not to move. It's just a little itch. Observe it. Yes, it's uncomfortable, but it too will pass. Misery, like happiness, always runs its course. Isn't that what Tree said? Or something like that. They're just words. What do they matter in the face of a flug. They won't squash a bug or scratch an itch. But maybe they'll help me to live through this moment. If I can get through this one, then maybe the next will be better. I don't think that's the point. They're all supposed to be borne equally with a good dose of calmness to wash them down. What am I talking about? I don't want this moment. I want to spit it out and wash my mouth. I want to fast forward to the one where the fly's dead and I'm laughing at its funeral. I warned you, fly. You're messing with someone serious. Weighed down in its tiny grave, surrounded by open mouths and gnashing teeth, the sky filled with a swarm of mourners stuttering into the jaws of flycatchers. Seen from above it's no bigger than a raindrop. Rows of fresh graves, as tears give vent to a flood of misery and open minuscule holes in the earth. Salt mingled with muck and rubbed onto the wound. If I could just move things along a little faster so that I can get through this. I'm doing it again. I'm wishing my life away. If I keep this up, I'll have no time left and nothing to show for the effort but a bale of wasted moments. I'm a fool. I just want to scratch my face! Is that really so bad? There are much worse things. Like the bomb in my chest that's ready to explode at any moment. Ticking away. Never resting for a second. You need to slow down, Time. You're always scratching and tearing at anything that tries to anchor you to the moment. Maybe the fly is walking on my face. Maybe its feet are planting germs in my pores. It doesn't matter. It is what it is. This is my moment. Live in it fully. Feel it in all its joy and misery. I won't run away. I will not scratch my face. I will accept my fate and live my life. I will weigh every second equally. I will learn to live better. I have made such a horrible mess of things. I can fix it. I can find Fool and make it come back. Things will be as they were before. We'll do time together. Coast on the euphoria. We'll glide over the ugliness and dive into the future, where life's always full of hope and promise. No, I won't. I don't need time. Who am I fooling? My bones ache for it. I can hear my blood sighing and slowing. I'm teetering on the edge of darkness. I can see the worms. I need more seconds to fill these loathsome minutes and topple them into the open maw.

The holes are dug and yawning to be filled. A graveyard of minutes. I'll cover them with earth and heap stones upon them, so that I never have to revisit these wretched moments again. Where are the seconds? I can't do this. Just a little more time. One quick score. Just one. What harm can it do? It'll be my last. I promise. The Woodcutters can help me. I just need to persuade them to wind me up good and tight. It shouldn't be hard. I'll slip a watch on their wrists. They've been down the same road I have. They know how it feels. They too must burn to escape from their misery. They're working on my cap now. It sounds like sleigh bells. Now's not the time to get distracted. Come up with a good excuse and sneak off. Tree will never know.'

Time gave his face a good scratch, startling the fly which had been taking a nap on his shoulder. In its fright it rose up in a clamor of buzzing.

"I knew it," Time stormed. "It was that damnable fly all along."

"Erm," he cleared his throat, "I think I might just go for a little wander in the forest. I need to clear my head. All that buzzing, you know."

"Can I come?" asked the boy.

"No!" Time hastily responded. "I want to see what the Woodcutters are up to. They've been working on that cap of mine. They may need me to try it on. I don't want to keep them waiting."

"I like visiting the Woodcutters," the boy said.

"Not this time. It'll be boring. You know how particular I am about my cap. It will probably take ages."

"Oh," the boy looked crestfallen.

"It's just that I'm planning a little surprise for you," Time floundered.

"What's the surprise?' the boy excitedly asked. "Well it wouldn't be a surprise if I told you. Gotta go. Toodle-oo, Tree."

Time trundled into the forest without a backward glance. He hadn't walked very far before he came to a fork in the path and a mire of indecision.

∞

I could go back, he reasoned. The way is clear and I won't get lost.

It's better to keep going, another voice argued. This may be your last chance to float once more on the ebb and flow of time. You've done it a million times before, there's nothing to be frightened of.

I want to change. I want a better life.

The forest fell quiet as Time poised on the moment of decision.

"Time." He jumped. The Woodcutters stood before him, their arms laden with coiled springs and the metal cap.

"I was just on my way to see you," Time told them. "But now that you're here it seems that I have found you, without losing my way."

"That was lucky. If you don't know the forest, it's easy to get lost. It keeps its secrets right out in the open, but it takes a long time to understand its ways. We can walk back together."

"Where does this path lead to?" asked Time, pointing at the right fork. "Oh, that's a slippery slope," the Woodcutters warned him. "It's best avoided."

"I wouldn't mind having a peep all the same," Time said.

"If you don't know what you're doing, you could really hurt yourself," said a Woodcutter.

"I'm no greenhorn. I've been down this path before. Look at me. Not a scratch."

The Woodcutters shifted the weight of the coils they carried.

Time nodded towards their loads, "That's nothing," he assured them. "Just a few springs that are easily replaced."

"We'd hate to see them shattered again, now that we've mended them. You were a harried soul when we first met you, Time, brimming with brine and vinegar. You represented everything we were trying to break free from. We don't want to see you hurt yourself, or anyone else, ever again."

"Don't be so prissy!" Time snorted. "I'm just looking for a little more time. Something to make the day go a fraction faster. I can't bear this slow death. Every single second carries the weight of an eternity. I can't see past it. This is what hell must be like, but here we're instructed to luxuriate in the torment. We don't even have the pleasure of screaming.

"You feel it too. I know you do. I see it in your eyes. Forced to live in your own heads. All that breathing in and out until you think you'll go mad. Peering and poking into filthy corners of your mind that should remain shuttered and secret, even from yourself."

Time slipped his hand into his pocket and pulled out a couple of wrist watches. "They're not much, but if you slide them on now we could slip away together. I know a guy who can get us much better ones as soon as we get out of here."

The Woodcutters backed away, but Time pressed them further. "They just need to be wound up tight. Once they're over the pulse, you'll feel the immediate rush." Time's hands shook as he held out the watches.

"Give them a try. One beat and you'll be hooked. We could make a run for it down the slope. Once I'm fixed up, I'll never let you go. You'll have time on constant supply and will never again have to endure the insufferable, unending moment."

One of the Woodcutters reached out and took the offering. He held it gently in the palm of his knotted hand.

Time panted, "Go on. Put in on. I'll be your master," he promised.

The Woodcutter brought it closer to his eyes and dreamily examined its face.

"You'll be mine."

He trailed it across his fingers.

"Slaves to Time."

The Woodcutter raised glazed eyes.

"All will be as it was before. All you have to do is put it on, Fool.
Time smiled.

The watch slipped slowly from the Woodcutter's hand.

"No!" Time cried, as it shattered beneath a boot. A deafening roar
filled his mind as time lay spattered on the forest floor.

"We're heading on, Time. What you choose to do is up to you."
The Woodcutters set off towards the clearing.

Time crouched at the fork, trembling and sweating, wracked once
again by the moment of choice.

∞

"I'm a lost cause, Tree," Time sat dejected beneath a canopy of branches.

"Only if you opt to be."

Time mulled and fretted. "It's decisions I'm uncomfortable with.
I've lost faith in my ability to choose. I don't know what's right or
wrong any more. When I lived by the clock everything seemed so simple. I just did what was expected of me and I bellowed out my chimes.
Now that I'm let loose in time, I don't know how to anchor myself.

"I am trying, Tree. But it's hard. I want to listen to reason, but
most of the time I just worry to the point where even thinking about
making a choice churns my gut. I used to be stronger than this. There
was a time when I lived by my wits and didn't need the affirmation
of another to force my fate. I've become so dependent, that I've lost
my capacity for independent action. It would be funny, if it wasn't so
pathetically pitiful. And here I am still, waiting for you to save me.

"Tell me what to do, Tree."

"Don't worry so much, Time. Once you choose to live a good life
the decisions you make may lead you in different directions but will
keep you on the same path."

"You're right, of course.

"I'm thinking too much and trying too hard. What I really need is a distraction to keep my head from boiling over.

"Though a decent meal would suffice. I'd settle for anything that doesn't include brambles and nuts."

∞

"Let's not make a meal of it," Time looked determined. "If we're going to breathe we may as well just get on with it." He lowered himself slowly to the earth, stretched his arms and rubbed his legs, jostled his bottom and wiggled his jowls. He tried another position, listed then shifted, before he eventually settled.

A sharp painful keening filtered through the clearing.

"Did you hear that?" Time demanded, immediately on his feet.

"At last," he exhaled. "Maybe something will actually happen."

"I think it was the wind," the boy responded. "Havn't you noticed the sounds it makes? Sometimes I think it's laughing with me; but there are other times when it makes me shudder, and I can hear the sadness of the world carried in its voice."

"No, you're wrong, boy. Firstly, wind can't feel pain," he counted on his fingers.

"How can you be so sure?" the Tree interrupted.

"Secondly," Time ignored it as his fingers poked the air, "the wind can't reach that high. That note was far beyond its pitch."

"Really?" the boy sounded skeptical.

Time jumped to his self defense to quell dissent. "Of course. I'm a musical maestro. I know such things. I might as well say it, though I am loathe to boast, but no one can follow a score as well as I. My timing has been described as impeccable. But, of course, you know all that."

"We do?"

"You heard me sing."

"Ah."

"What was that?" Time started. Eyes darted around the glade.

"I didn't hear a thing."

"You're not listening properly, child. You should get out there and see what's going on in the forest. This may be our one chance for a little diversion."

"I'm not sure, Time."

"It's an alternative to listening to me bleat on about my problems."

"I'm on my way."

"There! Surely you heard it this time?"

The boy stopped in his tracks. "I heard it!

"Could you make out what it said?" the boy demanded.

"I'm not sure, but I think someone's looking for their ball. You know how easy it is to lose things in the forest."

"I thought they said, 'All is lost.'"

"I suppose that would make more sense," Time conceded.

"It's coming from the North and it's getting closer," the Woodcutters ducked under a couple of low branches and entered the glade.

"We've been tracking the sound, but havn't been able to pinpoint its exact location. Our biggest problem is that it's completely empty. It's eerie, Tree."

"This is exciting!" Time clapped his hands. "We should make a plan. You three should comb the forest's darkest shadows to find the source and drag it out of hiding."

"What will you do?"

"I'll strategize."

"You mean watch from a distance."

"Is there any other meaning?"

The ragged sound silenced all chatter. It pitched and tumbled into a long, low wail. "Gone, gone, gone, gone, gone, gone, gone."

"What is that?" the boy asked the Tree.

"It is the sound of grief," the Tree responded, its branches drooping as though weighted by a great burden.

"Are you sure, Tree?" Time probed. "I just heard a few crows making a racket, "Caw, caw, caw, caw, caw, caw, caw," he mimicked.

"I wish you were right, Time. There is no need to track it. It is coming our way," the Tree added.

"Man the entrances and let nothing through," Time shrieked a command as he darted for cover.

"What should we do, Tree?" the boy asked.

"We wait. It will find us. There is no avoiding this."

"Gone." An empty gong, hallowed by the wind, reverberated throughout the forest. They all heard it clearly. Loaded with sadness, it dragged at their hearts.

"This will not do," the Tree muttered.

In the drawn-out moments of waiting, Time gathered sticks and sucked in his gut.

"What are you doing?" the Woodcutters asked.

"I'm disguising myself as a tree. It's called camouflage. It will give us the advantage of surprise."

"Duck!"

$$\infty$$

"Where?"

A flurry of birds crashed through the clearing in a cacophony of confusion, calling and shrieking as they screeched to a halt.

Wings flapped madly out of rhythm, and tail feathers stepped on their brakes as they tumbled and cackled towards the Tree.

"Easy now," yelled a commanding voice. "Landing zone approaching. Wind is holding steady at 40 knots. Angle west for a good headwind. Visibility is good and, yes, we have just been given clearance.

Pull up those feathers. Feet extended for impact. Prepare for a running stop. We have touchdown."

Feathers ruffled then settled on the boughs of the Tree and the branches of Time before the squadron broke into a tumult of disarray.

"She has lost her mind," they screeched.

"Thoughts scattered on the winds."

"Wailing and sobbing. She won't leave it down," they squawked.

"Wandering in the forest. Drowning in her mind."

"Help her, Tree. Grief devours her," they shrieked.

"Get off me!" yelled Time, causing a winged tumult above his head.

"Do I look like a lamp post?" he shrilled, as he spun arms and branches like windmills.

"Propel to the Tree," the commander's voice rose above the disorder, and the unsettled birds flocked to the upper boughs where their companions shuffled over to make space.

"Jackdaws 1, 2 and 3 prepare for take-off, you're heading out," the commander instructed. "Keep the target in sight. You're in position. I want a full load released. Deliver the package."

Time ducked, but he was too late as the birds emptied their bowels over his head.

"Good work, team. Come on home." The Tree's occupants erupted in cheers.

The Woodcutters doubled over in laughter, and the boy attempted to mollify a furious Time. "I've heard it said that it's really lucky," he said, in a vain stab at placation.

"My person has been defiled and I will have justice!" Time roared in defiance. The birds shifted uneasily on their perches.

"Enough of this nonsense," the Tree interrupted the clamor. "There will be no more attacks or talk of reprisals. Settle down and tell me what brings you here."

A hundred voices rose at once, each trying to tell their story, but meaning was lost in the confusion of words.

"Her grief has no bounds."

"She is shredding her heart."

"There is nothing to be done."

"She won't bury it."

"Her tears will never stop."

"She holds onto hope when there is none to be had."

"I will listen to each of you," the Tree counseled. "But I can only hear if you speak with one voice."

"You should send them all away, this minute," advised a disgruntled Time, who was wiping furiously at his head with a stained handkerchief.

"You best explain," a bird nudged its companion forward. A sigh escaped from a lined beak, and old eyes pierced the Tree with its round, unblinking gaze.

"We have our ways, amongst us birds," the hooded crow began, stilling every other voice in the clearing. "Every spring we lay our eggs and hatch our young uns. We instruct them to fly and to forage for food. We show them the world from the dizzy height of the clouds; and we help them to view the sky from the level of the worm. We give them the freedom of flight, and we bring them back to earth again, for we are wise enough to teach them both the joyful and sorrowful airs of the wind.

"We watch them grow fat in the summer of their lives, as we shiver in the inevitable darkness of winter.

"Life has its certainties as sure as it has its seasons. We are born in a husk and we return our bones to the earth that has fed us. This is something that we understand and that we accept as the cycle of nature."

"Yeah, yeah, I've heard all this before," Time muttered. "I thought we were in for something more interesting."

"One amongst us has lost this knowledge," the Old One continued. "She has suffered a great misfortune and it has unhinged her mind.

"It is a sad story that I have to tell you, Tree. This bird craved a chick more than anything else in the world. Last spring her eggs failed, and she struggled through the summer and the winter. Yet she maintained hope that the next spring would be better and that her time would come.

"It did. This spring she hatched a perfect chick. No baby was loved more. Perhaps too much. As the other mothers lined up their offspring on low-slung branches for their first instruction in flight, she kept hers safe in the nest, fearful that it would fall and hurt itself. We reasoned with her, and she promised that, when it was older and stronger, she would teach it everything that it needed to know. She gathered the tastiest, fattest worms she could find, and it flourished under her attentive care. It was clear that it would soon outgrow the nest and then, we felt sure, she would give it the freedom that the other young birds were already enjoying.

"She clucked over that youngster day and night. I will remember this spring as the season of her lullabies. Every evening we gathered in our homes and nestled under our wings to the croon of her mother's love song.

"Then early one morning, as she went hunting for the juiciest fare, our community was shattered by the most dreadful tragedy. The child, having watched its companions test their wings, was eager to try its own. A brave little thing, it crept to the edge of the branch and it threw itself into the currents. The fall was great, and it died immediately.

"The howls of the wind drove us from our nests. We flew to its aid, but its body was broken, and nothing could be done.

"The mother returned shortly after. Her song broke mid-note as she hovered above the scene, before plummeting to the earth where we were gathered around her fallen offspring.

"She rushed at us, hissing and cursing, blaming the world for the disaster that had befallen her chick. Then she scooped the poor mite into her wings and carried it to her nest, claiming that she would pour her life into its shattered form.

"There she stayed, refusing to eat or drink. She could not be consoled or reasoned with. It could be clearly seen that the soul had flown the chick's broken body, but she refused to accept it.

"That night her beautiful lullabies were replaced by a keening that spoke of the emptiness of the world. The stones cried themselves to sleep."

Time blew his nose loudly and wiped his eyes with his mottled handkerchief.

"We kept vigil around her nest to offer what little comfort we could and, come sunrise, we tried to persuade her to release the body so that it could be buried in the earth to nurture the soil which is the source of our nourishment.

"We failed.

"She held fast to the body and claimed that it stirred. Nothing that we said could convince her to act otherwise. Each day we have watched the darkness around her grow thicker. We fear for our sister, and we mourn for her loss. The child deserves to be put to rest and the mother needs the cleansing tears of grief and acceptance before she can be part of this world that we share.

"This is why we have come to you, Tree. We need your help."

"Where is she now?" the Tree asked.

"As we speak she travels through the forest to this spot. She believes that you will return life to her child, which is the only reason she consented to forsake her nest. She carries the chick with her."

The Tree responded, "Her pain runs deep and the forest buckles under its weight. We share her sorrow and will do what we can to support her."

"Thank you, Tree," the Old One sighed in exhausted relief.

"Of course we will help." Time was on his feet.

The wailing, which had fallen silent for a time, rose once again and drew closer. "We're coming, we're coming!" Time piped as he lurched in circles. "Though if you could take it down a notch, we'd appreciate it. I have very sensitive ears," he roared into the wind.

In a short time, the mother arrived with her offspring clutched to her breast. She was accompanied by black ravens that fluttered in her wake, voices raised in lament.

"Have mercy!" Time implored the group. "Let's not compound this tragedy."

"We're just doin' our job here, buddy," one of them croaked in response. "So a little respect, if you don't mind." The ravens elbowed past Time's protests and cleared their throats.

"We are gathered here today," one began in a funereal voice, pitched low and sonorous for maximum impact, "to celebrate the life of..."

"This isn't a burial!" the mother gasped.

The old hooded crow signaled the raven to stop. "Little sister, this is the Tree we spoke of. It has pledged its aid. Please listen to what it has to say. It can help you."

The mother's crazed eyes darted past the Old One to the Tree. "My chick is sleeping," she said. "It won't wake up. I need to teach it to fly. But it won't open its eyes.

"These old fools want me to bury it. Keep your death," she roared at them.

"I would never harm my baby."

"I know that," the Tree responded. "Even the wind in the forest has spoken of your love for your child.

"Come a little closer."

The mother stepped forward anxiously. The shadows clustered behind her. Waiting.

"My friends," the Tree spoke to the ravens, "it is time that you rested. Time will help you to find a comfortable roost."

They grudgingly fluttered to the branches indicated, and lined up like omens overlooking the scene.

The Tree turned its attention to the mother. "What is it that you would have me do?"

"You must make it fly."

She tore at her feathers as she spoke, pulling out clumps with her beak, punishing her body with her addled mind.

"Then you must help me."

Confused, frightened eyes pierced the Tree.

"I will do whatever it is that you ask of me," she rocked her child back and forth.

"First, you must set the child down," the Tree instructed.

Her gaze darted around the clearing, as though she expected the body to be snatched at any moment, but she complied with the Tree's direction.

"Now, I need you to visit every nest in the forest. At each you must ask for one feather to help your child to fly. But you can only accept it if the family has never been visited by Death."

"Is that all?"

"That is all. Return with a bale of feathers and your child will find its wings."

"You will watch over my baby?" she asked.

"As though it were a piece of my very own heart."

She darted into the forest, and quickly disappeared into the shadows of the trees.

"So what do we do now?" Time asked.

"We wait."

"Well, what about a little song to pass the time?" Time looked towards the birds, which let out a long groan.

"Here we go again," one said. "We're always expected to be the life and soul of the party."

"There's more to birds than song," another piped up. "No one ever asks us to discuss philosophy."

"Or philately," a magpie joined in. "I'm an avid stamp collector."

"Ah, forget it," Time grumbled as he threw himself down on the forest floor to wait.

∞

At the first nest the mother came to she explained that she needed a feather to help her chick to fly. A matronly bird clucked to her tale then plucked a tail-feather without a moment's hesitation. The delighted mother accepted it gratefully, before remembering to ask if Death had ever visited its family. Yes, the bird replied, this past winter it cast its shadow over our nest. The mother regretfully returned the feather and flew to the next branch, but Death had passed that way too.

She frantically flitted from nest to nest where each family willingly offered feathers she could not accept.

The day passed and not a single feather had been collected.

With clear eyes and a heavy heart, she returned to the clearing as darkness was falling. Time slumbered fitfully as the birds roosted in the Tree's many branches.

"Little sister," the hooded crow fluttered softly to her side.

"I understand," she whispered to the Old One and the Tree. She scooped the chick's body into her arms and wrapped it in her wings.

"I could not accept what had happened. I didn't want to believe that Death is as much a part of life as breathing. I love my baby so much." Her voice broke and tears fell down her beak.

Time woke and sidled up beside her. "Why don't you let me take a look?" he gently suggested. "I've been told many times that I'm a great healer." He awkwardly patted her feathers.

"There's nothing that you or anyone else can do," she sobbed. "Not this time."

∞

The long night eventually passed, while the Tree and the flock kept vigil. In the innocent blossom of the first light, the chick was returned to the earth, nestled between the Tree's giant roots.

"It will give me comfort to know that my beloved is close to you," the mother told the Tree.

"Next spring my new leaves will remember the death that gave them life," the Tree promised her.

Time bustled over. "The music was lovely," he said. "The crows outdid themselves. Though one or two were a little off-key."

"My dear, if I can be of service to you. If you ever need to talk," he trailed off.

"Thank you, Time. But if talking could help then it would not be so bad."

She turned to the Tree, "What should I do now? My soul is empty, and my nest is bare. I have nothing left." Her voice broke and she wrapped her wings tighter to hold herself from flying apart.

"Return with your flock. Let them help you. They care for you dearly. I will also be here when you wish to return. My branches are wide and will always give you shelter."

She bowed her head in assent, as the Tree nodded towards the old hooded crow. "I wish you a safe flight to your rookery."

A commanding voice filled the clearing, "We have a beautiful day for flying. Visibility could not be better and, with a decent tailwind, we should be back at base at 0800 hours. Straighten out those feathers. We have flight clearance. Wings in motion. 3, 2, 1 and lift-off."

The boy and Time clapped delightedly, congratulating each other on the flock's smooth ascent. The mother was soon engulfed by the mass of birds that filled the sky. In moments they were little more than specks on the clouds.

"I wonder what the world looks like from up there," mused the boy.

"I imagine it looks like Death has forgotten about it," a Woodcutter replied.

∞

"I'm no spring chick, but I have been restless of late." As he spoke, the Woodcutter set aside a delicate wooden bowl he had been carving and stared at the patch of earth between his feet.

"I don't want to leave the sanctuary of the forest and the home we have made here, but I also don't want to ignore the stirrings in my bones."

"What is it that you want to do?" the Tree asked.

"The right thing."

"Then you will."

"The trouble is, I'm not sure what that is.

"I've never fully escaped the Weaver's grip. I cannot shake it off. Even here.

"The more I see of the beauty of the world, the more my memories petrify me. My mind remains frozen in horror of her snare. How can I step out of the shadows to live fully in sunshine, knowing that others rot in darkness, tormented by her schemes and webs?"

He shivered in the early spring warmth, eyes focused on the knuckles that wrapped his index finger in their grip. Flesh and bone, his own, had once held his mother's hand. A small fist enfolding her finger. The same hand had wielded a pen. Then an axe. He could still taste the blood in his throat. The smell never fully dissipated. Beneath the clean forest air, it was still there. A pervasive stink that he could not scrub from memory.

He took a deep breath, emptying his voice of emotion as he began in a low monotone, "In the darkness, there is nowhere to hide. There are only tangled nets and dark alleys. Narrow lanes are lined with brutal structures. Faceless facades glower over the streets, with shuttered entrances and concealed orifices from which filth, blood and entrails spill into the gutters. Monstrosities tower as high as the neck can crane. A slat of sky, then rows of eyes hidden behind slits, watching everything. Nothing is beneath their gaze. Every glance is stripped and word sieved; and every miscreant thought is rooted out and dragged, bound and gagged, to the darkest recesses of the Spider's lair.

"Whispered rumors of what the walls conceal are as frightening as living in plain sight. Fear burrows beneath the rational, laying a lattice of tripwires in the mind. There is no moment of respite, or the promise of a soft lamp in a framed window. Lives are spent as rodents, bodies plastered to stone, scuttling through the shadows, fighting over filthy holes in which to shiver.

"Ignorance and oblivion are the only options in this wasteland. Honeyed directives ripple across the web, day and night, telling one what to think, who to envy, how to live, what to fear and when to die. Missives are posted evoking the Spider's many eyes, and the pleasures that she promises. Daily twitterings spin dire plots and stoke hate of Others, who threaten to destroy the state she has created. Flies are fattened on lies, then offered a cocoon in which to tremble in terror. Many weave their own prison, stupefied by falsehoods. In the absence of light, they look to the darkest shadow as both saviour and executioner. The Weaver is the Alpha and the Omega and, while her bite is feared, her oblivion is craved.

"In comes to all, in the end. There's little point in struggling. She feels every movement through her web. Enjoys, perhaps, the futile tremors of the condemned as they stumble towards dead ends. There is no path that is not of her making. The web is carefully, beautifully designed. The sole incandescence in this putrid realm. It is the perfect torment.

"Its kernel spans acres. Swept clean of ash and detritus, its frigid emptiness is more frightening than the crushing alleyways. In the center of her web the soul shivers alone, rigid in the glare of an interrogation lamp, accused and found guilty before a word is ever spoken.

"The Weaver is seldom seen, and yet she is everywhere. In the gaze of her underlings, the stutterings of the flies, in the whisperings that vibrate along the tendrils of the web. They fear her and hate her and give her their hopes and their dreams. She takes it all and feeds on last breaths, exhaled as screams."

The grip on his finger tightened in an attempt to still the rocking that accompanied his words. The Woodcutter gathered himself and looked at the Tree.

"I am no better than she. Here I sit in sunshine, like a glutton at a feast in a famine-stricken land. Surely it is wrong that I fill my belly with colour, knowing that others are starved of light?"

"You should not eat dust when there is bread to be had," the Tree responded. "There's light enough for everyone."

"Yet so many are still in darkness. Her flies are withering in her net, wrapped in shrouds, already half dead. I believe that I have the strength to help them; what I lack is the courage."

"What are you frightened of?"

"Of leaving this behind. The North terrifies me, and my heart falters when I think of returning. But doing nothing tastes like blood in my mouth. It reeks of weakness, and I want to spit it out."

"You are mistaken in two things," said the Tree. "The first is that you do not lack for courage. I have seen you battle your demons on a daily basis and win every time.

"The second is that the North will not douse your light. Wherever you travel from this forest, the darkness will scuttle from your radiance."

"You really think I can do it?" He gazed steadily at the Tree.

"I have faith in you. All you need is to believe in yourself."

"You will not be traveling alone." The second Woodcutter stepped into the clearing, "I won't let you have all the fun without me." He spoke with a smile, but his eyes were tinged with sorrow.

"You should not take it lightly, my friend. This is a dangerous road that we're choosing and there's no guarantee that we'll make it out of there in one piece."

"I'm not a fool. I understand the risks. Don't you know that I too have been tormented with thoughts of frozen souls filed away like so many useless pieces of paper than no one will ever read? It's time that someone set the parchment alight, so that something better can emerge from the embers.

"Besides, I want to see the Weaver's face when we tear apart her web."

"We have to do more than that. We have to put an end to it. Break a web and she'll spin another. It's the spider I'm after. Her lies must be stopped for once and for all."

"That's a bold proposal!" Time caught the tail-end of the conversation and twirled it. "Have you got a plan? She is a wily one."

"I'm working on it."

"I'm an excellent commander," Time volunteered.

"Are you saying that you want to come with us?" the Woodcutters looked dubious.

"Er, no. Well, not exactly. But I could stand on a hill at a safe distance and tell you how things are going."

"Can I come?" the boy's eyes gleamed, lit with faraway adventure.

"I need you here," the Woodcutter shook his head.

The boy's face fell. "I promise I won't be any trouble. Besides, the Wanderer showed me a thing or two. I can handle myself.

"Please, Tree," he implored. "I'm ready."

"You didn't heed me, boy," the Woodcutter responded. "Your part in this battle will be critical. But you won't be fighting on the front line."

"You can join me on my hill, if you like," Time offered. "We could have matching uniforms with lots of brass buttons, and you could carry the binoculars. What a lark we'd have!" Time beamed.

The boy's face fell like an empty sack.

The Woodcutter looked at him and seemed to struggle with his thoughts, "If we are to succeed, we need to show souls that they do not have to live in darkness. There is another way. You represent a life shaped by love and sunshine."

"I don't understand."

"The Woodcutter means that you represent hope, child." The Tree murmured to him through a rustle of branches.

"Then shouldn't I go with them?"

The Woodcutter responded, "If we are to bring light to the North, it is important that you shine with all your might in the forest. When we succeed in awakening the trapped souls, we will look to you to pierce through the darkness."

Time interrupted, "I get it! You need him to flutter like a flag or an empty prayer, muttered into the wind. He'll be our very own poster boy of the light. It's brilliant! Nothing sways souls like a sound bite." He pinched the boy's cheek affectionately. "They'll lap it up. We won't have to lift a finger. Fire the right slogans and they'll pick up the guns and turn them on themselves.

"I can see it now," Time waved his hands in front of the boy like a magician. "Picture this, a black poster, lit from above, stark letters, the colour of blood: *Better Dead than Dark.*

"Or, check this out: *Flies Rise Up. Death to Lies.* How's that for a slogan? Or, how about, *We can Fly?* A bit hackneyed. I have it, *Flies Flea your Fetters.* A play on words, that one. It opens it up to different types of winged insects.

"No, no wait. I'm on fire. This is it. This is the one: *Time's Flies are Having Fun.* It's perfect. We'll turn it into a party that everyone wants to join. If you're not in, you're out.

"They'll tear a path through the web to join us. You won't even need the boy. I'll take care of it myself. Take the flies under my wing, so to speak." Time chuckled.

"That's that settled then. So, when are we off?"

"We appreciate your enthusiasm, Time," a Woodcutter responded, "but the light has to come from the boy."

The boy hung his head, "What if I'm not bright enough?"

"Surely you're not hinging success on the boy's ability to be a beacon?" Time cut in. "If that's the case, and you're going to be crude about it, wouldn't it be better if you just lopped off her head and be done with it?"

"I had thought of that," the Woodcutter answered slowly. "What do you think, Tree? Is it really that simple?"

The Tree shook its limbs. "If you kill her you become her instrument: a sword shaped by her hand, which is the destiny she had planned for you all along.

"You will have lost everything and achieved nothing. Another head will grow. It will look no different to the one you severed.

"To eliminate the Weaver you have to take away her power."

"How?"

"Cut off its source.

"She weaves her webs, because people believe in her lies. She rules over darkness, because she has told them there is no light. She has taken away hope by offering death as the only choice.

"Shine your light, expose her lies and wake the creatures from their stupor. Power resides in her control over them. Help them to take responsibility for their own lives, and you will have stripped the beast of its venom."

"But how can we make them listen to us? We are just woodcutters."

"I am just a tree.

"The sum of what we are is the extent to which we choose to realize our potential. A woodcutter, or a tree, can be enough."

"I am just a boy. I will shine as bright as I can be."

"I'll feed you your lines," Time chimed in.

"Can't I just say what I feel?" the boy asked.

"Don't be ridiculous. You could come out with anything, and the last thing those flies need right now is the truth."

"The boy will speak his mind," the Woodcutter closed the discussion.

"Then I think I might sit this dance out." Muttering to himself, Time stalked to the edge of the clearing and flung himself down in a heap. "Amateurs!" he pouted.

Raising his voice, he blasted the Woodcutters, "You're fools to waste my talents. I am a great orator. There isn't a story I can't spin to my tune. There isn't a fly who won't hop to my ring."

"We're not looking to remove one ringmaster only to replace it with another. All we want to do is show them that there is another way of living. They are not bound by darkness."

"Give people hope and they're capable of anything!" Time hopped to his feet in agitation.

"Exactly," nodded the Tree.

"You can't be serious?" he exploded. "They welcomed her lies so that they wouldn't have to think for themselves. Now you want to give them choices.

"They're not like us. They're flies."

"We too are not alike. We are as different as earth and sky. But we share the same need of light. Without it, my limbs would wither and die. Without light, day would never follow night.

"The Woodcutters will defeat the Weaver by releasing the pendulum. Misery and joy, light and dark, both are part of life. They will restore the balance and let the North see that the world has capacity for love, as well as hate."

"Perhaps when you put it that way," he faltered. "I could root out my old commander's uniform. Officer's attire, I have been told, looks very fetching on me. The ladies love it, eh boys?" He nudged the nearest Woodcutter in the ribs. "Though all those medals tend to weigh me down."

"So men, when are we off?" he looked towards the Woodcutters.

"When our plans are made."

"That's where I come in."

The clearing swung a full arc as the Wanderer stepped lithely into their midst, wearing a flowing cloak and a dented smile.

∞

The boy whooped and flung himself into her arms.

"Where have you been? I missed you so much." He gasped as she twirled him in the air.

"I've come from the North."

As she steadied him on his feet again, he gaped at her in wonder. "That's where we're going."

She raised an eyebrow at the Tree.

"Well, not me personally. I'm going to hold the light as the Wood-cutters carve the path."

"Then it seems that I have rejoined you at the right time."

She placed her hand on the trunk of the Tree, breathing in its presence. "I have missed this place," she murmured. "But I fear that I bring you ominous tidings.

"I'm worried, Tree. Things have gotten worse. The Weaver has become more desperate and, as a result, more reckless. I came here to warn you that she's amassing an army of flies. We need to strike first before her swarms blot the skies."

"It seems we move not a moment too soon," the Woodcutters looked at each other, lines of concern etching their eyes.

"How do you plan to proceed?" she asked.

"With great caution," Time hastily responded, drawing his arms protectively about his frame.

"Nobody said anything to me about an army. This won't do at all. I'm not cut out for this sort of thing. Normally I send the Fool to battle, my banner chiming the hours until the dead can be counted."

"You're missing a Shadow," she glanced around the clearing.

"Don't get him started," a Woodcutter cautioned.

"When will you set out?" the boy asked.

"At first light," the Woodcutters told him.

"So soon?" the boy's shock froze him. "Why do you have to go so soon? Can't you wait a little while longer?" he looked at his friends, a silent pleading.

They shook their heads regretfully. "The decision is made. We cannot afford to wait, or the darkness will be upon us."

"I shall miss you," the boy blinked his eyes rapidly to dam the tears that would betray his youth.

"You will be with us every step of the way, guiding our path."

They turned to the Wanderer, "We would welcome your companionship on this dark road. It is a lot that we ask, but we need your help."

"You ask for nothing that I would not willingly give."

"Do we have to leave so early?" Time grumbled. "I'm not at my best in the mornings. I like to give the day a chance before I slice it into seconds."

"You must be getting soft, Time," the Wanderer playfully punched him in the belly.

"Watch it!" he spluttered. "I've just gotten the ticker back in shape and it's tocking along nicely, thank you very much. Check this out," he flexed his newly mended arms.

"Your work?" the Wanderer asked the Woodcutters. "He seems as good as new."

"I'm afraid so," they agreed.

"Fine. If you're all set on getting up at the crack of dawn, I'll set my alarm," Time conceded.

"No need," the Wanderer assured him. "I always wake with the light. Like clockwork."

Time snorted.

"So, what else has been going on here while I've been away?" the Wanderer asked.

"I've been abandoned and betrayed by my dearest slave," Time whined. "Misery has become my daily fare. I can't begin to tell you how I've suffered. But I shall try."

"No need to drag up the details," the Wanderer patted his shoulder, turning her attention to the boy.

"You've grown."

"At least an inch."

Together they examined the notch in the Tree that was made the last time she was there. Then he drew a wooden blade from his belt that the Woodcutters had carved for him and held it up for her inspection. She balanced it in her hands, then curled her fist around its hilt and slashed the air. It sang.

"It's a fine piece," she said.

He beamed as she handed it back to him. "I practice every day," he confided. "The Woodcutters play with me."

"It's not a game, boy."

His smile faltered, then failed. "I know that."

He looked at her, eyes stinging. His arm fell slowly to his side and the sword hung loosely in his hand. It was just made of wood. The world was too big. His friends were leaving. Darkness was coming. He was a small boy. The tide was too strong. There was nothing he could do. He was frightened.

She softened her words, "I am too serious today. Perhaps later we will play together, and you can show me what you've learned."

"It won't be enough," he whispered.

He knew that the morning would come. They would leave him. He could not hold it back.

She dropped to one knee and placed her hands on his shoulders, pinning him to the moment. "You are stronger than you know," she told him.

He could feel the tears swell. He didn't want them. He angrily shook them off and looked at her, beseeching. "Please don't leave me," he said. "I need you." His voice rose, despite his clenched fist, nails digging into his palm.

"I would never leave you," she said slowly, solemnly.

He wanted to believe her, but they were cleaning their axes and the laughter was gone.

"Then take me with you."

"You're needed here."

"I can't do it without you."

"You must be brave."

"What if the darkness eats them up?"

"It won't."

"You don't know that."

"I know that if we do nothing, we will lose everything that is important."

"It's not fair."

He hung his head and the tears dripped to the earth.

"Look at me," she said.

He held himself in a tight grip.

She said it again. He loosened, a little.

"You will be our light."

"What if I'm not bright enough?"

"You have the heart of a warrior, boy. You will be enough."

She sounded so sure, and seemed so strong, that the world felt safer. He nodded and, jumping back from her, balanced then brandished his sword as she had done. His smile returned, "Will you play with me now?"

"Soon, I promise."

She tousled his hair and turned to the Tree. "You're looking well," she said, taking in the new leaves uncurled like wishes across its boughs. "The colours suit you."

The Tree smiled and swayed, "There's still some sap in these old boughs."

"You've never been old."

"I remember what it was to be young."

"Do you miss those days?"

"Every season has its charms. I don't long for summer when I'm wrapped in spring. Though there are times when I miss being astonished. When you're as old as I am, firsts become scarcer and scarcer. However, experience brings its own compensations."

"There are days when I wake up and my leg aches." The Wanderer rubbed her thigh, remembering an old wound. "I'm not yet ready for the body's betrayal.

"Tell me the good things, Tree. What can I look forward to with age?"

The Tree thought for a time, "You'll cease to care what others think of you. The realisation that you can't please the world by changing who and what you are will come as a revelation. You'll start to be yourself, and you'll finally fill your own sagging skin with the ease that your body only displays in youth."

"Perhaps it's not such a bad trade off."

"You're not old, Wanderer!" the boy assured her. "Not compared to the Tree. Look at all its wrinkles," he ran his hand over its bumps and crevices. "I can feel your heart, Tree," the boy laughed as the evening beat slowly towards darkness.

In the last of the fading light, the Wanderer and the boy danced around the clearing, clanging blades and thrusting points as the Woodcutters looked on, their eyes sketching his every movement, drawing within themselves the memory of his laughter.

"It's time I took these ageing bones to bed," she eventually conceded. "We've got an early start and a distance to cover."

The Woodcutters invited her to share their log cabin, but she wrapped herself in her cloak, curled at the foot of the Tree, and fell deeply into the rhythm of the forest.

∞

The boy's lips trembled in the early morning light. When the Woodcutters finally wrapped him in their solid arms, he thought that he might break.

"I hate goodbyes," he whispered into their necks. He could have held onto them forever, if they had let him. But it was he who finally pulled back and reached inside his pocket for his heart.

The size of a chestnut and made of wood, he had poured all the knowledge he had gained from the Woodcutters into the simple design.

The veins stood clear in the pebble-smooth carving, so that the heart seemed to pulse in his hand.

"I just have one to give you," he smiled a little awkwardly. "I didn't have time to make a second. But I'll work on another, if you'll share this one for now."

He placed it in a rough palm, which closed over the gift.

The Woodcutters looked at the Tree. "It's the heart, isn't it? That's what it's all about."

The Tree nodded.

In moments, the companions had left the clearing.

∞

The weeks passed to the flutter of wings and commotion.

Birds arrived with daily news from the North: the Weaver had goaded her armies; the companions had arrived at her fortress; strong words were spoken; a scuffle at the gates; twanging along the lines of the web; messages intercepted; others delivered through dark-winged sentries; at the centre of it all the Weaver still plotted and wove deceit and dissent; darkness was holding, but feeling the strain.

Tales filtered through of daring feats in dark alleys, where light was brandished for a bright moment, before being doused by the spider-lings' venom, which dripped from the eye-slits in the watching walls. Cover was scant and many were lost. The insurgents forged ahead, drawing flies to their warmth. A woman was with them, it was said, who glimmered in the darkness.

Days stretched. The news wasn't good. The boy held faith that the light would penetrate to the cavernous centre, and that his friends would return to the forest before the season was out. He would not betray them by abandoning hope.

Every day he sat beneath the Tree, eyes closed, looking inward, and sent waves of love to the North. "I will not fail you," he promised, as he drew his energy together and focused his mind to a pinpoint.

"Every creature strains towards the light," the Tree told him, "especially those that live in darkness."

"What will happen if we cannot reach them?" the boy asked, though he knew the answer in his heart. He seemed to be growing up a little faster these days, and his eyes were often troubled.

"You must have faith," the Tree gently chided.

"What if they want to turn over and fall back asleep after we've gone to so much trouble to stir them?"

"The seed that lies buried in the earth all the long winter wakes with a longing for sunshine."

"Yet the passage through the earth is never easy, and there's no certainty at the end of it," the boy pressed.

"Without the effort, all the potential contained within the seed would rot to nothing," the Tree responded. "It is a risk worth taking."

"How can you be sure that we will succeed in drawing the flies to the light?" the boy asked. "The Weaver is very strong, and she can only be defeated if her subjects can be persuaded to stand against her."

"I cannot be certain. However, we are not toppling one web to cast another of our making.

"Our companions are simply waking souls who have lain dormant over a long, long winter. They have slept in darkness. Now they will learn that they have a chance to live in the light. We bring them a choice. That is all."

The boy shifted his position to ease the pins and needles in his leg.

"Make no mistake. It is a dangerous and difficult thing that we offer," the Tree told him. "Many will resist it, and resent us for putting responsibility for their destinies back into their own hands."

"Do you think that they will side with the Weaver?"

"It is impossible to tell. Nor does it really matter. Those who align with her will do so knowing that they could have chosen another path, not of her making. To live is to make difficult choices. In opting to cling to the darkness, they will have asserted their will and broken the Weaver's hold on them."

"Choice will bring chaos. If they fight, many could be lost. Even our friends," the boy's words trailed off and he swallowed hard, as he thought of all the lives dangling by threads.

"This is a war, and some will be trampled, but to have never even tried is certain death for all," the Tree responded.

∞

It came to them first as a whisper. The wind carried the news. Then the birds caught hold of its tail. Soon the whole forest was ablaze with excitement.

It was over.

The Weaver's grip on the North was broken.

Shards of the story were collected and pieced together. Lines crossed and jarred and converged in the centre of the web, where the final assault had taken place. There were claims that the Weaver herself had entered the battlefield, in an attempt to rally her flies. Thousands had swarmed and blotted the skies. But, despite the odds, the light had held.

Shutters had been prized open, revealing vaults filled with mummified forms. Reports were delivered of brittle figures, wrapped in sticky silken shrouds, that ached and moaned in darkness. Far too many were long past recovery and had simply dried like leaves and crumbled to dust when the first probes of light had penetrated. Many, it was said, were no older than the boy.

"They're coming home!" the boy's jubilation was tempered with sadness for the souls they had been too late to save. There was no sense of victory.

It was whispered through the leaves that stricken creatures were held in enormous grey voids, neutered of hope and shelved away, suspended in chasms on cold metal trays, row upon row, lined one upon the other as far as the eye could pierce the gloom.

Sitting in the center of her web, the Weaver had kept control of them all. Tuned to the faintest ripple of movement, she had shown no mercy to those who shivered or tore at their binds.

"That could have been me." The boy stayed close to the Tree as the news was delivered. Unable to grasp it, he tried to shake his head loose from the scale of the horror.

"You must face it," the Tree told him. "This has happened before. It could happen again. Knowledge and understanding must break this cycle."

"But I don't understand. It is said that the crypts are as big as cities and that they stretch all the way to the sky. How did no one notice?" Tears spilled down his face. "There were so many," he whispered in a choked breath.

"They became accustomed to living in the shadow cast by the vaults. They put their heads into their coats, hurried past them, and worried about what they would make for dinner. They severed their link with the world, and forgot about sunshine and seasons.

"In this way, the Weaver kept them in her web and, when their time came, she found a space for them on a metal tray beside the other hopeless souls."

"What will happen now?" the boy asked.

"It will take time, but the crypts will be destroyed, their shadows erased and each being will be awakened and given the chance to choose a path. This time, they will have a shot at happiness."

"And of our companions?" the boy asked.

"No news as yet."

"Why have we not heard from them?"

"The aftermath of war is a period of great confusion and uncertainty. There are still patches of dissent amongst the Northerners that need to be quelled. Some are looking for a leader to emerge from their ranks; others are weary of those who would tell them what to think. The light is getting through, but news seeps slowly out," the Tree told him.

"What can I do to help?"

"What I have taught you to do. Harness your mind, connect to the world and pour forth your love."

The boy sat beneath the Tree, cleared his thoughts and breathed in rhythm with the vibrations of the forest. Yet, even then, he was riddled with fears of loss, and held a shield before his mind refusing to delve into the space that words shy from. He remembered their steady hands, their arms around him, their last hug. He sat still, fighting off thoughts of last times. Loving the bones of them.

∞

The Tree watched over the boy and felt a tremor in its roots, its leaves and its limbs. Once again, the world was turning.

Spring was waning and the sun was gaining ground with every passing day. Chicks that had hatched in its eaves had already learned to fly. Mothers looked less harried as their broods ventured further from the nest.

The Tree felt the newness ripen and find its place in the world. Broad leaves opened fully, hiding nothing.

Everything changed, and yet it had happened so quietly that it might have passed unnoticed.

"What's your favourite time of the year?" the boy asked the Tree.

The Tree fell silent and thought for a long, long time.

"There is a moment that hovers between the havoc of winter and the renewal of spring. It's the instant before the phoenix rises, when chaos is reduced to dust and expectations have yet to be formed. It's perfectly still and utterly silent, and it exists outside of all that was, that is, and that will be."

"Is that what death will be like?" the boy asked.

"Perhaps," the Tree responded.

"My favourite season is spring," the boy announced.

"That," smiled the Tree, "is how it should be."

"Mine too," a gentle voice lilted into the clearing. The boy's gaze followed it to a smile that made his knees tremble.

It might just have been a trick of the light, but it seemed to the boy that a ray of sunshine had been woven and clothed and sent to join them in the woods. He had never seen anything so beautiful.

The woman's eyes softened as she looked about her, as though returning home after a long absence. Beneath a traveler's cloak she wore a fine, white tunic which was clasped at her waist by a simple plaited belt. Her hair fell loosely in waves down her back. A carved wooden heart rested at her throat, its veins pulsing in the dappled glow.

It almost hurt to look at her, but the boy was unable to lower his eyes.

He watched as she slowly moved towards the Tree, spilling light with every soft movement. He blinked and wiped his eyes to clear his brain and settle his vision as the woman and the Tree blurred and merged into one image.

Body and branches erupted into a blaze of colour. Shadows disappeared as every limb, leaf and hidden place in the forest was suffused with light. The world was radiant.

"It is done," he heard her murmur. "I am the sunset and the dawn; the last night of winter and the first day of spring. I will give freely the eternal moment to those who thirst for minutes."

The light faded and it was day once more.

"Who are you?" the boy asked. Words swelled like blossoms.

"Don't you recognize me?" she asked, her eyes carefully neutral.

The boy shook his head.

"You're not looking at me," she gently admonished, as she leaned back into the Tree's embrace.

The boy carefully examined her features, her cloak, and finally his eyes fixed at her throat.

"Where do you get that heart?" he asked.

Her fingers protectively touched the beautiful carving, and her eyes brimmed with sorrow as she looked at the child. The boy's heart contracted, and time locked in her gaze. He wished with all his being that he could reverse the moment and un-ask the question but, for all that, he could not look away.

The world gathered itself around her words. "I've come from the North. The battle was won, but the casualties were many. This is the spoils of friendship."

"You found it?" the boy asked, fighting to still the tremor in his voice and the sting in his eyes.

She shook her head, "It was offered, and accepted, with love. They said that you would see it and understand that the war had been worth it. Despite the great losses."

"The Woodcutters?" he asked softly.

"They fought bravely."

"Are they coming home?" he asked.

"It's where we all eventually end up."

"I'm not sure that I can wait that long," the boy said. "There is a hole in my gut and I can't seem to fix it."

"That's what the heart is for," she said, removing it from around her neck and gently placing it in his hand.

The boy held onto the Tree for support. "You knew?" he asked. The Tree murmured in the boy's ear. Soft, whispered words of comfort.

But all he could hear was the keening of his own voice telling him they were gone.

∞

"It doesn't make any sense." The boy covered his eyes with his hands, blocking out the words, the world. He bowed under a cloak of sadness, greys and thick weaves, smothering his breath, unable to face the fact of their absence.

He had no faith in a Nirvana fit for such warriors. All he saw was a gaping hole where the Woodcutters should have been. He encountered no moment of truth or redemption from which he could shape some semblance of reason. It was wrong. He berated the Tree with his grief.

"If this is some test, then let's agree that I've failed it. I can't go on. The world doesn't make sense to me. Every day there are miracles. Look at what spring has snatched from the mouth of winter. That flower was reborn. But my friends are gone. Explain that to me," he demanded, voice ragged.

He had let them down in their last moments, when they needed him most. His love wasn't enough. Words wormed into his mind to torment him.

He curled up and finally fell asleep, writhing through troubled dreams as the Tree and the woman watched over him.

∞

Darkness descended and words dissolved.

∞

He could hear their voices in his head, "Ah, boy," as they hid behind a woodpile and, later, laughingly ruffled his hair. But he feared that too would fade and he'd have nothing left to cling to but dry parchment and mannequin figures. He buried his head in their worn shirts, inhaling the scent of resin and sweat, and feared the moment when their essence and smells would be reduced to stick insects in a dream.

His memories were corrupted with imaginings of their last moments. The woman told him what she could. They had embraced before the final assault. They had entrusted her with their heart. She had not seen them fall. The battle was brutal, and the numbers were vast. There was no space for hope. She had found their bodies in the rubble, within a few feet of each other. He pictured torn clothing and throats stuffed with screams. Their eyes were open, she said, looking at the light. Did they even know they were dead? he wondered.

"Some moments are harder than others. I keep getting punched in the gut when my head is elsewhere, and I don't see it coming. It makes me gasp."

The woman stroked the boy's head.

"Will it ever get better?" he asked the Tree.

"The sadness that weighs you down will never get any lighter. So, you will have to get stronger," it counseled the boy.

"It's crushing me. I can't get out from under it, let alone carry it."

"I cannot take this burden from you. It is yours to bear. But I will help to hold you up," the Tree promised.

The boy nodded, his eyes dark pools of pain.

∞

"What happens to love when it's ripped away? I loved them. I love them."

"They're in your bones," the Tree told him. "Who you are is shaped by having loved and been loved by them. They are part of you now. Love doesn't go away because the beloved is departed."

"Why did they leave me?"

∞

The days lightened, the sun ripened, and the boy grew stronger.

He looked around him and the pain lodged a little deeper. Colours seemed faded, but he could still make out their hues. He spent time with the woman, seeking answers that couldn't be found in the questions he asked her.

"How did they die?

"Were they in pain?"

They were dead. His heart told him that was all that mattered.

He tried to still his addled thoughts and focus on the shapes before him. But his mind prowled the litter of discarded futures. A fog enveloped his path and he struggled with the chaos that he could not contain within himself. It spilled over his every moment. There were instants when he forgot his loss; but laughter turned bitter in his mouth as he was assaulted with his treachery. Time and again he returned to the Tree, where he sat in its eaves, breathing in and breathing out, attempting to clear the clutter and confusion. The woman often joined him, both a point of quiet and a disquieting riddle that he had yet to solve.

"The Woodcutters entrusted you with their heart," he said, working through a puzzle. "They clearly loved you very much.

"Your cloak belonged to a friend of mine, and was once worn by a Shadow. I never thought that it would give it up. It was the first thing that seemed to give it substance. Who are you," he wondered, "to have gained such trust?"

"You know the answer, but you prefer to chase questions. Look closer," she instructed him, as she wrapped the cloak around her a little tighter.

"You are the brightest being I have ever met."

"Don't be fooled," she cautioned. "The brightest light casts the darkest shadow."

"There you go again," he grumbled, "talking to me in riddles."

∞

He found himself looking at her when he thought she didn't notice. She was the clearest, stillest creature he had ever seen. Curled at the base of the Tree, her chin resting on her knees, she could have been mistaken for a child. She seemed brand new. Yet she knew so much.

She bothered his thoughts. He felt that he should recognize her, but his mind couldn't put the pieces together.

She was patient with him and did not seem to mind his staring. By times she would catch his eye and smile. At others she became wrapped in the Tree's thoughts, swept on an inner journey that led her to spaces that he could not yet fathom, where time seemed to have no meaning.

The Tree told him that he needed to persist. That he was still learning, and that he too would reach places within himself that he had not yet imagined. But he envied her ability to follow the flow of meaning, and was exasperated with his own painfully laboured progress.

When he asked her how she knew so much, she shook her head and told him that those who claimed great knowledge were the biggest fools of all.

He quizzed her about where she had met his friends. What they had done together. What they had spoken of. Had they talked of him? Were they frightened, he wondered? But, more than anything, he puzzled over how she had ended up with his heart and the Wanderer's cloak.

Her face lit up when she talked of the Woodcutters. Yes, they were frightened, she said. But this is what made them brave. They could neither have lived, nor died, any other way. They loved him, she told him. But he already knew that.

The Wanderer, she reassured him, was safe and well and walking amongst blues and stars. The boy longed to see her again. To feel her gaze appraise him. He recalled her voice, telling him that everything would be okay. That he was strong enough. He wanted to believe her. He also burned with questions about her part in the conflict. It was she, it was rumored, who had forged the path to the center, having spirited the web's plans from the depths of the Weaver's lair.

"It is the Wanderer's story to tell," the woman smiled when the boy harried her for details of his friend's daring. "I can only attest to her courage and compassion." She paused, caught in her thoughts, and said, "I glimpsed her in the heat of the final battle. Light poured from the point of the sword she held aloft. She was fierce, and she shone. She faced the Weaver without flinching. It was the spider who dropped the challenge, before scuttling back to the shadows."

She smiled as she spoke of the Wanderer, and it was clear to all who cared to look that there was a tremendous bond between the two women. When pressed, she explained that the Wanderer had shown her great kindness and that she had helped to free her from the shadows.

The boy jumped on the clue offered. "Were you amongst the souls who had been trapped by the Weaver?" he wanted to know. As she shimmered before him, he rejected the notion even as the words had been formed.

"I was indeed lost," she responded. "But not in the way you think." She shuddered, but her eyes never wavered.

The boy dwelled on all that she told him. It was a great comfort to him to know that the Wanderer was in her element, laughing up the world. He missed her desperately, but knew that she would return. For now, they were each on their own paths. Though the distance was great, he felt her closeness. An hourglass had been broken and, in the matter of friendship, space and time had no role to play.

He wondered at love and concluded that absence did not diminish it in any way. It simply made it sharper. It might cut you, if you weren't careful. But he didn't want to be careful. Love mattered, whether it hurt or not.

Without the Woodcutters, the Tree, the Wanderer, and now this strange woman, his life would seem empty. Even Time, he admitted to himself, had his moments.

The woman spoke little of Time, though she had spotted him crouched on a hillside overlooking the battleground, hiding from view of the fleeing souls.

"Was he alone?" the boy asked.

She shook her head. He had a legion of followers, looking for a new life and a rule book by which to strangle it.

"After he accepted that he had lost his Shadow, he cleaned himself up. It was hard, but he was getting braver and seemed ready to lean on himself. He must have fallen in the end." The boy lowered his head.

"In many ways, Time is a victim of others' yearnings," the woman replied.

"I think he feeds on others' weaknesses," the boy said, a lick of anger singeing his voice. "It makes him feel stronger."

He briefly recalled the Shadow, a pitiful creature that barely hovered on the edge of his memory. It had never seemed more than an illusion to him. A trick played by a grisly entertainer, paid for by the crowd's horrified gasps.

"The Shadow was real, boy," the woman told him. "Look closer."

∞

He did. All he could see was light. It blinded him to the point that he could no longer make out the woman's shape, her form. She became as unreal as a spectre. Blood and bones melded into a daydream.

I see you.

It can't be.

I know you.

I know nothing.

∞

"Don't be frightened of what you see," the woman cautioned. "When confronted with something your brain can't decipher, then you must open your mind's eye and trust in your gut. It understands much, much more than you will ever know with your senses."

The boy struggled within himself. The woman and the Tree waited patiently as he grappled with what he had grasped, and what he had yet to admit.

Spring hovered on the rim of summer. The year was almost done. So many lessons were still to be learned.

Then one day, as the last of the youthful buds blossomed into bosomy flowers, the boy nestled into his favourite branch of the Tree, and took a breath.

"I see you," he said to the woman.

She smiled deeply. "That is all that anyone can ask of another."

The Tree settled comfortably into its roots. The boy tentatively gathered his thoughts. His words came haltingly, at first, but grew in certainty and strength as he spoke.

"You are the riddle and the answer," he said.

"You are sorrow and you are joy.

"You are all things in one form.

"You were the Shadow and now you are the Light."

"You've grown, boy," the Tree nodded. "Just a notch," the boy conceded.

∞

The truth had been there all along. From the very first moment he had seen her. Now that he recognized the woman, he couldn't fathom his previous blindness. Nor could he get his mind around the transformation.

"We are all a balance of light and darkness," the woman explained. "Our decisions shape what we become. Our very humanity is carved by what we do, and the choices that we make."

"But you didn't have a choice," hot tears welled up in the boy's eyes. "Time captured you and made you his slave.

"And I looked at you and saw nothing but a Shadow." He hung his head, wretched with shame.

"You're wrong, child," the woman's voice was tinged with deep sadness. "I was a slave to Time. But it was I who chose Time as my master."

He began to protest, but she held up her hand and continued. "I took the watches from Time's grip and closed the manacles around my own wrists."

"He made you do it," the boy persisted.

She shook her head, "I worshipped Time. I would not allow him to leave me."

"How did you escape?" the boy asked. "Time would never have let you slip from his grasp. He needed you. We saw him after you got away. He was a wreck."

"Time never had the power to hold me. It was I who had put my life under lock and key. I escaped Time's tyranny when I decided that I no longer wished to be a slave."

"It can't have been that simple," the boy countered.

"It was difficult," the woman conceded. "But once you set upon the right path, the world reaches out to help you.

"It is true that I had starved my soul for so long, that I had faded away to a Shadow. I despised what I had become, and willingly embraced every torment. I was little more than the wraith that you saw.

"Then I met the Tree. It looked at a Shadow and it saw me."

She leaned against the Tree. Dappled light shifted through its leaves. Her hair lifted gently in a soft breeze. Sunshine rippled across limbs and eaves.

"From that first encounter, my life changed. Slowly. I was so consumed by Time that I didn't believe it possible that there was still light lurking within me. But, little by little, Time lost his hold on me. I witnessed so many small acts of kindness in this forest, that I began to believe in love again. I watched the Woodcutters fight their demons and reveal the beauty in a piece of wood. I felt the Wanderer shiver when she carried me to the fire and wrapped her cloak around my shoulders on a bone cold night. I heard you defend me when the Weaver and Time fought over my wreckage, like dogs over scraps. I even witnessed snatches of love in Time's deep regard for the Tree.

"Through all of this, the Tree never wavered. Never once did it doubt me and, strengthened by its certainty, I began to piece the broken parts of my soul back together again."

"I should have done something," the boy struggled to keep control of his shaking voice. "I thought of you as a Shadow. Of course, I pitied you. But I never looked at you. I never once tried to get to know you. I saw darkness, when I sought the light. And so, I looked away."

"It is easy to love that which is beautiful. It's much harder to wade through filth and grime with the small hope that a battered soul's still clinging to the wreckage. However, we all learn from each other's journeys. It's how we grow."

"I should have held your hand."

"It wasn't your job to save me. I had to do that for myself."

∞

Warm days and sudden showers set the forest alive with giggles and whisperings. Come evening, the scent of wild garlic, mingled with trodden grass and musky earth, filled the glade. The fading light stretched its tendrils a little further, peeling the day in an unbroken loop before finally melting into night's embrace.

The Tree's leaves spread wide, providing a canopy of speckled green shadows for those who sought shelter beneath its eaves.

A warm breeze played with the boy's hair as he chatted with the woman from his favourite perch.

She often smiled at his questions, but never failed to answer as honestly and openly as she could.

Her legs tucked beneath her, her shoulders resting against the Tree, she was alive and at home in the forest.

"I can't picture you as the Shadow that crept into our lives," the boy confessed.

"Don't be blinded again," she counseled him.

"Will there be others?" he asked.

"No sooner did I cast aside the manacles, than another turned the key."

"You saw this?" he asked.

"In the North hoards hounded Time's heels, snapping for his attention. They tugged at his chains and bowed before him."

"So nothing really changes." The boy sounded defeated, weary at the notion that another Shadow was carrying Time's bags and bending beneath his assaults.

He wanted the Tree to banish Time from the forest, but the Tree refused to bar the way to any creature that sought its counsel.

"Time will come, as he always does," the Tree told him.

"Then how can we make him change his ways?" the boy asked.

"Time is made up of minutes and hours, seasons and years," the woman chimed in. "It is the nature of Time. We cannot change that, any more than we can change the nature of a tree.

"Our power rests in our freedom to choose the part that Time plays in our lives.

"I sought Time out and cast him in the role of tyrant. I counted my life in minutes and blamed every misstep and forgotten friend on the bell that rang out the hours.

"I saw others living clockwork lives, waiting for the future to come and break them out of their misery. Trapped by inertia, and tied to Time, they simply ended up counting down the minutes till their breath ran out.

"They died without ever having really lived. They knew neither failure nor success. Love was nothing more than a phantom, as they had long ceased to care for themselves. They crouched and muttered in the shadows, and watched as Time stole all their best lines. When the curtain fell they roared their last, cursing Time for running out on them."

"Time could have refused them," the boy countered.

"Perhaps. But when lives that have lost all value to the owner are pawned off as gifts on an unwilling recipient, it becomes easy to be careless of the empty token, no matter how precious, or fragile, it is."

"He didn't have to stamp on it," the boy hotly declared. His cheeks were pink, and he held onto the Tree for support as his anger simmered.

"We all walk with our own shadow. Would you welcome another's trailing behind you?"

The boy reluctantly shook his head, uncertain of his mind and suspicious of his emotions.

"Every creature has its place in the world," the Tree reminded him.

"Even Time?" the boy asked. "If we could get rid of him, then souls would take responsibility for their own lives and stop flinging themselves under his feet leaving a trail of roadkill."

"Without the passing of time, the seasons would blend into each other," the Tree responded. "Without its steady course it would be easy to forget that every moment contains a beginning and an ending. To live is to change. Time's unceasing counter spurs us towards failures."

"Isn't that a bad thing?"

"Not at all. Success and failure are both symptoms of having tried. To live fully is to take risks. To fail again. To do better. Hiding in a corner, and shivering in the face of life, is the only defeat.

"The knowledge that time will pass can inspire us to take control of our lives and value each passing moment. We can choose to live in the light, without regrets and without shackles, rulers of our own destinies."

The child mulled over what the Tree told him, struggling to contain his anger and understand the workings of time.

"There is light and dark in all of us," the woman reminded him, as evening fell and the Tree's shadow stretched across the forest floor.

$$\infty$$

The woman wandered in the woods, trailing her fingers across flower petals that opened their secrets to her caress. She passed through mossy glades that hoarded the morning's dew in their deepest crevices. She drank from the spring that watered the Tree's roots, and tasted earth and leaves and clear, cold skies. Her path led her to a meadow, where the grass reached her thighs and coated her with sap and burrs and the stuff of the forest. She felt the sun on her bare arms, and her head swam with the weightlessness of the heavens. With each step the fresh growth sprang back into place, as though it had never borne her weight. The wind carried the smells of heat and honey and bales of green. A thousand insects hummed and whirred and sizzled in the air. Bird calls plotted her passage and trilled in bushes. A long, lonely skrawk echoed across the land, far above the tree line. The woman's breath and heart and mind and limbs entwined with the life of the forest. With a simple certainty, she understood that she was part of the world and the world was part of her. For a precious moment, in a clearing in the forest, she knew that she could fly.

∞

The boy sat amongst the Tree's roots, eyes closed, wide awake. His heart was cradled in the crevice between his collarbones, secured by a leather tong.

The softness of the boy's face had been re-etched in harder lines, which displayed a new strength. His hair, as ever, remained an unruly mess, and a smile hovered around his mouth, even in repose.

His chest rose and fell so softly, that the flicker of his small life could easily have gone unnoticed. Except, of course, by the Tree, who felt the boy's breath as it felt its own roots and leaves and limbs.

The Tree filled the sky above the boy. It touched the East and the West, the North and the South. It stretched towards the heavens and delved deep in the earth, its compass never wavering, not even for a moment.

It had witnessed many comings and goings over its years, and it had grown in stature and strength. Yet, even now, it never stopped probing further, always towards that which lay just beyond its reach.

It pondered the boy's growth and, once again, marveled at the miracle of birth and death and all that lay between. The forest ferns had all uncurled from their long sleep, and their laced leaves glanced against the Tree's trunk in delicate clusters. Chicks that had nested in its eaves now gathered in the evenings to chirrup and gossip. And, that very morning, the Tree had heard a faint chime at the forest's northern reaches. Time, it was certain, was passing, and would soon be amongst them.

The wind drowsily grazed against the Tree's broad leaves, causing a gentle flutter amongst the tallest branches. Insects droned on and on, holding forth on blades of grass that had sprung up at odd angles around its network of roots. The stream that fed the forest trailed lazily across mossy stones, brushing against languid limbs that dangled in its water.

Spring's fever was hushed, its work done. The season had eased into summer.

$$\infty$$

A leaf fell from the Tree and tickled the boy's face as it drifted on a passing breeze. The boy smiled as he breathed in and out. The Tree settled into its own murmur and joined the boy's rhythm. The woman stood in the tall grass, her face open to the sun. The moment past as another was born, and there was real peace and happiness and harmony in the forest.

THE END

Acknowledgements

The urgency to create is intrinsically tied to the willingness to fail. As is so often the case, my book was conceived with gleeful abandon. Its delivery was strained and difficult. It didn't quite fit. Yet, buoyed by a mixture of quickening courage and thickening hide, I pushed on.

I am indebted to my first readers for the significant part they played in padding both my mettle and my pelt. My brother, Michael Sorahan, read with care and called me often to discuss an idea, or a line that piqued his interest. His delight in the story reinforced my belief in this unconventional allegory. He was one amongst many who offered insights and encouragement, who included: Ruth Donald; Áine Kelly; Mairéad Ward; John Greene; Damien Brennan; Deirdre Walsh; Elaine O'Mahoney; and Mary van Beuren.

I'd also like to thank Luke Gerwe, editor and supporter, whose enthusiasm for my work was matched by his keen eye and expertise.

I am also grateful to my teachers, both in and out of the classroom. I wish to acknowledge in particular, Declan Kiberd, the finest mentor and scholar I have ever encountered, who inspired his students to have faith in their own ideas. A generous and rare trait.

The ideas explored in this novel ripened over the course of my travels. During this time, I met numerous people who cultivated my mind and guided me towards my path. The opportunity to learn and practice Vipassana meditation in retreats in Dehradun in India and in Shelburne, Massachusetts, in the US, played an important role in the evolution of this story.

My book was also shaped by those who nurtured me as the tale unfolded: my dearest friends, who took pleasure in my joys and were always no further than the end of a crackling telephone line, regardless of distance and time zones; my loyal and loving champions, Neil and Michael Sorahan; Mairéad Ward, with her steadying roots and steadfast embrace; and my beloved Catherine Gilmer, a warrior woman, who left an indelible mark on my story.

I am forever grateful for my family. My earliest memories are laced with love and the smell of clover. I recall wood fires, stray creatures, epic tales told around the dinner table, and easy laughter. My parents placed great weight on hospitality and on learning. Dad, a master storyteller, passed on his love of language. Mum, the strongest and wisest person I have ever known, instilled in me a belief that I could fly. My siblings, who have carved their paths with courage and determination, continue to be an inspiration.

This book would not have been written without the support of my partner and fellow wanderer, Will Chin. We have shared countless adventures since our paths first crossed; and it is my abiding joy that we journey onward together.

Finally, a special shout out for Lyra, without whom the night sky would be empty of stars.

About the Author

Róisín Sorahan is an award-winning Irish author, currently living in the United States. She has published numerous stories about her wanderings across six continents. Prior to becoming a nomad writer, she pursued a decade-long career in public relations. She holds a Master of Letters from Trinity College Dublin, specializing in Samuel Beckett. *Time and the Tree*, her debut novel, was awarded the Readers' Favorite Gold Medal for Inspirational Fiction.

For more information,
visit **www.roisinsorahan.com**